NAVIGATOR'S SINDROME

By Jayge Carr

NAVIGATOR'S SINDROME
LEVIATHAN'S DEEP

glumly. The Guild had broken men for lesser sins than overcharging its members.

Volubly servile, he escorted her to a vacant niche and bowed himself away. As soon as he slipped back into his customary position behind the bar, he realized he had a far more immediate worry than the Guild, awesome as that monolithic power could be.

The Gilded Cage was more than it seemed. Merely bilking spacers (though on a Low-Tech world like Rabelais, the simplest High-Tech item might be worth more than a man could earn with his hands in a lifetime) could not have afforded enough profit for the exotic drinks, lush women, and sybaritic imported luxuries the Gilded Cage supplied. But hidden among the blackened beams and swinging oil lamps of the bar's ceiling were a series of holo relayers that repeated all actions in the bar to a set of far more luxurious lounges some distance away where, among other pleasures, the Privileged could watch the antics of the offworld animals in complete and unsuspected privacy. The Arena rooms came high, but for many jaded tastes, it was a favorite diversion.

Unfortunately, the bar had been comparatively quiet; no knife fights, no waitress forced to dance naked on a table, none of the usual or exotic amusements.

When the light on the bar that only he could see—thanks to the black light contacts in his eyes—flickered imperiously, Zaqanna the bartender hurriedly slipped through the door behind the bar and across the storeroom to the transmatter plate that was activated by his hand alone. He stepped out in the main corridor of the Arena lounge and hurried to the door whose frame was still blinking angrily to his contact-augmented eyes.

"Lord Singh"—he bowed casually—"did you notice those two Bythi in the center niche? They're just drunk enough to be ripe for murder. I've ordered Kithal to flirt with the noseless one. Did you ever hear how the Bythi duel? *Most* amusing, lord. They cut off their own fingers, joint by—"

"Worm," the man sprawled on the fur-heaped couch drawled, one hand idly stroking the small body beside him, "I want the woman who just came in, the woman dressed in black."

"Lord"—Zaqanna shook his head—"she is a Navigator."

"A Navigator." The lord shrugged. His ancestors had been Gene-Altered dominant; he was all gold in color, skin, eyes, hair, the last of which flowed in thick heavy waves to his broad shoulders, despite the fact that he was in late middle age. The GAing should have prevented fat; nonetheless he had developed a paunch, flabby jowls, and the beginnings of a double chin. "A spacer, you mean. So? Taming that pride will amuse me—until your duel."

For the merest moment Zaqanna toyed with the idea of luring the woman somehow to the lord c'holder; if the autocrat managed to lower that proud head a trifle—or all the way—he wouldn't grieve. But she no doubt had offworld protections, and though the lord's bodyguard, within easy call, had offworld weapons, too, there was still the Guild to consider. Whether the woman won or lost, he would have made a powerful enemy, one he couldn't afford.

"I regret, lord." Zaqanna spread his hands, empty. "She is a *Navigator,* and we cannot risk offending the Navigator's Guild. But if you are bored, I have a delicious little creature you have not yet tried, daughter of one of my women and a spacer. She has—"

"Worm, I don't usually have to repeat my orders. Name your fee for the woman in offworlder's clothing whose every move is a challenge."

"Lord Singh, her price would be no more starships coming to this world. No more imported luxuries, stargoods, the profits from the offworld markets—or the starweapons. She is a *Navigator,* lord, and the Navigators protect their own; and without Navigators, no ship will land here. That is far too high a price to pay for a mere woman. I have so many others. Have you tried my fiery Zulaika yet? I—"

"I want *that* woman, worm." Alerted by the threat in its master's voice, the sleek red hunting z'par curled by Golden Singh's hip raised its head, the fronds that ran from just above the eyes down the lithe spine unfurling and pulsing bright crimson. "Hush, Nemesis." The c'holder reached over to stroke the fronds, despite the needle-pointed quills that stiffened them. "You, worm" —to Zaqanna—"you have procured me male spacers, for my gladiatorial school, and other uses. Must I teach you your trade, worm? Get *her;* my patience wears thin." The z'par's high keen counterpointed the menace in the last words.

"Lord." Zaqanna was firm. "I cannot. The risk is too great."

"Then get her under contract—you've done that, too. Will these touchy Navigators you babble fearfully about protect a contract-breaker? Do it openly, or however you please—just—*do it!*" His

CHAPTER 1

She called herself Jael. Arrogant in her Navigator's black, she strode into the spacemen's bar, steeped—like all such bars—in the fumes and vices of a hundred worlds.

Silence rippled out from her entrance, phrases broken off in mid-syllable as elbows dug into ribs and heads jerked around; drinks froze forgotten partway to gaping mouths. The boldest of the men smiled, or nodded, or half-rose hopefully. The rest merely stared bemused at the vision in noli me tangere black. She stopped, disdainful gaze slowly swinging around, piercing the room's dimness. *No!* Then shoulders turned back to her, shrugging, the jangor-tangor game resumed, new rumbles of conversation, laughter arose.

The head bartender leaped away from the clot of cargo handlers he'd been serving. "Your pleasure, honored star-finder?"

"Stock you Mare's Milk of D'Gedd, dispenser of sweet forgetfulness?"

"My pleasure to serve, honored star-finder. If you would condescend to sample it, to ensure that it meets with your approval . . ." He prided himself on his ability to identify any accent; instinctively, he analyzed hers. That odd sentence structure, the formality which he had automatically echoed, the turn of vowel—the Nucleus Worlds. One of those overbred half-myths from the Center, was she? But the Center accent was overlaid with —by the Thrice-Weaponed! He almost knocked the dusty, priceless flask off the shelf. The Love Marts of the Third Arm! Cupidity warred with fear. The worth of so striking a woman, Third Arm (but how *could* she have escaped?) trained. . . . But there was the Navigator's Guild. . . .

He set the Mare's Milk in front of her, with proper reverence, and got down a shot-gold Rth's-egg chalice. Unsealing the flask, he filled the goblet barely a third full, and then, holding the fragile vessel in his two hands so that their heat could release the rich

scent, he slowly swirled the greenish-white liquid around until it
thoroughly coated the inside of the goblet.

He offered the chalice to her, and she leaned over it, long, slender hands below his but not touching, and drank in the fumes. But
the carved face rose quickly, and he knew this one had known
Mare's Milk many times before. No chance then, even if he dared,
of stupefying her with a second or third serving.

"And what owe I you for this prize, master of this house?"

He licked dry lips. "Your Guild fees all, most honored star-
finder. If you would only press your ident here . . ." Humbly, he
offered the small qualifier.

Jael, still somewhat under the fumes, laughed. "Think you I
know not the penalty for falsely assuming the garb I wear, owner
of flesh?" Her gray-green eyes flicked over the women scattered
around the bar. With another laugh, she reached for the emblem
hanging on a chain around her neck. At her touch, the chain
unlinked; holding the emblem, chain dangling, she pressed it with
practiced ease into the small qualifier, being sure her own skin
touched also. The silvery ankh on her cuff flashed brightly, but not
as brightly as the golden assent of the qualifier. Jael laughed
softly. "See you, soul-less one. In good standing."

"Good lady, I never doubted. How else may I serve you?" His
face was round and guileless, pink-cheeked and smooth-skinned.
But his eyes were small and hard behind thick bronze lashes.

"Comfortable privacy only, dispenser. If these niches behind us
have privacy shields, one of them will do."

"Lady, I have sweet-scented rooms upstairs, two with imported
grav nullifiers, finely adjustable, and your choice of a marble bath
or—"

"Dispenser, are the niches shielded?"

"Sheets of the finest synthetics, food to tempt the most traveled
and discriminating palate, and skilled—"

"Dispenser." Her smile remained, the voice was soft, but his
sales pitch abruptly ceased. "A third time ask I, are these niches
equipped with shields?"

Sullenly. "Yes . . . lady."

"And, dispenser"—still the clear contralto voice was soft—
"when I have finished here, present you the bill, and I will pay it.
All of it, dispenser. I have what your world values. And seek not
to overcharge my ignorance. I will report your price to my Guild
before I leave your world." He understood the threat and nodded

NAVIGATOR'S SINDROME

JAYGE CARR

DOUBLEDAY & COMPANY, INC.
GARDEN CITY, NEW YORK
1983

To the men and women of Medical Center Hospital, without whose skill, care, and downright bulldog obstinacy, neither this book nor its perpetuator would exist. The said perpetuator is grateful; it remains to be seen if the book's hapless readers will be.

Library of Congress Cataloging in Publication Data

Carr, Jayge.
Navigator's sindrome.

(Doubleday science fiction)
I. Title. II. Series.
PS3553.A7629N38   1983   813′.54
ISBN 0-385-17221-4
Library of Congress Catalog Card Number 81-43446
Copyright © 1983 by Margery Krueger
All Rights Reserved
Printed in the United States of America
First Edition

hand lay on the z'par's shoulder; the merest nudge, and the animal would attack.

Zaqanna stood erect, considering; then, slowly, he nodded. "I will try, Lord C'holder. But you must be patient—it will take time. Days, perhaps tennites." The lord smiled, relaxing back against his furs. "Anticipation sharpens the appetite. Just get her, worm—and don't worry about your fee."

Zaqanna bowed. "As the lord c'holder wishes." He flicked a glance at the child lying silent beside Golden Singh. "If the lord is dissatisfied with Hadeen, I can fetch Zulaika—or perhaps the lord would prefer another. . . ."

"Dissatisfied?" The c'holder glanced down, frowning; his left hand frozen in the act of caressing the delicate bare back. "This one, worm. What is its contract worth?"

"Three hundred years, lord. Lovely, isn't she? And yours alone. Raw clay—"

"Half that for a whimpering bore, worm. It is now mine."

"Two hundred years, lord. That blue hair alone would fetch a fancy—"

"Done, then. I'll not haggle like a trademan. Done, at two hundred years. It is mine, to do with as I choose."

"Yes, lord. She has other costumes. I will have them wrapped and—"

"No need." The lord pushed disdainfully, and the body rolled off the lounge (the z'par dodging back just in time) to lie limbs askew and wide-open, unmoving eyes staring at Zaqanna. "Just get rid of it."

Zaqanna stared down at what had been one of the children belonging to him by contract, daughter of a woman belonging to him by contract—and quite possibly his in literal, physical fact. She had had great potential; he regretted he had not valued her higher. But the lord grew bored quickly with his playtoys, and was usually willing to contract them back cheaply; Zaqanna had taken that into account in setting the fee. He knelt and picked her up by the long blue feathery hair. "Yes, lord." He bowed, the body dangling from his hand, legs dragging. "Will there be anything else, lord?"

"That ruby-eyed one, if you still have her. She's less dissatisfactory than most. And—" He stroked the z'par, ordered his wants.

At the door, Zaqanna was stopped by the lord's voice. "Worm,

I've changed my mind. Put *that* in my carriage. Nemesis deserves a treat after his disappointment tonight, don't you, my gallant warrior?" At the sound of his name, the sleek z'par sprang to alertness. Lord C'holder Golden Singh caressed the scaled head with genuine affection. "Yes, and we'll have another treat soon, won't we, my bravo? A proud one. Shall we share the chase, good Nemesis? And the spoils. . . ."

Zaqanna shuddered—but only when he was out of the lord's sight.

CHAPTER 2

There were more protections in the portslum of the world called Rabelais than Navigator's black. A tall, rangy man whose hair had once been a disciplined sweep of tawny shot with gold and was now dun and unkempt, sauntered through the streets, not yet deserted even though the ring had set and it was a couple of hours until sunrise. He seemed to have no purpose, no goal, he simply journeyed on a drunkard's random walk, his feet aiming now here, now there. Yet he wasn't drunk. Despite the haunted, sunken eyes, he was zero Kelvin sober, not a trace of alcohol or drug in his system.

The "between-the-lines" gang seemed to materialize out of the very mist.

The lone man stopped because it was stop or push his way through the living wall.

One of the men stepped forward. A black river of dried blood meandered down one side of his face, and little buzzing midges seemed to be trying to find a drink in it. He held out a dirty hand, palm up. "You got any IPCs?"

"No." The man whose clothes of washed-out gray matched his hollow eyes shook his head.

"Port-chits?" Unlike the IPCs, interplanetary credits usable on any world, port-chits were Rabelaisian, issued by and redeemable by a consortium of c'holders with large interests in the port or its various functions. They were valued in multiples of hours of standardized, unskilled labor, and were the closest thing to money on the planet, though used mainly by offworlders at those establishments that would accept them in place of some sort of contract.

"No."

Infinite contempt flashed from eyes that thought they had seen everything. "You signed one of those plasmaed contracts?"

"In a sense."

He spat, the liquid landed with a faint pock. "And they let you loose, without a keeper? Tell another, spacespawn."

A one-shouldered shrug. "I've a talent. They keep me. When they need the talent, I do what they want. Otherwise, I'm left to my own devices."

The ex-spacer—for he was wearing a well-known uniform, though its insignia were worn and/or torn away—flicked a glance at his fellows. "Anybody believe him?"

The man at his left spoke with a distinct planetary accent. If their victim had been curious, he might have wondered why an obvious civvy had landed and been stranded on Rabelais. But he didn't. He wasn't a spacer himself, after all, and he was here, wasn't he. He hadn't such luxuries as curiosity left, anyway. "Nye, I don't believe him. Everybody knows about these—bloodsuckers. Nye, he's off a ship or has signed a contract or is sliding between the lines." He didn't have to add the obvious. Like us. He gave the man in gray a cynical up-and-down look. "He's thin, but he don't look hungry. He's dressed plain, but not ragged. Not sliding, then. And if he'd signed a contract, he wouldn't be wandering around loose. Nye. Off a ship."

"I told you I signed a contract. Not a standard one, one with special clauses. A contract, nonetheless."

The line of men shifted, and he was surrounded. The ex-spacer with the dried blood on his face smiled, a predatory flash of teeth. "He's lying. Let's see what's really in his pockets."

For the first time, a hint of expression flashed across the man in gray's face, though what it was his opponents couldn't have said. With trained speed, his foot slashed out, the hardened toe sinking into the ex-spacer's body at its most vulnerable point. His victim let out a strangled bleat like a ram getting its throat cut and doubled over, clutching where he'd been kicked.

The man in gray, face again impassive, twisted slightly, stiffened hand slamming toward the man who'd spoken second, smashing horizontally across the bridge of his nose with an oddly soggy crackle, as though a butcher had chopped through a side, meat and bone giving way to the sharp knife.

And then three other men flung themselves on him, and he was borne to the ground, his body thrashing but not unseating his enemies.

It was several minutes before the leader could get back enough breath to ask, in a thin tight voice, "What's the take?"

"Nothing," a subordinate reported. "He wasn't lying about that. "No IPCs, no liner scrip, no offworld currency, no doss-stick, no vals, no nothing. No local chits, either."

The leader cursed. Then he bit out, "Put him against a wall."

It was mud brick and rough and must have ground cruelly into the man in gray's back, but he only stood, arms held by two of the gang, facing the still-pale man he had hurt so badly. "You think you're cute. Come on, spacespawn. Where'd you stash it?"

The man in gray only smiled.

The ex-spacer pounded a fist into the taller man's gut, and his victim, gasping for breath, doubled over as far as four hands holding on to his arms would let him.

"I said"—fist raised in threat—"where's your stash?"

Silence.

"You want a knee—or maybe you got nothing to hurt?"

"I have no stash. I told you—I signed a contract."

"And I told you, I know how these freer-than-free hypocrites work. Once you've signed a contract, that's it. If you'd signed a contract—"

Incredibly, the man in gray only sounded bored. "I told you once, not all contracts are the same. If you've a talent or a skill, they're willing to pay high for it." His lip curled. "If all you have is muscle and the luck of being from a High-T culture, and maybe the gadgets any of us might own—"

"Talent." It was the man with the new broken nose and the planetary accent sneering. "Like my sister." Hurt throbbed in his angry voice, revealing him as younger than he looked. He gave the helplessly held man a sneer. "You don't look the part, but I suppose—what kind of c'holders do you please? The women? The men? Kids maybe, that seems about your speed."

"I doubt you could please any of them. Most c'holders are quite"—his lip curled—"fastidious. I—"

"Dry you!" The youngster attacked, fists flailing, and the man in gray was beaten back against the wall.

"Stop that!" The leader pulled him back. "At least until we have something useful out of him."

Their victim spit blood and choked a little.

"All right, spacespawn." The leader was tired of playing games. He drew a knife, space issue, not vibroscalpel or ultraheat, but plain etersteel, with an edge to split hairs. "Tell us where your stash is, or I start cutting. Not your throat, then you couldn't tell. But maybe I'll spill some of your guts, eh? Take a while to die, maybe somebody here might even be able to sew them back in. Eh? But it'll hurt. Shall I start with your guts?" He ran a thin line down the other's body, not pushing hard enough to cut—yet—just leaving a dent in the thin fabric.

The man in gray stared over his head, not speaking a word.

"Naze." It was a man who hadn't spoken up to now. "It's no go."

"Wha—"

"He's vacuumed to his ears, man. Look at the way he took Jeroa's blows just now. Vacuumed, frozen, eating space. You could slice him in microlayers, and he'd only laugh."

"That true." It was an animal's growl.

"No." A mirthless laugh. "Cut me, and do I not bleed."

Naze slid the sharp knife along the gaunt cheek, and blood followed. "Yeah, but they's all kinds of snow." He sniffed. "Breath vile, but nothing on it. Not that rotgut they brew, that's for sure."

"I suggest," the tall man dressed in gray said in the same dispassionate monotone he'd used all along, "that you let me go and try for more fruitful game."

"Sharrup!" A snarl of unadulterated hate. "And maybe we'll get our goodies another way. Maybe we'll just cut your throat."

"That's contract breaking. I told you I signed—"

"So maybe we believed you lied. Other contracteds aren't strolling around loose—" Perhaps it was the very lack of fear in his would-be victim that made him a challenge, so that the ex-spacer drew closer, knife threatening. Until suddenly his eyes met the blank ones of washed-out gray, and something in their depths made him flinch back, voice an oath almost forgotten except among a few spacers, those whose roots went all the way back to the original manhome. "Mother of God! You *want* me to slit your throat!"

"If you say so," the man in gray agreed politely. "Though what motive you envision for so pointless an act . . . Perhaps, having taken an instant dislike to you, I want to see you tortured to death in a public square. That's the standard punishment here, I understand, for—"

"Haryd," Naze appealed to the man who had only spoken once.

"Don't risk it, Naze. He just might be telling the truth. You know these crazy dunghillers only keep from smashing us under their thumbs 'cause we haven't broken any of their crazy contracts. Yet. We better keep him alive."

"All-lll right." Naze thrust the knife back wherever it hid. "But he won't like it."

He only used his fists and his knees, and when he left, the man in gray lay crumpled on the muddy ground. But his broken mouth still curled in a cynical smile.

CHAPTER 3

The six men playing jangor-tangor in the large niche close to the door seemed engrossed in their game. But when Jael the Navigator left the Gilded Cage, much, much later, one of them casually flung a handful of port-chits on the table and sauntered out.

Once through the door he hesitated, peering after the already distant black-clad figure. His hand went to his pocket in a habitual gesture, his fingers touching an object like a doubly flattened teardrop, its surface worn smooth as synthi by the passage of countless fingers. He brought it out and flipped and caught it. In his palm, a darkness darker than the center of a dustcloud—but in its center was a winking, beckoning brightness. Still he hesitated, lip caught between slightly yellow teeth—and from within, Zaqanna's angry shout, followed by the snap of a whip and a woman's howl of agony. His hand clenched on the small artifact, then he dropped it in his pocket and hurried after the almost invisible black-in-black vagueness, guided more by the crack of heels on cobbles than sight, his own thick-soled boots carefully noiseless.

It was the solemn hour of the night, and a light mist further hazed the dim, gauzy ringlight. He had to follow more closely, and even his breathing sounded loud in the hush.

But his prey strolled along, with all the time in the world, confident in the protection of her Guild black. He started to catch up with her—and then held back. He had to be sure. . . .

Once his boot skittered a loose pebble, and she whirled at the sudden sound. But he had leaped for an alleyway as soon as he felt the pebble move, and when he peeked cautiously out, she was strolling idly on again.

Guildsman black or not, this was the portslum, haunt of the evil and the desperate and the greedy, savage and primitive—and dangerous.

The mist thickened, and he closed the gap. She rounded a corner; he followed—

—and recovered consciousness, hands and feet bound, in almost total blackness.

"Be a little less ambitious next time, cutpurse," his would-be victim's amused voice spoke in his ear. A rustle, and a sound of footsteps moving away.

"Wait!" He forced the syllable through a swollen, painful throat. He had a vague memory of something slipping around his neck as he turned the corner. He even felt a rueful admiration for the way she had so efficiently turned the tables on her pursuer— and a vast disgust at himself, for bungling his mission. He had gambled—and lost. Unless . . . "Wait, Navigator! The shields in the Gilded Cage are faulty."

He could almost hear her shrug. The footsteps continued away. "Wait. He's never tried for a Navigator before. He must want you very badly, to risk the Guild's retaliation." The footsteps were very faint. He forced loudness from his abused throat desperately. "Break local law, or what passes for it here, and even your Guild cannot protect you."

Silence.

"Zaqanna knows his world well—and uses its peculiarities. If he claims you by contract-right, your Guild would be willing to pay a fine, but Zaqanna won't be willing to accept a fine. On this world, nothing comes before honoring a contract; your Guild will have signed some, too. They will give you up, because it will be simpler than fighting a whole world, especially for a lawbreaker—a contract-breaker, here. And the penalties for contract breaking—you'd better listen to me, Navigator—before it's too late!"

Still silence, and he thought she'd gone too far to hear him at all. Then boots slushed through soft filth toward him, and he could feel her bending over him in the darkness. Her voice was clear and cold. "I think you'd better explain all that."

He relaxed, heaved a sigh of relief. "There's a sharp corner of something sticking into my back. Sit me up, will you?" In the dark, all he could see were her eyes, enormous, staring at him.

Then a bright but contained light flared in his eyes; automatically he squinted and turned away. Ruthlessly the light probed, he could feel its cold breath exploring his face.

He would have been far more worried than he was if he could have realized what she was seeing; he underestimated the changes shadows and squinting made on his square, pleasantly commonplace face. In light, his rust-colored hair and slow freckled grin (the grin mostly absent lately, the freckles all too often lost in an angry flush) provided saving notes of humor; in the sharp glare, the short scar jagging one side of the neatly clipped beard deepened into sinister significance. (Like most spacers, he paid no attention to planetary fads; his hair and face were his own, and though the scar would remain only until he had saved enough High-T credit to have it removed, he had never considered biosculpting himself into bland—if handsomer—conformity.)

The light flicked out, and he blinked away hazy spots.

"I could have killed you, cutpurse. But I didn't. If this is some sort of trick—" She sat him up, then he felt her fumbling with his clothes. "That's a cryowire you feel, cutpurse, and I've taken the wraps off. If you think to hold me here until your friends come—one twist, and it'll cut clean through. If I am attacked—or if you cannot satisfy me that your information is worth this delay—I'll have your manhood and then your tongue."

"I'm Hannibal Reis, master of a small freighter. Zaqanna—that sly-tongued villain from the Gilded Cage!" He choked, controlled himself. "Zaqanna *took* a member of my crew, just as he's planning to take you."

"My hand is on the wire control, cutpurse. Go on. How did he take this other?"

He could feel the sweat rolling off his face. There was a faint nimbus around her head, so close to his. "The same way he intends to get *you,* Navigator. Oh, that girl didn't appeal to his fellow feeling as a woman, the way she did you. I heard *plenty,* through Zaqanna's faulty shields. Plasma, for all I know, her story's true. This world is—fierce. No, my broth—Rowan was young, naive. She appealed to his chivalry, offered him eternal gratitude if he'd help return her to her family. Oh, she played him like a sonar, she did. Plasma, if only I hadn't been stuck with that conniving cargo protector! If only—" He bit down in anguish. "He came back to the ship, and I wasn't there. *I—wasn't—there!* He left a tape, that's how I know what happened. He said—never mind. I told you this world is fierce, didn't I? It has no laws, no laws whatsoever, just contracts. And contracts must be honored, or the whole thing will fall apart. So they make examples of contract-breakers. Horrible examples. They're *savages,* vindictive—brutal. They took Rowan, and—" A pause. "Do you know what the penalty for interfering with a man's contracts is, Navigator? As long as he holds her by contract, she is his *property,* like his boots or his wines, until *he* acknowledges a new contract."

"Um." She sat back on her heels, but he could feel her hand, bulky around the cryowire control, still resting on his thigh.

"I couldn't hear all you and that female Judas goat said, but Zaqanna is very skillful at editing. I've learned a lot about him, since . . ."

"That will do him no good. I carry a Personal. And when the two records don't agree, we'll all three be psyched."

"Not her, her evidence is worthless, she is a contracted, a bondswoman. But you and him, yes. And when the two psychs don't agree—" He heard her breath draw in, a sharp hiss. "Zaqanna has connections. And in any port, even this one, especially this one, there are broken psychers, ready to sell their skill. He'll probably use one anyway, as a precaution. But when the two *minds* don't agree—it is *you,* the accused, the apparently guilty, who'll seem to have a motive for altering records, for altering your own mind. . . ."

Again a pause. He could almost hear her thinking. "You know much about this business, cutpurse."

"I *owe* Zaqanna. And I've been looking for a way to erase the debt."

"And if I return to Guildhall and report that a woman of this world offered me inducement to steal her from her master, and I but spoke as to draw her out fully?"

"It might protect you," he said grudgingly. "That and the black you wear. Especially if you ship out at dawn and never come back." Her whole body jerked, and for a horrible second he thought she'd triggered the wire. But her control was excellent.

"Call you me a coward, cutpurse?"

"What's that girl, or what he'll do to her for failing, or Rowan, or me, to you, Navigator? You've a skill you can sell high on a thousand worlds. Why risk being dragged naked to the auction block—"

"You said this world, this no-laws-but-contracts world was fierce, cutpurse. So tell me: if Zaqanna dies or is condemned, what will hap with that girl?"

"I don't know. I suspect she'll be sold again to pay his fines or

debts or whatever. If she can get word to her family—assuming her
tale is true—they might be able to redeem her."

"And if not, almost any master would be an improvement over
this animal Zaqanna. A miserable world, cutpurse, where a
woman's only choice is between bad and worse ways to sell herself."

"This is a *free* world, Navigator." He couldn't help the sarcasm.
"Everyone equal, women as well as men; no law, no sin, no crime,
no—"

She spat, he heard it land with a little pock. "No law, so no
rape, no robbery—no murder."

"Just contract breaking. Kill a man—and you void his contracts.
Steal—and you risk voiding contracts. As for women—they're as
free to defend themselves as to accept a contract. On other
worlds, there's marriage, pairing, communes—affection at any
level. In a sense, they're all contracts. Only here, they're not hypo-
critical about it." He couldn't have said why he was playing devil's
advocate for a world he despised; except that that cursed ability of
his to empathize with both sides of any question told him that
there had been a glorious ideal here once; only the devilish perver-
sity of human nature had soured it.

"Contracts! Tscha! I said, bad and *worse,* cutpurse. A *stink-
hole,* this. But there are worse than this, I admit. Much worse.
We've spread too far, and too fast, and in too many places, re-
verted to animality. . . ." Lower. "The evil, spread so widely, entrenched so deep . . . how can one fight against it?" Briskly,
louder. "What am I to do with you, cutpurse? If this tale of yours
is true—and I would believe any vileness of that sweet-faced seller
of artificial joy—then I am in most dire peril. And I owe you, for
your warning. But if the vileness is yours . . ."

The stink of the alley made the gorge rise in his throat. He
wondered, irrelevantly, if he would ever be able to cleanse it out
of his clothes. Suddenly he laughed. "You've a problem, haven't
you, Navigator. How long has it been since you've trusted any
man?" He chuckled again, amused. "Did you know, I posted notice at your Guildhall for a Navigator, until this with Rowan made
me take it down. If you and I had met under other circumstances,
we might have reached agreement. Though I doubt it. We're too
small a crew to have an icestar among us, skilled Navigator or
not." Again he thought he'd gone too far, but after a long, long
second she, too, laughed softly.

"You almost make me believe in this freighter of yours, cutpurse."

He shrugged, mentally. She was doomed, of course, but maybe he could profit from her downfall. There was still Rowan to revenge.

If she didn't cut his throat, that is.

CHAPTER 4

Yes, I'm familiar with that c'holder, no problems there. And you're—how old did you say?

Twelve, lady.

Young enough to be trainable, that's for sure. (A hesitation.) Old enough to make such a life's decision?

Yes, lady!

(A smile.) I think you're right, son. Well, then, let's make it all square and shipshape, shall we. Name, Lysander, age, twelve local, close enough to stans, I think we can just call it twelve. Father's name?

I don't know, lady—

"Not again!" The girl-woman dressed in regal white paused in the doorway, frowning, some thirteen years before Lysander had his crucial interview on the same night that the Navigator who called herself Jael walked into the spacemen's bar and changed the course of so many lives. The roots of events are seldom single or simple, and ripples from seemingly unconnected events can cross and recross, their effects lingering beyond the span of individual memory.

The naked man in the woman's bed sat up, blinking. He'd been waiting a long time, and the silence and gentle firmness of the petal-stuffed mattress had been irresistible. He hastily knuckled sleep out of his eyes and spoke. "I have been ordered here by the Lady C'holder Medee Oriflamme."

The girl—she was barely fifteen, though her poise and self-control made her seem older—took two impatient steps inward from the doorway. "So I gather." Her voice was dry. "You're not likely to have passed my guards else." One delicately arched brow tilted abruptly. "You *are* one of the Lady Medee's contracteds?"

His mouth twisted, though her voice, like her face, was calm, almost soothing, like the stroke of a hand over soft plush. Yet he knew well what she was seeing, he didn't need any of the Lady Medee's many mirrors to know that "homely" was the kindest way to describe his crude-hacked, mismatched features. Still, a lady c'holder had spoken, and he answered. "Yes, I am, Lady C'holder. I was recommended to her by her friend, the Lady C'holder Isis Wistern."

It was the girl's turn to twist her mouth, as though she tasted vinegar. "That—" She swallowed the rest. It was habit by now, swallowing her opinions, even in front of contracteds, whom most c'holders regarded as nothings, objects bound by and no more important than words on parchment. Finger tapping restlessly against her chin, she gave the man a careful up-and-down assessment; eyes of so pale a bluish-gray they looked almost silver in the dimly lit room narrowed thoughtfully. His body was well made, lean yet tightly muscled, tapering from broad shoulders to an athlete's flat stomach and narrow hips. But that face—both her sister and her sister's crony usually demanded outstanding good looks in all their personal servitors. This man didn't seem their type at all. "You say my sister sent you?"

"Yes, Lady C'holder." He hadn't moved after that first instinctive sitting up. Now he dropped his head, his eyes fixed on the coverlet beneath him, its simple geometric pattern so different from the florid rococo favored by this lady's sister.

"To my bed, specifically. Not for muscle, you're not a skilled, a controller, or anything else."

"Lady C'holder, I am trained as a guard. For tonight, I have been ordered to please you." Through his lashes, he appreciated the slender form draped in simple white. The thick lashes hid his thoughts, which were, that for the first time since he had entered the household of the Lady C'holder Wistern (already with a reputation as an unusual toy, ugly but surprisingly proficient), he would take pleasure in his duties, give her joy because he wanted to, because something in those haunted silver eyes had plunked on the strings of his heart. But she was a contract-holder and he a contracted. In all the history of slavery, gulfs, castes, classes, there had never been a higher barrier between two people.

"What, precisely, did my sister say?"

He caught that overwide lower lip between his teeth, and then started, "Lady C'holder, your sister said—"

The bleakness in both face and voice caught her attention, and she waved a dismissing hand. "Never mind, I can guess."

If she hasn't been turned on by any of my pretty ones, maybe an ugly one will turn the trick! The Lady C'holder Esme Oriflamme bit her lip, hearing the cruel words as if they'd been spoken aloud. "Perhaps," she muttered to herself, but the man sitting on the bed heard, "she'll send a cripple the next time." Her eyes were flashing with angry fire, but he knew the anger wasn't directed at him, her gaze passed over him as though she saw right through him. With a sigh, she reached up and unclipped her nightcloak, and the girl standing silently behind her caught it before it could fall and hurried to hang it neatly in the wardrobe.

"Nialla." The c'holder was reminded of her servant's presence. "I shan't need you any more tonight, dear. Go get some sleep."

"Yes, Lady C'holder." The girl sketched a curtsy, her eyes all the while boldly surveying the man on the bed. She gave a wriggle as she moved through the door drapes, and threw a glance over her shoulder at him, and he, smiling, couldn't help a brash wink in response. She was such a pert, vital little thing, all innocent attraction.

The c'holder caught the byplay. "I don't need you, either, contracted. Leave now."

He would be punished hardly for his "failure," and he knew it. Nonetheless, he obediently slid toward the edge of the bed. As she came toward him, he said softly, "I wish you would let me do for you, Lady C'holder. Anything."

This girl's sister would have had him severely punished for deviating from her orders a hair's breadth. There was even the possibility of a charge of c'breaking. But he hadn't spoken from fear of punishment for failing in his assignment, but because of a sudden surge of pity. He hadn't even recognized it as pity, this was a contract-holder, and c'holders were gods on earth. Yet at some instinctive level, he had recognized loneliness, deep and bitter, and had made the only gesture he could to assuage the pain he didn't even realize he sensed.

It was the element of sincerity in his voice that made her hesitate, then call out, "Nialla!"

The pert head crowned with a mass of black curls popped back through the opening in the door drapes. "Yes, Lady C'holder?"

"I had forgot something. Come back for a bit, Nialla. Be sure the curtain is fast behind you."

"Yes, mistress." She almost danced in, a gay and mischievous sprite, her unbroken spirit a telltale for what life in this lady's household was like.

"I had forgotten how severe my sister's temper can be. Has she enjoyed the services of this contracted long?" An old saying went, It's hard to be a hero to your valet. Likewise, it's hard to keep secrets from servants. Most c'holders regarded contracteds as things, objects, furniture, but this young girl was well aware that minds and eyes and knowledge existed behind willing (or seemingly willing) hands.

"Long enough. You know your lady sister. Send him back now and—" An expressive grimace wrinkled the gamine features.

The naked man on the bed felt his eyebrows soar upward. Never, never had he heard a contracted speak so of a c'holder. And *to* a c'holder!

"Pest!" The lady's neat white teeth worried her unpainted lip. "I'm tired."

Eyes wide, he leaped the rest of the way off the bed, totally willing to leave or stand up all night, to give the lady the rest she needed.

She sighed, again, gave him a quick, somehow impersonal, assessment. "You look as if a night of rest would do you no damage, either."

He had taken two steps toward the door when it hit him. "Here, lady?" If he stayed the rest of the night, he wouldn't be punished.

She shook her head, mouth suddenly tight. "I—prefer my privacy. However, there are soft rugs in the alcove there"—she gestured—"and a curtain that can be drawn." The last was an order. She turned her back to him, and the dress she was wearing began sliding down, and he hastily averted his eyes. Perhaps it was memory of his honest concern that caused her to add one final statement: "Tell my lady sister whatever you choose. I shall deny nothing."

"She may send me back again." He didn't know why he said that.

He couldn't see her sparkling eyes or sudden smile. "For your sake, I hope so. You look as if more than one night's rest wouldn't come amiss."

"As you say, mistress." She was a c'holder. He couldn't say, I'd gladly give up my rest for you.

She pulled the silskin coverlet over herself, the pleasurable feel against her skin the compensation for the added weight and warmth. "Be sure to draw the curtain tightly. If you must make sounds, I'll not have them disturbing my slumber."

"Yes, mistress."

She snuggled down. "And, Nialla—"

"Yes, mistress?"

"You're free until smallrise, Nialla. And—get some rest yourself, dear."

"Yes, mistress." But she didn't leave. Instead she stared at the naked man, head cocked, with much the hopeful air of a hungry blackwing watching a hole, in hopes a fat worm would venture out.

Jaw dropping, he looked from the slight figure barely making a hump under the thin coverlet to the freckled sprite smiling perkily at him. If she'd said it aloud the message couldn't have been clearer. But— *Dare we?* his expressive face asked.

For answer, she caught his wrist and drew him into the alcove, drawing the curtain. Her mouth at his ear, she whispered softly, "You needn't worry. Any child I bear will be under contract to *her*. And she protects her own."

"I can't worry," he replied, equally softly. "Not about that." He was a contracted, with certain duties laid out *very* specifically. The fate of the children he sired was one thing he couldn't afford to be concerned about.

"If you want me to leave now, I will." Suddenly, she was serious, the dancing black eyes solemn. "It's one thing I've learned from her. If a thing isn't offered freely, it's worthless."

"I don't understand."

Her merry grin flowed over him, leaving delicious tingles in its wake and somehow enclosing them in a private world of two. "I don't expect you to. It's taken me a long time." Another elfin grin. "She's a good teacher, though she doesn't realize it. But for you, now, it's simple enough. Do you want me to go, or to stay with you?"

He shook his head, as though to clear fog out of it. When he grew older, he would realize that a beard would soften some of the crudity of his features. For now, he was clean-shaven, and his smooth skin, though burned to a hard brown and pulled taut over the outthrusting cheekbones, looked somehow young and vulnerable. "I—I regret. I still don't understand."

She tossed a dimple at him. "All you have to understand is this.

For tonight, the choice is wholly and completely yours. I stay with you, or I go. Whichever."

He hesitated, reached up a hand to touch her softly rounded young cheek. "Do *you* want—"

She couldn't tell him that none of the male contracteds to her mistress had pleased her. Nor that, like most women, she yearned for a wooing, a courtship, a time to be sure—and then a permanency. Those who could have offered her such a permanency, she had not wanted to. Yet now, something protective and compassionate in his attitude toward the girl-woman she both loved and admired had matched her own feelings and set off something new and sweet deep inside her. "Only if you want."

His other hand came up, so that he was cupping her face. "I'm not very attractive." He didn't add what they both knew: that they might never see each other again.

"Something else she taught me, without meaning to. It's what's within that counts. The lady's sister is far more beautiful than she —on the outside."

His smile was wry. "Yes." Then again, more emphatically, "Yes."

The curtain was very thick.

—my mother was attending her mistress lady c'holder to a party given by her lady's sister. The party got—as my lady's sister's parties sometimes get, and my mother was separated from her lady. She was found, unconscious, many hours later. She never remembered what happened that night, indeed there are gaps in her memory, especially around that time, that persist to this day. She's tried, she's said many times that she senses there is something most important for her to remember, but she cannot. (Anxiously.) This won't bar me, will it? Not knowing?

Of course not, son. It might be helpful to know, for various reasons, medical, for example. But not to worry. It's what you are that counts. Study and work hard, and if you've the talent, you'll be a Navigator some day. And if not—though your tests show you have the potential—well, the Navigator's Guild takes care of its own. All its own.

But this was Rabelais, that unique world of unlimited freedom. Here the Navigator's Guild took care of its own—if it could.

CHAPTER 5

Jael didn't cut Freighter-master Reis's throat, after all. She even loosened his bonds before she left.

His freighter was old, but lovingly kept up. But one of its flaws was that the galley couldn't brew a decent cup of kaffen. Every time he'd get the plasmaed thing adjusted properly, he'd have to pick up a new supply from another world, with that world's adaptation of the original plant, or worse, a half-native hybrid, or, ultimate horror, a native substitute, and it all had to be done over again. On newer models, there were galleys with miniature anlabs that could add or subtract molecule by molecule, until they built a product to their owner's taste. But such were products of the High-T nucleus worlds, too rare and costly for an old, small-haul freighter. He tasted his second cup, gingerly, frowned, made another minor adjustment to the galley.

"Freighter-master Reis, you bespoke a Navigator at Guildhall." The voice was as cool as when she held his manhood in jeopardy. He turned slowly, looked her up and down as if she were a stranger. In a way she was; he hadn't gotten a good look from his corner seat in Zaqanna's dimness, and the alley had been almost dark. He felt his mouth pursing in a whistle. No wonder Zaqanna, that dealer in flesh, wanted her. Tall and supple and slender yet curved under the tailored uniform. Hair hidden under the billed cap. But the face—her face—yes, Zaqanna had known . . . Not pretty, but beautiful, bone-deep perfection of plane and line and proportion, hard-won character—but not cold, no, not cold; the passion was there, under that duril-hard layer of control, under that touch-me-not air that both challenged and excited.

Whose every move is a challenge, the golden lord had said; Reis, had he heard, would have corrected him—whose every move and expression and feature are a challenge.

Automatically, his left hand went to the pocket holding his lucky piece; he gripped it tightly, its smoothness soft against his work-callused palm. Should he or shouldn't he try once again to recruit her aid? He couldn't flip the artifact under her nose, and he decided, as he so often did, to wait and see. To cover his hesitation, he took a long gulp of the hot kaffen. He choked and grimaced, and one arched brow went up in that smoothly sculptured face. "You've had a trip for nothing, Navigator," he said. "I have no opening."

Her eyes narrowed. "Yet no *Guild* Navigator has recorded accepting your commission."

He glared at her over the mug. What she was accusing him of was dangerous; he could never survive being blacklisted by the Guild. "Navigator." His weariness showed in his voice. "I've had to sell much of my cargo, at a loss, to pay fees and fines. I wait now in hopes of a charter. I cannot afford to pay your Guild's high fees, for one of you to wait with me."

She nodded. It was a desperate gamble, and they both knew it. The longer he waited, the more of his paying cargo would go. And after the cargo, the ship's spare stores. And after them . . .

"I will pass the word of your need about at Guildhall. We Navigators hear much. Perchance we can be of some small service."

"I thank you, Navigator," he said formally. Again he started to refer to what had gone between them the night before, and again he hesitated and finally kept silent.

"It is nothing." A pause. "Perchance, since I am here, you might show me somewhat of your vessel, master. Then, if you should acquire your cargo before I have found a satisfactory berth . . ."

He shrugged. "If you wish. But—favor for favor, Navigator. This is a small ship, and we cannot afford—" The hand with the mug in it gestured toward the double crimson stripe that slashed across her left shoulder. "—afford a class Double-A Navigator."

She shrugged a weary shoulder. "This is a poor world, Low-T, ships are few and most bring their own Navigators. A Double-A might be willing to accept a lesser berth and lesser fee for the chance to find better opportunities elsewhere. Under the proper conditions."

He knew, suddenly, why a Double-A was stranded on this backwater world. On long voyages, female crew members were, as a matter of course, expected to be—compatible. But not this little bundle of duril control. No, sir! Had her captain been fool enough, and besotted enough, to make it an order—which she refused, citing her Navigator's right to privacy?

"I had a fever," she interrupted his thoughts, "and missed my last berth. My record's at the Guildhall. You'll not be able to better it."

"A Double-A." He smiled wryly. "I doubt it. But the time to talk terms is when I have a cargo to haul. May—may I offer you a cup of kaffen before we tour my ship?"

It was a small ship, old but well automated, running on a minimum crew, all of whom took double or triple duties in stride. Not including the needed Navigator, he had six besides himself at present; two of them, the first pilot and the assistant engineer, women.

At the airlock, he warned her. "Don't build any hopes, Navigator. Even if I get a cargo, this is a small ship. Compatibility among the crew is very important."

Her eyebrows went up. "Your crew, master, seemed most competent. Especially your first pilot and that pretty engineer. With a competent crew, I foresee no compatibility problems. But we're demanding a landing berth before we go into hyper. Fare-thee-well, Freighter-master."

Chewing his lip, he watched her move easily across the ill-kept, rutted field until she could hitch a ride on a swaying, rumbling cargo-tub. Then he slammed the port savagely home and returned to the galley for more kaffen.

His second pilot was in the tiny galley, slurping kaffen and munching a sweet bread. "Now that," he announced, licking crumbs off his full lower lip, "is the kind of Navigator I like to ship with."

Master Reis slumped into another extruded seat. "Sorry, Liu. Even if we snaffle this one, she'll insist on Navigator's privacy."

The dismay on the pilot's face would have been amusing, if it hadn't echoed his own feelings so accurately. "Ah, no—no! Reis, you jest. All that lovely, lovely—it goes to waste. Ahhhh—" He couldn't think of a curse vehement enough.

Master Reis nodded glumly. " 'Fraid so."

Liu growled.

"Navigator's privileges." Reis had reminded his pilot of what he needed no reminding of. Ships depended on Navigators. No computer, no matter how advanced, could cope with the eternally varying parameters of hyperspace. But a highly trained, highly talented Navigator could link with a computer and the team of machine calculation and human judgment and intuition could bring a ship safe to port. Usually. But the strain on the human half of the partnership was high, the emotional price extreme. Hence, Navigator's privileges, Navigator's privacy. The strain had to be compensated for somehow. Most Navigators were either sexless or satyrs. The smart captain made sure the Navigator was always happy, even if it meant giving up his or her own personal preferences. Or, alternately, that the Navigator was kept insulated from the rest of the crew, away from the human squabbles, the inevitable stresses and strains of people crowded in close quarters for too-long periods of time.

When you started with the reality that Navigator talent, that knife-accurate intuition, was rare and that Navigator training was long and arduous (and also that most Navigators cracked under the responsibility, sooner or later—luckily, usually on the ground) then you could see why the Navigator's Guild sold its precious product for all the market would stand, and insisted on and received all its rights and privileges.

Every Guildhall had its sad quota of broken Navigators: some held, kicking and screaming, in loving restraint; others who refused, utterly, to navigate again; and still others who simply couldn't be dragged aboard any ship, ever, for any reason.

But the Navigator's Guild, that rope between the stars, was powerful, and even a broken Navigator could rise high. For an unbroken Navigator, a Double-A, even stranded temporarily, the sky was, literally, the limit.

He couldn't keep Liu much longer, either, Reis thought sadly. Liu had come aboard the Scalded Cat originally because of the opportunities for learning the small craft afforded. Now he had served his apprenticeship, and there were better opportunities, aboard bigger ships, waiting. Reis didn't mind, though he would miss Liu. Both men had profited, Reis getting a crewman cheaply, Liu getting the experience he couldn't have gotten near as quickly elsewhere.

Reis's teeth ground against something metallic. He stared, puzzled, into the thick mug. There was something in his cup.

He remembered suddenly, the woman, picking his cup up to sniff disdainfully. Had she put or dropped something in it then?

He knew what it was as soon as he rolled it out into the privacy of his cabin. A Navigator's Personal. Navigators always recorded every move they made aboard ship, so it could be analyzed back at Guildhall. Most simply wore their tiny recorders constantly aboard, editing out the nonessential or personal bits later. In many Navigators, habit was strong enough that they wore their Personals constantly, on ship or shore.

Personal evidence was acceptable in any court of law.

But she didn't have her Personal any more, he did.

Now she had nothing to deny Zaqanna's altered tape.

Maybe her Guild could save her, maybe a minor house on a minor world wouldn't or couldn't bother.

He tossed it up and down, as he so often tossed his lucky piece, lip caught between his teeth; then he stopped and examined it more closely.

Navigators never simply dropped their Personals carelessly in pocket or pouch. They were hung on a chain (no ring or other attachment visible), or sealed to insignia, hatband or the like (no seal or magnetite, either), or carried *inside* something—locket, charm, even cuff links—hollow and habitually worn. Yes! That broken, twisted-together double wire that had also fallen out of the cup. As though a broken catch had been wired temporarily shut—until the wire gave way, too, spilling the container's contents.

Then she wouldn't know where she lost it. He remembered a cool voice in the darkness, interrogating him while immense cold threatened.

Serve the frozen-hearted bitch right if I just tossed it in the disinter and forgot I ever found it. But the disinter shaft was at the end of the corridor and before he reached it, he'd had—as he so often did—second thoughts.

Zaqanna was the real enemy. With him occupied with this, just suppose . . .

Besides, she had come to his ship freely, so maybe the Guild had already squashed Zaqanna. But—suppose not. Suppose they had merely been able to force a trial, under Guild auspices, or worse, local. Then she'd *need* the Personal.

And she who needs must pay.

A very unpleasant smile spread over his face.

CHAPTER 6

Actually, Reis had overestimated Zaqanna. They were waiting when Jael returned to Guildhall.

Zaqanna had edited the tapes most skillfully, actually altering words very rarely, but it all had taken time. And then time to wait for an Adjudicator's Court to open, and to lodge there his complaint. More time to collect a squad of enforcers and march to Guildhall. Still more time there, to argue with the feeble oldster who was Hallmaster.

Jael walked right into the middle of it.

Zaqanna, of course, with his innocent face and husky enforcers; and a dozen or so Navigators: those who preferred to spend shore leave at the Guildhall, and the stranded scaff and raff.

Jael's arrogance and aloofness had won her few friends among her fellows, but Guild honor and privilege were involved. The argument was heated.

"What's all this?" The calm voice cut through the squabbling, and they turned to see her framed in the outer doorway, eyebrows raised in amused incredulity.

The Hallmaster shuffled over, squinting through his nearsighted eyes. "Greetings, sister." Then, angrily, formality over, "Navigator Double-A Jael, you have been accused of suborning a debt-contracted."

She laughed.

"It amuses you, does it." He frowned. "The penalties are high, and you know our custom. Offend against local mores, and there is little we can do."

"You mean"—her voice was husky with anger—"little you will bestir yourself to do. Guildhalls have been removed for less than this shameless false accusation."

The oldster paled, and she controlled a flinch. He was a strandee, one of those who could never bear to go aboard ship again. He could never threaten the local rulers with loss of Guildhall, loss of shipping. And if the locals were aware of this, then she had lost much of her Guild's protection. She wondered if the captain who had left her here had known. Probably he had. Probably he had chosen this world, knowing. The fever had been genuine enough, a common hazard of breathing, eating, drinking the products of world after world.

But most captains would have given her a few days' leeway, instead of grabbing any Navigator they could snatch and taking off.

And—there were drugs that caused fever.

(She had had her revenge already, though she couldn't know it. The Navigator the captain had chosen was a youngster who had cracked once already. A week after lift-off the captain found her swinging gently on a noose in her cabin. The girl had been dead for hours. The captain did what he could; other ships had lost their Navigators from one cause or another and limped safely back to port. But he wasn't so lucky.)

The argument moved into one of the lounges, and Zaqanna was forced into showing the altered holo.

A holo record made while a privacy shield was on. Jael was calmly sardonic; most worlds would not consider that evidence at all.

Zaqanna had an answer. "Only those parts you yourself permitted were recorded."

"I permitted?" The finely arched eyebrows arched even higher. "Strange. I wasn't aware I permitted my privacy broken at all."

Zaqanna smiled, his pale blue eyes glinting. "Here, drunkenness is not held an excuse for contract breaking. Whether you remember or cannot because you were intoxicated—"

"*I was not drunk!*"

"Then there is even less excuse for what you did."

"Be quiet, be quiet." The oldster was querulous. "Let's see if your holo confirms your accusation, groundling. If it does not . . ."

Zaqanna's smile broadened.

The holo started black, just a voice. "Your pardon, mistress. May I break privacy to serve you?" It was a young female voice, high and trembling with nervousness.

"Who—oo is't? Whadaya wan'?" The answering voice was low, slurred—but recognizably Jael's.

"I am Leany. I bring you a second bottle of Mare's Milk, and sweetmeats specially chosen to heighten its flavor. Frosted Driquil nuts, and—"

"I have 'nuff. Go 'way."

"Please, mistress. If you don't wish the second bottle, the sweetmeats are yours, contracted for. Master Zaqanna selected them carefully to complement the Mare's Milk. At least try them. Besides the Driquil nuts, there are—"

"Don' itemize!" The voice sounded far less drunk when angry. Then a heavy sigh. "Aw ri', aw ri'. Bring'm in." A mutter, of which the only distinguishable word was "privacy."

"I have your permission," the young voice insisted.

"Ye', ye'." Impatient. "Bring'n your local whassits, girl, for Mother's sake, an' stop *dribblin'!*"

The holo appeared, showing the inside of the niche. It could have been made of native natural materials or cheap imported synthi; the details were lost under a coating of grime and abuse.

The two long seats were padded, fairly new cushions striped a vivid orange and crimson, and long enough to seat four or even five or six crowded together. Jael was sprawled on one of the benches, upper body raised on one casual elbow, one leg swinging idly over the side. There were few physical evidences of her private debauch: a sheen of sweat on her forehead, the short mane of tawny-and-dark tiger-striped hair tousled, possibly by the removal of her cap; the high tunic collar opened and her lower legs and feet bared by the removal of her lined ankle boots (carelessly kicked under the table) and trouser legs unseamed to the knee. (Her revealed bare feet were noticeably non T-norm. Long and slender and delicately boned like the rest of her, they were also obviously prehensile, ending in four finger-length, equally opposable toes. At the bottom of occasional swings, the leg stopped long enough for the finger-toes to bend around and scratch busily behind the ankle.)

The serving wench was short but buxom. (Imported drugs ensured the latter.) Her knee-length hair (more drugs) of brassy yellow (local dye) swung free, and her other wares were coarsely flaunted in a costume that consisted mostly of small patches of thin crimson material tied precariously together over a black fishnet body stocking through which her white skin gleamed even whiter. Her high spiked heels were matching crimson, as was the heart-shaped patch by her mouth.

"Privacy," Jael's voice snorted in the dimness of the lounge.

"You gave permission," Zaqanna answered smoothly.

". . . serve you," the wench was saying. "May I adjust your table's height? Is there anything else you desire? I am yours to command. May I—"

"Puddown tray 'n go."

Zaqanna rotated the holo slightly, so that both the quarter-life-size figures could be clearly seen. When the waitress leaned over to put the tray down, there was a chorus of amused comment from the audience. Her top had been artfully designed to gape open as she moved.

"Oh!" Something fell under the table and the girl fished for it, giving her audience flashes of full buttocks clad only in coarse-meshed black net.

"Leave't, girl." Jael sounded more amused than irritated by the performance. "Better still—jus' *leave*."

The girl rose, panting slightly, full breasts straining against the thin material. "Mistress, can I not serve you? I am well trained, and most inventive. Anything you desire . . ."

"*Any*thing," Jael drawled, with a cutting undertone of mockery.

"Anything." The girl nodded eagerly. She took a couple of steps toward Jael in the narrow aisle between table and bench, hips swinging more than the spiked heels could account for. "Whatever you wish, mistress, whatever. Truly, I can give you such—" Her voice pleaded with an undernote of fear.

"Enough!" Jael snapped. "Stop 'miliatin' yourself, girl—if you got 'nuff spirit lef' to be 'miliated. I don' wan' you, or that tawdry 'scuse for pleasure you offer. Say I 'gain, for the las' time—*go!*"

"Please, please, *please.*" Voice and girl alike trembled. "Would you prefer a boy? Zaqanna has a pair, one golden as spring sunshine, one black as—"

Jael was obviously sobering rapidly. She sat upright. "No, I don' wan' a boy, either, curse you!"

"A man. A man, then," the girl babbled. "Zaqanna would be most pleased to himself—"

"I wager he would!" Jael snapped to her feet, to stand, trouser legs flapping, bare feet straddled, weight equally balanced on the balls of those prehensile feet, hands hanging loosely. Drunk or sober, it was a trained fighter's stance, and reeked of danger and hair-trigger temper.

Desperation blinded the girl to her peril. "Perhaps you prefer to watch." Her words ran over each other in her haste. "Zaqanna can arrange that, too. But to speak your pleasure—"

"My—*pleasure*—is that you leave before I—break—your—neck!"

The girl shuddered. "Better that than what *he* will do to me," she said simply.

The fight drained out of Jael. "I am a *woman,*" she said bluntly. "Surely that animal cannot expect—"

The girl hugged herself and shuddered. "He accepts *no* excuses. And—and there are those who will—who will contract to participate in one of Zaqanna's punishments. And more who will—want to watch . . ." She held out her hands, trembling. "Please, mistress. Something. Anything . . ."

Jael smashed a fist into her other palm, then spread her own hands out wide. "Will it satisfy him," she asked, "for me to pay 'ported liquor prices for a glass of colored water for you, plus some reas'n'ble fee, for your *time,* to—to converse with me, when you might be servin' others?"

The girl licked crimson lips uncertainly. "I—I don't know. I'll have to ask."

"Best 'ask' firmly." Jael shrugged and turned away. Over her shoulder she added, "I'll not pay for the use of bought unwillin' bodies, yours or anyone else's. Not *ever*."

"But I'm willing, I'm willing. Whatever, truly, mistress . . ."

Jael spat contemptuously. "Bought, I said. Be silent, or I pay for what I used 'n go, 'n you can settle with your black-livered master however you can."

"Oh, no, mistress. I'll be back shortly." The girl disappeared through the misty barrier that should have meant a complete privacy shield and was instead only a flimsy translucent light curtain.

Jael stared after her for long seconds, face blank, eyes narrow. Then she reached down and drained what was left of the Mare's Milk in the opened bottle in one long swallow, throat working to force the thick liquid down.

"By the Turning Wheel!" Someone in the audience paid tribute to the feat.

The empty bottle slid out of her hand, landing on the floor with a soft *thunk*. Then, with a low moan, Jael slumped onto the bench, face buried in her hands, arched, trembling back eloquent of anguish and despair.

The girl was soon back. "Permission to reenter," her voice came softly.

Instantly, Jael was erect, the cynical observer, the cold, controlled Navigator again. "Permission granted."

The girl set her tray on the table and said with a giggle, one conspirator to another, "He's overfee'd you so much for my drink, he daren't charge for my time, too. But I can't stay too long."

"Good."

The girl plopped herself down on the other bench and sighed. "Even a few minutes' peace . . ." Jael snorted. "Say, tell me, mistress, if I may be permitted to ask, how did you get to be a Navigator, anyway? A woman, I mean." The girl stretched luxuriously. "Isn't that unusual?"

"Out here, perhaps." Jael sounded abstracted. "In the Nucleus, there are roughly as many female Navigators as male. Navigator talent is rare enough; they can't afford to pass up any potentials, especially for something as irrelevant as sex."

"Irrelevant," the girl snorted in turn and sipped her drink, making a face. "At least he could put some sweetener in it. You'll not find sex irrelevant *here,* I can tell you." Jael shrugged, letting the younger girl lead the conversation. "But, truly, mistress, how did you become a star-finder? I've heard it's very difficult, and takes many years' training, and some rare skills."

"Um-hum." Jael cracked open the second bottle.

"And were you contracted young? Did your parents contract for you? How—"

"Girl." Jael's mouth twisted, there was an edge to her voice more than the questions warranted. "I'll not pay Zaqanna's robber's prices for the time it takes to tell my tale."

"Do you think *I* could become a Navigator like you? Do you think—"

"No." Uncompromising.

"I would do anything, anything to be free of Zaqanna, mistress!"

"Sounds to me"—it was impossible to tell which of the younger Navigators was speaking—"as if Zaqanna's debt-whatever-you-call-her was trying to suborn the Navigator."

Zaqanna wished he could have edited that portion of the tape more; but it wasn't the significant part.

"Girl," Jael was saying, "I'm not even sure this Guildhall *has* testing equipment. They all should, but—" A shrug. "But if they do recruit, *anybody* has the right to take the tests. Anybody. If you're not allowed any time to yourself, the Guild will *pay* for the time testing takes."

Leany made a face. "Zaqanna has to know."

" 'Fraid so. The Guild has to be very careful."

Leany thought it over, chewing her lip. "I'd better not. He'd be so angry at my trying to escape him, that if I failed . . ."

"Why should he be angry? The Guild will pay him, or fee him, or contract with him, whatever you call it on this world, for you, if you score high enough on the tests. They don't haggle, either. They won't accept someone whose obligations can't be cleared away, but they're always willing to risk a generous amount for a potential Navigator."

"Is that how you—"

"No, as it happened. I—I navigated a yacht safely to a Guild port by myself. More luck than anything else, it was, but in such a case they don't bother with testing." (A planet-buyer's private yacht, fully automated, sybaritic luxury marred only by browning stains that were a constant reminder.) "Just as well, if they had, I'd be dead. Well, personality stripped, it amounts to the same thing. Laws! A world can have too many laws, as well as too few." A feral grin. "Though with too many, there's always the chance of a technicality, a loophole." A snort. "The Guild lawyer proved I was underage, and the Guild stood guardian for me. And I've been a Guildswoman ever since." (I *might* have made it myself; Mother knows, I'd just escaped from a far worse cage than a civilized world's jail. . . .)

"I'd just be changing one master for another." Leany bit her lip. "And Zaqanna's anger . . ."

"Like that, is he. Best not try, if you're that afraid. But—no risk, no gain. And Guild life isn't slavery—whatever you call it here—or even close. Oh, there are rules, but they apply equally to all Guild members, and most of them act in your favor. You have to pay back the cost of your training, and whatever obligations they took care of for you; but Guild fees are generous, it doesn't take long. And after that, you're free, or as free as anyone can be, in this best of all possible universes."

"Free of Zaqanna," the girl murmured.

"If you enter training and fail," Jael went on, "you still have to pay back what you owe, but the Guild will find you a useful place. It just takes longer to pay back, that's all."

"I'm afraid." The girl shivered. "I can't take the tests, I don't dare . . . if the Guild wouldn't protect me, if I failed the tests . . . I'm not very smart . . . only . . ." She wept, a child's easy tears. "I can't stand it, I can't, I can't!" She grabbed Jael's wrists, the tears streaking her makeup into a red-and-black clown's mask. "Please help me, please, please, for pity's sake, for whatever you hold sacred, help me out of this trap!"

Jael slapped her face, lightly. "Calm yourself!" The sniffles damped down. "Now, girl, I'll help you if I can." Here Zaqanna had made a cut. Jael had gone on, ". . . without breaking these contracts your world holds so sacred. I'll not place myself in jeopardy beside you."

"Oh, thank you, mistress, thank you!" Leany caught Jael's hand, covered it with tears and kisses.

"A little less water," Jael commanded. "Now, tell me. What is your situation here? How did you come to this place?"

CHAPTER 7

It was a commonplace, sordid little tale, old as the human race. Leany, pampered only daughter of a small-time merchant, had led a very sheltered life. Then—she met a young man. "My parents disapproved of him, so we met secretly." She was seduced by his glamour, his aura of sophistication as much as by his charm and good looks. They ran away together. "We hadn't any choice; my parents were about to contract me to someone else."

Leany's cavalier seemed to have powerful contracts. They wound up in a coastal pleasure city, in a suite in a luxurious hotel. He gave her—on promissory contracts, it turned out later—clothes, jewels, furs, expensive offworld imports. It had been heaven.

Until one day Lucifer disappeared, with all the portable goods, leaving behind a pile of unfulfilled contracts and a frightened girl with a single contract, worse than worthless because it obligated her for all the others.

Her parents were half a primitive continent away, and her father rarely had anything to spare, making just enough from his small, short-term contracting to keep his family.

So she offered the only valuable she had, herself.

To her surprise (but Jael only nodded grimly) her contract had been sold, not to one of the luxury hotels as a potential hostess, but to a caravan owner. Of course, in the days before the caravan left, she was constantly being rented to the highest bidders. It was her first experience with perversion and sadism, and it was a sickened, terrified girl who was caravanned farther and farther away from her parents.

"And they charged me with all kinds of brokerage fees for drawing up the new contract and consolidating the others into it and then re-contracting me to the caravan owner. But all the fees I must have earned in that horrible place—they were never taken off. I don't even know who received them. I didn't even realize they should have been taken off, that they hadn't been. I didn't know anything, I—"

The tale went on and on. Zaqanna was the third holder of her contract, and the most brutal.

"Let me see if I have all this straight," Jael summed up. "You're legally—" Leany made a noise. "All right, no laws, not legally. You *are* a debt-contracted. You're obligated for many more years' standard labor than you could possibly live." Leany nodded. "But Zaqanna could reassign your contract, if he chooses, for whatever value is acceptable to him."

"Don't even ask. He won't reassign, he says it's too much trouble breaking in new women. He says he'll reassign when *he* chooses, and I'd better make sure he doesn't choose for a long, long time, because the best contract offers around here are from the specialty houses. I'd kill myself before I'd go to one of them, only they won't let you kill yourself, they—"

"So he keeps you in line with that threat, does he?" Her tone promised Zaqanna much, none of it pleasant. "But you're a debt-contracted, so if someone pays—comes up with a contract worth more than your debt, Zaqanna has to accept it and release your contract, right?"

"Unless he's contracted for more than the worth of the original debt himself. Then you have to fulfill both, the original and the difference. And—Zaqanna's added a rider to my contract. You see, each year a c'holder holds a debt-contracted's contract, they're supposed to subtract a standard year's earnings—or more, if they feel that that contracted has been worth more—from the total of the debt. But Zaqanna claims that my living expenses— what I eat and wear and my living space—are worth more than what I earn. So each year—I owe *more*. And if I get pregnant"— tears smeared the painted mask even further—"he'll own them, too. And I know he'll somehow arrange it—I don't know how—I'll owe and owe and *owe*. . . ."

"Sweet." Jael ignored the tears. "Well, then, girl, let's see what we can do." This was where Zaqanna had done the most editing. He cut out all Jael's careful qualifiers, made her promise to "rescue" Leany no matter what, turned her bitter curses into threats against himself, and put anti-contract and general anarchy into her mouth.

In the end, Jael had promised to meet Leany in an alley behind the bar, to "talk some more."

"And did I return, master of falsehoods? Was I in the alley at dawn?"

(How disappointed he had been when she hadn't appeared; he had hoped for more damaging admissions. But he had decided he had had enough—including the satisfaction of a punishment ar-

ranged for Leany, with several of his patrons eagerly participating
—to show for his time. The altered tape would condemn Jael.)

He opened his mouth to say that Jael had come to the alley—
Leany would lie on his order—but something in her tone stopped
him. If she had, through luck or guile, an unbreakable alibi for
that time, a proved lie or faked tape would tear his whole case
apart.

"No." His voice was smooth. "You disappointed Leany—"

"Or you," she interpolated smoothly.

"Leany," he repeated, "whom I have already punished for her
disobedience. No doubt you were—ah—unavoidably detained." His
tone implied, "drunk under a table somewhere."

Jael, remembering a dim alley and a furious man interrogated
under dire threat, smiled thinly. The smile confirmed Zaqanna's
belief that she had an alibi, that he had narrowly avoided ruining
himself.

"It matters little, though," Zaqanna went on. "The damage to
the contracted has occurred. The evidence here is irrefutable." He
tapped the holo case. "Your Navigator has condemned herself,
utterly."

"False, altered evidence," Jael snapped, "and I can prove it!"
Everyone stared at her. "I was wearing my Personal. It will show
what truly occurred."

Zaqanna paled, then congratulated himself on his foresight.
He had arranged for the psycher as a precaution for the formal
judgment; he would have the man ready this very night! (Though
how he hated to have his mind tampered with!) Even if the
woman knew enough to demand that her evidence be formalized
before an adjudicator, and demand it *now,* he had plenty of
under-the-table contracts. The second deposition of evidence
would be delayed a day or two, however long it took, until he was
ready. The woman's Personal would do her no good, no good
whatsoever.

But Jael had jerked off her chain, to stare in horror at the single
dangling ident. "But my Personal was on—" she gasped.

Zaqanna smiled inwardly. So the sessions with the psycher
would be unnecessary, after all. He had a fine memory for detail,
and he remembered the chain, empty except for the glittering
ident.

"In a pocket, sister," one of the Navigators suggested.

"No, I always—" She frowned, but began systematically probing
them anyway.

"Perhaps"—the Guildmaster quavered—"you forgot to put it on when you left for a—ahhhhh—for a night out, sister."

"I'm sure I had it on," Jael asserted stubbornly. "I always wear it. I—" She stared at the chain fiercely, as though her need would make the missing Personal suddenly appear. She searched her pockets again, and the magneclosures on her wide belt, piling the contents of all on a small table. Her sleeves were rolled up to the elbow; she rolled them back down (Zaqanna had already noted the large ankh cuff links on the table) and unseamed the front of her tunic and removed it. When vigorous shaking produced nothing, she began a meticulous, muttering, inch-by-inch inspection of the inside.

Underneath, she was wearing only a thin stretchy top. Zaqanna's eyes roamed happily. The merchandise-to-be was *prime*. (And no need to ruin that delicately symmetrical perfection with the drugs, either. This was connoisseur's fare, at least for a while. Not like Leany or the other bar-wenches. He'd dress her in opaque but thin materials. Lots of draperies, but clinging here and there to the curves suggestively as she moved. That was the way, with this one. Not everything out on display, leave the client the pleasure of anticipation, of unwrapping his new delight slowly. . . . And he himself would have to test her paces, to be sure that he used her in the most advantageous manner. . . .) His tongue came out to wet his full lower lip, leaving it pink and glistening.

Jael caught him appraising. Their eyes held until, with an angry gasp, she jerked the tunic back around herself. "I don't need the Personal." She bit the words out individually. "That tape has been altered. I demand to be psyched. A psycher will prove—"

"But you can't expect to remember precisely what you said," the oldster reminded her. "That's why psycher evidence isn't called if recordings are available."

"But . . ." She turned, hands spread wide in appeal, to her fellow Navigators. "Don't you understand? I have Navigator's Syndrome. I would never risk offending locals. I would never risk —*I can't stand being closed in!*"

The other Navigators nodded. Claustrophobia, usually mild, was common among Navigators. The mind rejected their awesome responsibility, connected it with the ships they guided, where the quarters were often cramped and small. Navigators lived balanced on the knife-edge of sanity—and sometimes one of them fell off.

"I'm sorry," rumbled the burly, grizzled chief of the enforcers, offworld dissonance pistol holstered on his right hip, shortsword tilted for easy cross-draw on his left. "But I have a warrant, and you've shown no evidence to contradict it. I regret, Lady Navigator, but you must come with me."

"No." She backed away until she was stopped by the wall. She pressed herself against it, hands flung away from her body, fingers spread wide, as though she would grow roots to fix herself there forever. "No! To be *locked up!* Never!"

Zaqanna licked his lips again. Such a lovely panic reaction, so easily triggered. He had clients who would consider such an added fillip, spice to their pleasure. Then he looked again. She was trembling, eyes wide and blank, a sheen of sweat on her smooth forehead. The hearing was set for several days away, and she might well break enclosed in a cell for that space of time. And why waste her breaking, when it would be worth much to the proper client. He pulled the chief enforcer's head down, whispered in his ear.

"No!" the man exploded.

"But I'm sure the Guild would stand surety." Zaqanna's voice was synthi-smooth, and would have warned anybody less senile than the oldster.

"Of course," he sneered, insulted.

"So, then." Zaqanna smiled at the chief enforcer. "You have your orders. I am the offended party, and if I am satisfied with lesser measures, you may not quibble."

The man pulled himself up to his full, considerable height. "I take orders from the Palace of Contractual Magistrates, not from *you.*"

"You would disturb Chief Adjudicator Lyhunt at his deliberations for something so trivial? Well, it's your back, man. But I'll tell you what he'll say. He'll say the choice is mine, since the offense is against me."

The grizzled peaceman glared down at him, knowing that he spoke truth. Especially if Zaqanna (he added "the slimy" in his thoughts, having known him from other occasions) had a chance to "trim the adjudicator's quill" before that worthy passed down his fiat. "I have none with me."

"Then we will wait while you have them fetched."

The chief enforcer growled under his breath, then glanced at Jael, now well guarded by several of her fellows. She was still crucified against the wall, cap askew, hair plastered in sweat wisps to her face, breathing in panic gasps. He felt a surge of pity, knowing she wouldn't last an hour in one of the tower's cramped, fetid cells, much less the long wait until the hearing. But whether sly Zaqanna's alternative was any kinder . . .

A jerk of his head brought one of his squad to his side; a quick order sent the man scurrying off.

Zaqanna didn't intend to have his property-to-be damage itself. He moved toward Jael, surrounded by angry Navigators. "Calm yourself, my dear," he cooed. "There will be no cell."

"What do you mean?" snapped one of the Navigators, a tall, wraith-thin albino with angry pink eyes.

"I have made arrangements," Zaqanna said. "There will be no cell."

Jael collapsed into a chair, face buried in arms, shoulders shaking uncontrollably, but the albino continued to glare suspiciously at Zaqanna. "What do you mean?"

"Normally, with the evidence so strong, a cell in the tower would be mandatory." Jael shuddered, and he patted her shoulder, his hand lingering. "But a Navigator is special, above certain tawdry suspicions. And, besides"—the hand moved slowly over the shaking shoulder—"I couldn't bear to waste such loveliness . . . in a cell. . . ."

Jael looked up, eyes dark with sheer hate. "No!"

"My dear, my dear," he chided gently, chortling inside in gloating anticipation. "You will be free to stay here with your friends, if you wish. I want you to understand, that though my honor, my contractual duty demanded"—the chief enforcer snorted—"demanded certain acts, still, personally . . ." His hand cupped her chin, caressing, and she jerked it angrily away. "For you, nonetheless, my doors are always opened." (The enforcer's eyes opened, too, in sudden comprehension. That poor woman!)

"Tsha!"

Zaqanna smiled. "You have many days, my dear, to change your mind."

The messenger arrived a few minutes later, with a pair of gaudy metal loops. The chief enforcer approached Jael, who shrank back against the tall albino. The enforcer knelt. "Lady, you must," he said gently. "Give me your hand." She licked her lips, shrank further back. "Lady Navigator," his voice was firm, "it is this—or the cell."

Hesitantly she extended her right arm, the partially rolled-up sleeves exposing a delicately boned wrist and the lower part of her sleek forearm. He slid one of the metal loops around it, a wide band striped in raucous crimson and jet, and adjusted it. "Not tight, not uncomfortable?" he asked, and she shook her head. "Yes," he nodded, "it moves freely. Do not try to take it off, lady, it can be removed only with the proper equipment. If you try, you will die, and these your friends who stand surety for you will be contract-breakers in their turn, and gravely punished. Do you understand?"

She seemed dazed. "My friends . . ."

He nodded. "Your friends stand surety that you appear before the lord contract judge's throne. This is a reminder merely, but it must not be removed. There is an explosive in it, to prevent its removal. Keep it on all the time, do you understand?"

"Explosive . . ." There was a glint in her eye.

"Your friends stand surety," he reminded roughly. "*Your friends.* . . ." He rose. "Tavern-master, shall I wear the other. . . ." But Zaqanna, with a smile, held out his own wrist, and continued to smile and hold out his wrist until the peaceman, sighing, put on it a similar loop, striped gold and jet.

"As long as the two bracelets are close together," the enforcer spoke loudly, to no one in particular, "the reminder will not bother the accused. Attempt to escape, to leave"—he would not look at Jael—"and it will begin to pain. The farther apart, the worse the pain. Do you understand?" A pause. "Lady Navigator, do you understand?"

Numbly, head bowed, she muttered assent.

"My duties are complete." He spoke stiffly to Zaqanna. "If I may be excused."

"Of course. I will commend you to the Lord Contract Magistrates' Court for your devotion to your contractual duty."

The sound of the squad's feet was still echoing when Zaqanna bowed to Jael and said, "With your permission, Navigator, I will be going also. Just remember what I said—for you, my door is always open." When Jael remained stubbornly silent, he bowed again. "Until we meet again, then," he murmured and turned and glided easily out the door.

"Animal," the young albino spat after him.

Opposition unites even the most disparate of individuals, and despite their differences, the Navigators had a strong esprit de corps. The council war had lasted perhaps ten minutes when Jael gasped, "My wrist! It's starting to hurt. My *arm*—"

"But you haven't run, you've stayed right here," the albino objected.

"I haven't moved"—knowledge was bitter in her eyes—"but Zaqanna is moving away from *me*."

CHAPTER 8

"You're crazy, Ryker, you know that." The yellow-haired girl Leany was trying to repair the damage to the man in gray's face some hours after his encounter with the "between-the-lines" gang.

He put a finger into his mouth, wriggled a tooth and, with a slight wince, pulled it out and tossed it onto the floor.

" 'Tract you," she screeched at him, "don't you muck up my carpet." It was, or had been once, a lovely thing, handmade, a pattern whose elegant interweaving of unicorn and nymph, willow grove and satyr went back into antiquity. Now it was faded and worn, stained in a dozen places by dirt, food, blood, and others unidentifiable.

"If you want me to leave . . ." He shrugged and started to get up. He had been lying on her bed while she swabbed at his blood-smeared features with a wet rag, but when she jumped to pick up the bleeding tooth, she left him room to get up and he used it, sitting up and sliding his long legs over the bed heaped with bedraggled furs and quilts.

"Zaqanna wants you available," she spat at him.

"Does he?" A shrug. "Another dirty, eh?" Again the one shoulder moved in a weary shrug. "All right. Where am I to wait?"

Her mouth curled. "Here's as good a place as any." It wasn't an invitation, and both knew it. Zaqanna had been willing to assign Ryker a room of his own in the complex above and behind the bar, or even in the much more luxurious rooms that catered to the most powerful of the c'holders. But Ryker simply shrugged and walked away from any room that had been offered. If he wanted to sleep, he simply lay down wherever he was, as long as he was out of people's way. Sometimes a storeroom, sometimes an alley, or any empty room that was handy. So "Ryker's" room had remained an unused waste, with nothing inside but the minimal furniture Zaqanna had provided, and used only when Ryker happened to be tired and in the vicinity, and even then he was as likely as not to curl up on a crate downstairs or even in an empty booth. So the room that had been Ryker's became simply another of Zaqanna's rooms.

Leany had tried her talent on him, as she tried on any who might possibly be useful to her someday. Ryker was immune, though. Not that he passed up her offer. But it was as if any simple bodily appetite were totally unimportant to him. He ate, if somebody shoved a tray of food in front of him and told him to eat it; and he used Leany, or any of the others, if she offered, in the same impersonal manner. To Leany, it was the ultimate insult. That a man might use her as he'd pick up a rag to wipe his nose on. Necessary, for that instant, then tossed aside and forgotten. She had only one weapon available, and she wielded it mercilessly.

"Want some of your Elysium?" she sneered sweetly. "Can't have any of it now, Zaqanna wants you *available.*"

As usual, the weapon slid as if blunted over his imperturbability. "It isn't time. And if it were time, all the Zaqannas on this miserable dungheap of a world couldn't stop me." It was said with the same impassive emptiness of all his words, but Leany knew from experience how true it was.

She gave him a slow, animal smile. "Aren't you ever tempted to take it sooner?" Zaqanna used drugs—occasionally—to keep his contracteds in line. If necessary, of course, if the contract wasn't enough in itself—he wasn't wasteful. He collected new victims with drugs, likewise, rarely, but he didn't like to. A vacuumhead wasn't reliable, he'd said. And it was true, where the drug became the be-all and end-all—

Ryker was the exception. He rationed himself. Zaqanna had large supplies of Ryker's Elysium—cut to almost innocuousness, it made a pleasant, safe buzz, though most people preferred something stronger . . . and safer. Zaqanna didn't even bother to be careful of the drug in its uncut state; his clients and contracteds were acutely aware of the danger, and Ryker controlled his craving. Fanatically. Now he drawled what he had said often before. "You know the answer to that, woman." He didn't even sound impatient.

"What difference does time make? If you have to have it, you have to have it."

"I don't 'have' "—he put the word in quotes—"to have it. I am not physically addicted."

"But you want it, don't you?" Her voice was a mellifluous coo. ". . . want it so bad you'll do anything for it. Isn't that the same thing?" He'd never opened up quite this way or this far before. She wasn't curious, and she didn't care for anybody but herself. Still, knowledge was power. And she needed every little grain she could get.

"No." His voice was still unhumanly monotone. "No, I won't do anything." Again a shrug that was an almost imperceptible move of one hollow shoulder. "What you people do to each other —I couldn't care less."

"Even me." Her voice sulked.

"Girl, you give me something you regard as trash, don't expect me to value it any higher."

Her lush lower lip stuck out. "Some people do." Which was true. She was often in demand. As far as Zaqanna favored any of his contracteds, he favored her—and would continue to, as long as she remained in demand.

Ryker sat up on the bed piled high with the most sensuous of furs and synthetics, sprinkled religiously each morning with musk and subtle incenses. "You've hooked another one, haven't you."

She smiled, her pink tongue darting out to wet her lower lip.

His mouth twisted and then smoothed back to its usual controlled line. "What would you do if one of them manages to take you off? I wonder. Pulls you out of this cozy nest and into the real universe?"

She licked her lip again. "Nobody beats Zaqanna."

"Somebody might, someday."

"I'm not worried." Then, remembering that Zaqanna had wanted Ryker "available": "When did you eat last?"

He rose to his feet, swaying slightly. "I don't remember."

"Come on then. Pipi will still be on duty in the kitchen."

"All right." He absentmindedly pulled on the torn tunic of offworld synthetic, and she sighed, knowing she or one of the other girls would have to mend it eventually. In some ways he was worse than a child. A child would at least say when it was hungry, complain of cold and ask to have clothing mended or replaced. Ryker simply walked through the hours of his life, existing until the time when he allowed himself his one anodyne.

Or was it an anodyne? She had asked Zaqanna once what it was like, and the man had only shrugged. "Deadly," he had said.

Then, "Don't you touch it." She had known better than to make
the obvious comment, that Ryker hadn't died, but Zaqanna saw it
in her eyes. "Take a single grain"—he made the threat in the dry
voice that was Zaqanna at his most menacing—"and I'll assign
your contract before you come back down. It is deadly. And po-
tently addictive. Ryker—I don't know how he manages it. They
say it's an experience that makes life itself seem like a drab nothing. Elysium is so unendurably beautiful that the user can never
stand coming down from his high. So he takes it constantly, burns
his body out. All but Ryker, who controls it, c'breaker knows
how. You've seen for yourself, though, it's left him nothing to live
life with. Nothing is important to him but the next dose. So I'm
warning you, 'tracted. Taste this particular forbidden fruit, and be
reassigned. And you know where."

She hadn't had to be warned twice. Zaqanna never made empty
threats.

Leany and Ryker were still in the heat of the kitchen when
Zaqanna finally returned, oozing smug satisfaction like a cat with
cream *and* yellow feathers still on his chops. Ryker wouldn't move
until somebody pushed him, and Leany knew that as long as she
was at least appearing to baby-sit the offworlder with the important talent, she probably wouldn't be ordered to any more dis-
tasteful duties.

Zaqanna dropped onto one of the chipped but sturdy wooden
benches—nobody needed to be impressed *here*—with a contented
sigh. Leany, without waiting to be ordered, scurried over to the
large hearth-oven where a simple vegetable stew was kept warm
continuously, and spooned a generous portion out onto a large
plate, plonked it in front of Zaqanna and added a tall mug of
golden pale.

Zaqanna tucked in hungrily, wiping his chin at intervals on his
sleeve. Only when the plate was almost empty did he slow down,
chewing thoughtfully, eyes narrowed and staring at Ryker, who
was sitting with long legs asprawl on another bench and gazing, as
he so often seemed to, at nothing in particular. "I won't need him
for now, but keep tabs on him until I say different, just in case."

Ryker didn't even blink. It was Leany who asked, "Why?"

Zaqanna took a small bite and savored it slowly. "Pipi can do
better than this." He spoke as to himself, and Leany flinched.
Then, going on, speaking his thoughts aloud as he sometimes did,
because, after all, contracteds weren't people, just things, and

Ryker didn't care, would forget anything but his own private purgatory/paradise in seconds. "I thought I'd need more proof. Now I'm not so sure. I dislike having him—but I daren't be caught short. Keep him ready. Don't let him have any of the Elysium."

Ryker's head came up. "I'll take it when the time comes."

"You signed a contract."

"Read it again, dunghiller. You to supply the Elysium, I to have it at stated intervals. I'm due tomorrow. I'll take it tomorrow." He didn't add, Or else. He didn't have to. He had learned about this world, all its peculiarities, before coming. He knew exactly what he was saying. There was only one thing important in his life, and he would have it. Not Zaqanna nor his whole world could stop him.

Zaqanna shrugged, recognizing an immovable object. "I doubt I'll need him. . . ." Then, to Leany, "Last night, was she wearing any kind of recorder, did you notice?"

Leany shrugged. "Offworlder magics? How would I know?"

"What was she wearing?"

"Clothing. She'd taken her shoes and cap and outer tunic off, she had her insignia and a glittery bauble on a chain around her neck. I doubt she was wearing anything beneath the undertunic, and her sleeves and pants legs were partly unseamed. If she had something in a pants pocket I might not have noticed it, but otherwise—"

"The bauble on the chain was her ident. Nothing else with it?"

"That I saw."

"Yes, that's how I remember it. But she might have had it in a pocket, it might have been on. I'll not feel secure until it's found." His lips pursed. "Perhaps I'll have a word with the c'holder contracted to keep the Guildhall clean. And—pass this word, Leany. Ten years' standard off the contract of whoever brings me the Navigator's Personal. And a year off to whoever tells that person about it."

Her eyes gleamed. She'd go search the booth first— "What does it look like?"

He grimaced. "Offworlder bauble. Small. Doubtless with the emblem of the Guild on it." A pointing finger with a coil of wire wrapped around it.

"Navigator," Ryker drawled, as some of what they were saying had penetrated. "You're reaching high this time, dunghiller. The Navigators' Guild protects its own."

Zaqanna smiled. "The reward will be high, offworlder. And"—a sneer—"I'll see you get your share."

Ryker shrugged, eyes turning inward again. "I get what I want regardless. Always."

Zaqanna was thinking aloud again. "It'll be a fairish wait until the adjudication. I won't bother with your skills until after you've recovered from the Elysium. Then—*if* the Personal hasn't turned up—I'd best make absolutely sure."

Ryker didn't even bother to shrug.

"Mind-meddler," Zaqanna growled in disgust. "Does it give you a sense of power, to lay your fingers in other people's thoughts? Like those who contract for my Arena rooms, who like to see and not be seen?"

For once Ryker responded to a taunt, his voice its usual unvarying monotone. "The word you want is voyeur, dunghiller. And no, I've seen rot like what's in your mind too many times to be amused, amazed, insulted or even interested."

"We understand each other." Zaqanna stood up, spine stiff, head thrown back.

"I understand you." And Ryker withdrew into his solitary world.

CHAPTER 9

It didn't take the Navigators long to figure it all out. The port and its satellites *sprawled*. But the old, pre-Rediscovery town, crowded for safety within its high-walled citadel, was compact. Even when population pressure had forced the inhabitants out, the habit of building high and close had remained. There were no distances within the city proper to compare with the vast port. And Zaqanna's tavern was on the far end of the sprawl from the Guildhall. Jael, unfortunately, was young and healthy and enjoyed walking.

"You'll have to get a room near the tavern," the albino suggested finally. "If you're close enough to him, it won't bother you."

"It's still getting worse," she gasped. "I can't stay here!" She fled blindly through the door.

"We'll go with you, find a place for you to stay." The albino was right behind her.

But there were no rooms, close enough, available. Zaqanna had passed the word.

Even if they could have gotten it, a room wouldn't have been much help. Zaqanna was a very busy man. He delivered delicacies, in person, to various c'holders; he visited space-cargo warehouses from one end of the port to the other; he personally selected goods from the various farmers' marts, the contracteds' exchanges, numerous scattered wholesalers. And sooner or later, the invisible leash that joined them would grow unbearable, and Jael would trudge on until it eased—until he moved again, tugging her behind him like an overlong tail of a kite buffeted by the winds.

So Jael walked the streets. Her fellow Navigators stayed with her in shifts. They soon realized that the enforcers had been ordered to watch out for them. If they stopped in a doorway or alley mouth or blind corner merely to lean against a wall, sooner or later, usually sooner, an enforcer came along. "Move along, move along now, no loitering." If their eyes held furtive pity instead of sadistic glee, their voices were firm; they had their orders.

The Navigators learned to linger long over their meals, or cups of the local brew, but soon the sight of an enforcer was enough to make Jael lurch to her feet, flinging Guild chits carelessly toward the table as she fled, her honor guard scurrying to catch up with her.

The albino broke. He went to Zaqanna, offered him any fee he would name for a room in the Gilded Cage, a period of rest. Zaqanna laughed. He was pleased at her endurance. The longer she held out, the longer m'lord c'holder's games with her could be expected to last, and the greater his own gains. And there were others showing interest in the offworld woman, too; he was anticipating more and more being able to combine pleasure with a windfall harvest.

He told the albino he couldn't take a fee from any of the Guild without prejudicing his case. But, he said, smiling broadly, he admired the lady personally. She was welcome to share his room with him—anytime. He laughed softly, triumphantly, slyly. The boy—despite his height he was young, barely out of training—stormed out, cursing.

Only once did the enforcers' hazing run into a hitch.

Threading his heavy-booted way through tables toward the

Navigators, a burly enforcer tripped over the outstretched paw of a hunting z'par, curled bonelessly at its master's feet. The beast howled, and so did its master, springing to his feet and shaking the hapless enforcer until his sword rattled in its sheath.

"Clumsy clod! If you've harmed Nemesis, I'll have your hide for a rug and your empty skull for a goblet. You—"

Jael and the other Navigators had likewise leaped to their feet, but the two men and the animal, bounding around his master and uttering a high, excited keen, blocked their exit.

The angry beastmaster was blueing the air with curses, finishing with "What right had you to enter a c'holders' establishment? What is your name and station? I'll have you broken for this, you—"

"Sire, Lord C'holder," the enforcer stammered in the first break in the angry tirade, "I was only following orders, sir; doing my contractual duty, sir." He pointed at Jael and the others. She tried to wriggle behind the golden-skinned beastmaster and out, but he wrapped a long arm around her shoulders and held her. "*These* people, sir," the enforcer finished.

"They are c'breakers?" The golden c'holder frowned. "All of them? And you, single-handed, have been given orders to place them in custody? It seems improbable."

"Us—custody!" the Navigators exclaimed, all trying to explain to this sudden champion how innocent they were, how they were being unjustly persecuted, how unfair the whole shoddy procedure was, how—

Only Jael was silent, even when the young albino, stuttering on his fury, displayed the banded wrist.

"I see," the golden autocrat cut through the multitongued accusations. "Worm," he said to the enforcer, "are any of these other than the woman accused of contract breaking?"

"N-no, great C'holder." The enforcer was trembling.

"And she is in mechanical custody. *What are you doing here, then?*" The z'par howled, reacting to the anger in his master's voice. The enforcer tried to flinch away, but the closely packed tables blocked his retreat. "I repeat, worm, *why are you here?*"

"S-sir, *please,* sir, orders, s-s-sir, there've been c-c-complaints . . ."

"They didn't fee their shots?" The aristocrat's voice was silky. Elaborately, he glanced down at the Navigators' table, where a pile of Guild chits spilled over the glassily smooth polished surface in a long streak.

The enforcer gulped and managed to get out, "L-l-loitering, sir. Possible-delay-of-contract-fulfilling-by—"

"Loitering? Loitering! You're harassing respectable contractors for *loitering?* Do you think to put me under custody, too? I've been here longer than they have, you worm, you clot, you—" He shoved, and the enforcer staggered away, falling over a filled table, to the curses of its inhabitants, who had been watching the show openmouthed. The lord didn't give him time to recover; he pushed, shoved, kicked the unfortunate enforcer, his tunic and skin daubed in red and green sauces, his hair and beard embellished with assorted chunks of edibles, out of the café and into the street, all the while cursing loudly, the z'par counterpointing with a melodious trill.

"And you'd best keep your distance," the c'holder shouted after the enforcer, who was limping hastily away. "I'll not answer for Nemesis, if you come too close to him again."

"I wish you hadn't." Jael stood beside him, right hand absently rubbing at the banded left wrist. "I prefer to fight my own battles."

"You prefer to be driven from a half-eaten meal? Odd tastes you offworlders have." He had expected to be thanked; he had even had hopes of simplifying matters, eliminating the middleman, so to speak—his anger thickened his voice.

"I'd rather not have others interfering in my affairs."

"Interfering? Why, you ungrateful—"

"Ungrateful? You meddled, sir, uninvited, in affairs that were none of your concern. Now you're in trouble, too, and mine is the fault. I don't like debts I can't repay."

"Debts? Have I asked for a contract?"

"Asked? You're a man, aren't you. Well, if you're fined over this, send a message to Guildhall; I've still some credit left."

"Sister," the albino protested, "you are discourteous. This gentleman defended us, and you are practically accusing him of—of some evil motive."

She wiped her forehead wearily, and sighed. "My apologies, noble sir. I plead exhaustion. If I have wronged your motives, I am sorry. But others of your world have not acted in a manner that makes me think well of any of you."

He glared down at her from his superior height. Then he lifted her left arm. She tried to pull it away, but he was stronger. He kissed her left wrist, where the pulse beat just above the striped bracelet.

"If you owed me any debt"—he was smiling—"you have just paid it, in full. The clay between us is wiped smooth."

"Generous of you." Her voice was bitter.

"Sister!" the albino protested again.

"What I did"—the golden-skinned c'holder was still smiling—"I did for Nemesis' sake, not yours. That clod deserved worse than he got. You needn't feel indebted in the smallest degree."

(That night, as sometimes happened, an enforcer didn't return from his rounds. Two days later, a headless flayed body was fished up in the nets, far more gnawed on than even a couple of days in the water might account for.)

"I don't." She smiled, with visible effort. "But I appreciate what you did, nonetheless."

"So you say, offworlder." He turned to retrace his steps to his own table. *None of my business,* his tense, proud back proclaimed.

"So I say and mean," her soft voice followed him. "I thank you, sir, for your good intent."

But when he turned once again, she was already out into the street, drearily putting one foot in front of the other, moving in the slow, methodical plod of total exhaustion.

"We do thank you, sir." The albino bowed before hurrying after her.

The golden lord watched them go, his hand on the z'par's head. "Good Nemesis, good boy," he murmured, smiling softly.

"Sister," the albino dared to comment, "you were discourteous to that man. He might have helped. You are not usually so foolish."

"Brother, a fool is one who computes a run before reading the instruments," was all she answered.

Not unnaturally, the enforcers were infuriated by their loss of face; the hazing grew vicious.

Reis heard about the hazing, of course. In a sense, a spaceport is a small town. His first impulse, to go to her and demand a price for the Personal, had waned as his temper had died. But he wasn't just going to *give* it to her, either. Let her stew a day or two, he had decided; they wouldn't be able to snatch a Navigator the way they took Rowan. Let her suffer a day or two, or even three. . . .

Gratitude had a much nicer ring than brute force, didn't it?

But when he heard about the band, and the escort, he realized that returning the Personal to her in public, so to speak, would be

the equivalent of having the town crier announce in the square
that Zaqanna had better get his mind in order before the hearing.

Yet it didn't have to be given to her directly. Any Navigator
would do. Except that the next Navigator he saw—and, he quickly
learned by a judicious question or two, all who dared emerge from
Guildhall—was being paced by an enforcer, almost but not quite
treading on his heels as he moved along. Everyone else was giving
the pair a wide berth.

Giving the Personal to another Navigator would be the same as
giving it directly to her.

He had the sense not to comm Guildhall; he was certain the
surveillance included more than the part that showed. Yet even if
they dared scan Guildhall itself, the Navigators had protections. . . .

Reis hesitated, chewed his lip, cursed, and tried to keep himself
and his crew as busy and as far away from the Guildhall, the Navigators, and Zaqanna and the Gilded Cage as possible.

Surely it would be safer in a day or two—or perhaps three.

It wasn't.

CHAPTER 10

Neither Golden Singh nor the Navigators noticed the gaunt man in
gray who had been propping up a wall during the affair in the out-
door café. Yet he had been there, watching the whole with eyes so
blank and unseeing that, if anyone had glanced at him during the
brief but noisy confrontation, they would have dismissed him as
blind.

But as Jael brushed by him, in her Navigator black and bristling
with suppressed fury, it was as if something clicked behind those
flat mirror-silver eyes, and the entire scene was replayed, analyzed
—and absorbed.

He straightened and moved after the little clot of Navigators,
mouth pursed, a slight frown wrinkling the high forehead.

It was not young Nikady, the wraith-thin albino, who noticed
him following, but an older man, tough and stocky, face and
depilated head tattooed in a devil's mask of scarlet and blue like a
Terran mandrill monkey. He dropped back slightly, bent over and

made as if to shake a pebble out of his shoe. Though his eyes were apparently bent down and absorbed in his task, he still gave a long hard assessing look at the tall shambling scarecrow of a man who followed so close behind.

Mouth tight under the flamboyant tattooing, he caught up with his friends, and, one by one, passed the message to the other three men standing guard.

"Ric and Parsival and Djarum and Ansel will be catching up with us soon to take their turn," Nikady the albino commented in a whisper.

"Aye." The hard, truculent mouth beneath the tattooed mask twitched tautly. All three men had said essentially the same. Once the next shift had taken over, they would be free for a while. Usually, they would simply return to the Guildhall for some much needed rest. But not this time.

Nikady's communicator buzzed. "He's moving again," a tinny voice announced. "North for now."

"All right, acknowledged, out." Louder. "Take the next good right, sister."

She didn't even nod. The communicator buzzed again, and young Nikady gave precise directions to allow the next shift to intercept them, then looked up, question in his eyes, at the blue-and-crimson mandrill face of the Navigator called Spyro.

"He dropped back when the buzzer first went off," that worthy said very softly.

"Just another curiosity-seeker." Nikady was equally soft-spoken.

"I don't—" Jael took an abrupt right, and her four honor guards followed, almost in military precision.

As they turned the corner, Spyro said, "I'll just peel off and be sure."

"Carefully."

"Aye." A frown twisted the monkey mask into a grimace to haunt nightmares. "What a world!"

"None of us want to stay here."

"No." Spyro stopped, and took his shoe off again, and pulled a small tool off his belt. He was kneeling, frowning down at what he was doing when a double shadow fell over him and passed by. "I say," he raised his voice but used a casual tone, "would you stop and lend a hand?"

The double shadow came back and stood still. "What do you want?" said the deadest voice he'd ever heard emerge from a human throat. Spyro looked up, startled. The binary sun was high over one shoulder of the man, providing brilliance to spotlight details as well as the doubled shadow. The man standing over him with unnatural stillness was tall and gaunt to emaciation. His clothes were frayed in places, but offworld. The long, unkempt hair almost concealed that there had once been stylish glitter-threads inserted, rooted in the scalp, and their lack of length suggested that the hair had once been worn in a different and shorter cut. The bleached pale skin was mottled with bruises or dirt or both, and the eyes were deader than the voice.

"Just a hand for a second. My sole's come loose and I was trying to use my heater to fuse it back. But I need one hand to hold it in place, one to steady the shoe itself, and one to aim the heater. That's three. I'd be glad to give you a chit or two for your time. Or feed you."

Ryker simply gazed down at the kneeling man impassively. "I'm not hungry."

Spyro didn't believe that. "You're offworld, too, aren't you?" He wedged the shoe between his knees and pretended to be fiddling inside. "Stranded here, eh?"

"No. Choice."

That brought the devil-monkey head up, and fast. "Choice?!?" he echoed, incredulous, his usually facile tongue deserting him.

"The one world in the galaxy where one can do whatever one wants openly, because there are no laws, no scruples, no morals, no ethics, no customs, nothing and no one to outrage," Ryker said.

An atavistic fear made a frisson like hungry spiders run up Spyro's back. An old saying his mother had sometimes quoted ran through his mind. "Take what you want, God says—and then pay for it."

He didn't realize he'd said it aloud until the other man said simply, "Yes."

"What do you want, then?"

"Nothing I haven't got. Now."

Spyro jammed his foot back into his boot and rose. The other man had a head on him, and reach, but if it came to a fight, Spyro would break him into little pieces—and they both knew it. He clamped a muscular hand around the other's bony wrist. "I think I want to talk with you."

"I go in that direction." He nodded toward where the group in Navigator black was still plainly visible.

His reaction—or lack of it—was all wrong. A normal man would have bristled, pulled away, protested, done something, anything, except just stand there impassively, as though the rough hand prisoning his wrist were a midge that had landed there by accident and would fly away in a second, leaving his life without a ripple to mark its passage. Spyro had a sudden horrible thought. His hand jerked away as though the gaunt wrist had suddenly turned red-hot. "You signed a contract here?"

"Yes."

"I had not meant to hinder you in—in contractual duties." The Navigators had learned a hard lesson.

"You have not. And if you wish to walk beside me, and converse as we walk, that is surely your privilege." The voice was still impassive, monotone.

"My privilege, yes." Spyro rose to his feet, fell in beside the seemingly aimless amble that nonetheless, thanks to overlong legs, ate up distance. "But you don't have to converse back, do you?"

"Neither of us is constrained to anything." Already they were cutting down the gap between them and the group in black. And Spyro saw, with a sigh of relief, that another group in black was heading down the street toward the first. He would have reinforcements, and soon. Although what even four could do with this scarecrow zombie of a man . . .

Then something about the wording of what the other man had said clicked into place. "You have questions of me?"

"Why not? There are few enough offworlders here on a permanent basis. If another is to join our . . . happy crew . . ."

Spyro spat out a curse. "Not if we can help it."

"You may not be able to prevent it." Somehow the very evenness of the short sentence made it an insult beyond insult.

"We'll interdict this world."

"It's too Low-T to care. Except for the privileged ones, most of these people have no knowledge of any other life. They won't miss the offworld luxuries they've never known."

It was only what the Navigators told themselves. "They'll care all right. When they add up what they're losing." It was bluff, and a hollow tone in his voice said he knew it.

"Which of the Navigators is at risk?"

Spyro answered automatically, not realizing, as Leany or Zaqanna would have instantly, how uncharacteristic Ryker's behavior was. "Our sister, the Lady Navigator Jael."

"A woman." An almost imperceptible pause. "It could be worse. Women know what to expect in such situations."

Spyro's reply was unprintable.

"Yet I believe I heard—certain accents are unmistakable. It will not be the first time—for her, will it?"

Spyro's fists clenched. Navigators were the pampered pets of a thousand worlds. It was hard to remember that, on this one—

Nikady and his two companions fell in step with them. The young albino flicked a glance from the clenched fists to the equally clenched mouth. "Spyro?" The other two were poised also, ready, only waiting for a signal.

"He's signed a contract here." Spyro bit it out. The others blinked, gasped, let out short exclamations of amaze and commiseration.

"Voluntarily," Spyro added.

"Arrrrrgh," one of the new pair spat.

"He assures me that we won't interfere with his contractual duties"—Spyro's voice was heavy with bitter irony—"if we merely walk along beside him and supply the courtesy of light conversation."

Viciously, "That's a relief." Toki was older than any of his fellows, a wiry wisp of a man, his head crowned with a cotton-candy nimbus whose color was an accurate barometer of his emotional state. At the moment it was prussic acid-green laced with dried-blood maroon; even as he spoke, waves of grim knife-gray rippled through it. In a couple of planet days he was scheduled to ship out, and he didn't like not knowing what would happen until he was lucky enough to cross the path of someone who had stayed. There was no form of faster-than-light communication but the FTL ships themselves, so the ships carried all the news. And when or even if the fate of his sister Navigator would catch up with him— He was so jumpy he made even Nikady seem calm by comparison.

"Curious, are you?" It was the fourth Navigator, Estaban Xavier, hitherto silent.

"Curious?" Ryker tasted the word. Curiosity was an emotion. He had nothing to spare that might be labeled an emotion. He shrugged. "No, not really. But it is unusual to hear a Third Arm accent away from the Third Arm. At least," he amended, "not on an off-the-way world like this." Men and women of the Third Arm were sometimes sent—suitably enchained—to other areas to recruit, to advertise, to satisfy clients that couldn't or wouldn't make the journey in person.

"No," Nikady muttered. "The only use for worlds like this they have is to raid them. And who hears much during a raid."

"As the Lady Navigator could doubtless bear witness." It wasn't a question.

"Shanghai!" Nikady spat it out. Two of the others looked surprised, but the silent one merely nodded.

"How do you—" Spyro frowned.

"When she was so exhausted a couple of days ago, and I carried her. She was having a nightmare—reliving it, I think." His mouth twisted. "Shanghaied. Her parents were likely the real booty. Judging from their daughter, both must have been something spectacular."

"They like 'em young, in the Third Arm." Spyro's fingers twitched, as if searching for a victim.

"And ripe," snarled the older man, his nimbus a disgusted mud-brown. "Young to train, ripe to use—may Shiva eat their black souls!"

"If they have any," Nikady snorted.

"Shanghaied as a child to the Third Arm." Ryker might have been reading a street sign out loud. "And yet she is now a Navigator."

The quiet one spoke a second time. "Don't ask." The other three stared at him. "The Guild is not so large that paths cannot cross and recross. She probably does not remember one face among many. I—can not forget." Eyes like golden champagne met one startled gaze after another. "Don't ask. You'll sleep better. Suffice it—she escaped."

"You never said a word." Nikady almost accused.

"I meant not to now. Her story, not mine. Please, brothers, as we are all brothers, forget I said anything." He remembered Ryker. "And you?"

Ryker simply kept walking.

"And *you?*" He tugged a sleeve to gain attention. Oddly, they might have been brothers—or one a distorted fun-house-mirror reflection of the other. Height to a centimeter. Features similarly aquiline, saturnine, cynical, deep-carved. Thick waving silver-gilt hair and a dull lank gray mop. Gauntness contrasted to svelte yet muscled litheness. When the two gazes met, thick lashes on heavy lids dropped to veil eyes of sparkling gold until they, too, could have been gray.

"I what?" Ryker was far away, though his body jogged along.

"You will keep silence about what you have heard just now." Estaban Xavier, usually so quiet, even among his fellows, persisted. The double suns gave his silver hair the gleam of a new-minted coin.

"I have heard nothing that bears repeating."

Again the hungry spider frisson went up Spyro's back. *Not human,* he thought. Then, eyes fixed on Ryker's skeletal form, he bit his lip, remembering some High-T mechanicals he had seen once. Designed to look like a human, to walk and talk and act like a human, yet there had been a hollowness about them, a lack of depth and self and—humanity. This man—if he was a man— reminded him of those mechanicals. As though he were—were programmed, and nothing that happened could break or shock him out of that programming.

Or as though—his eyes narrowed. As though he actually weren't human. Out here? It seemed impossible. And yet, he simply didn't react. If he was such a mechanical, how could they tell? And—did it matter?

Ryker could have told him, it did. That little scrap of humanity left in him was all that stood between the Navigators—all of them —and total disaster.

CHAPTER 11

The Rabelaisian C'holder Golden Singh had been balked, temporarily, of something he desired, and his spoiled soul demanded reparation. Now he had arranged an hors d'oeuvre, a lagniappe, a pleasant way to wile away a boring afternoon until he could make ready to attend a particularly amusing orgy that another c'holder had spent much time and ingenuity devising. Yet that was tonight —a vast and boring abyss stretched out between—and this was now. He shifted slightly on cushions stuffed with softest down and scented with rare wild musk, and reached impatiently for a shimmering goblet filled with golden nepenthe. He sipped—and spat. Pfaugh! Too sweet! He'd have a word with his wines mistress. His lips curled. A word—not enough. He'd bring her along to the orgy. Finisch would no doubt be able to arrange a . . . suitable position for her. He frowned slightly, trying to remember what she looked like. He replaced his contracteds so often . . . yes, lovely, he demanded that. Tall and willowy and hair like a river of night shot through with gleaming gold. Tsk! Why hadn't he made use of *all* her talents before—

The door behind him opened. "Golden," said a voice that was a pout made sound, "it's far too hot for arena games."

He didn't bother to turn around. Medee Oriflamme, her wire-thin body barely swathed in blush-pink gauzes that were far more seductive than simple nudity, glared at his back. Then she swished through, ignoring or stepping on the several contracteds who hovered, ready to jump and make themselves useful at the snap of a finger or even in anticipation of their c'holder's thoughts before they could be expressed.

"Have some nepenthe, C'holder," he drawled, still gazing dreamily out over the empty arena before him. "It might sweeten that tongue of yours."

She flung herself on a cushion, and a cloud of spice and lemon reached his nostrils. "A new scent, C'holder?" He reached out a languid hand, and she placed her wrist on it, so he could bring the pulse point to just under his nose. He sniffed, nodded, and laid a casual kiss on the inside of her wrist, before sliding into a more comfortable position on the heap of sensuously covered cushions.

"I said, it's too hot—" He flicked her a bored glance, before turning his attention back to the oval of packed beige sand. Above, the sky was clear, so brilliant a hue it hurt the eyes. Heat waves shimmered above the smooth sand, but the box had a canopy, and contracteds were moving large fans over buckets of ice, normally brought with great difficulty from the peaks of nearby mountains. (In Singh's case, the ice was produced by an offworlder machine that cost the time of a dozen contracteds to run a muscle-powered generator.)

"The nepenthe is cool"—he ran a casual finger down the sweat beading on the goblet—"and the show will be interesting."

"Yes." She flounced into a knees-drawn-up position on her heap of cushions to stare down into the empty arena. "I see how interesting it is."

"The show is still being prepared," he informed, idly crumbling a sweetcake and licking lavender icing off his fingers. "They're a trifle reluctant."

"Oh." She reached over and sampled the icing, with a petulant frown. "Why aren't we watching the encouragement, then? Better than nothing."

"Boring." He rolled over, gave each of the contracteds crowded into the back of the box an assessing glance, and gestured a young girl to his side. She came eagerly. She was new. He arranged her as he wanted her, and added, "They're having inductor receivers implanted. I wasn't planning to use them this soon."

"Untrained. How *dull*, Golden. None of the finer points to appreciate." She, in her turn, examined the clot of contracteds in the box. "You and you." She pointed. "Run down into the sand and amuse the c'holders still arriving."

The first one pointed to merely shuddered, but the second said, "In what manner, Lady C'holder?"

"Do I have to spell everything out? Use your ingenuity—if you have any. Ask the programmer. Let us be amused." Her slender tongue came out and she licked the coral-colored icing off another cake. "I like this topping, C'holder. Would you ensure that your cook gives the recipe for it to mine?"

He was not paying much attention to her. The girl he had gestured over was weeping, tears of pure pain.

"The recipe, Golden," Medee repeated, more sharply.

He freed his mouth long enough to say, "Yes, of course," and continued what he was doing.

"You two." She gestured out toward the empty oval. "Down. And make it amusing." Then she added, as they were scurrying out, "Don't damage each other without permission. You're only an *entr'acte*, after all." To Singh, still thoroughly occupied, "If it wasn't ready, why'd you have me come?"

The girl gave a howl of agony and he pushed her away. "It'll be worth waiting for." He shifted again so that he could gaze out onto the arena. The two Medee had chosen were running onto the sand. They had paused long enough in the outfitting room to pick up weapons. A programmer was with them, evidently rattling off last-minute instructions. "Strip, you idiots," Singh called down. "We want to be able to see the bruises."

The two below were using padded clubs. The bruises were spectacular, but, except for soreness, neither would be impeded in performing other duties.

Medee laughed gaily as a blow from one lifted the other off her feet and threw her backward in a flailing sprawl. "The knees," she shouted down. "The knees are exquisitely sensitive. And the soles of the feet."

"You see," Singh smiled, golden teeth flashing in the brilliant sunlight, "sometimes an untrained pair can be entertaining by their very ignorance."

"Is that what you're planning for this afternoon?" She spoke absentmindedly, her eyes still intent on the arena, wet pink tongue licking already glistening lips. The combatant standing up was making full use of his strategic advantage; his victim on the ground threshed and screeched, but he wasn't giving her a minute's respite to regain either feet or weapon.

"Yes." He tried a sip of ebony Nun's Agony, and nodded slightly. Very good. Perhaps he wouldn't take his current wines mistress to the orgy after all. Not when she could find a treat like this. Perhaps he'd just give her—a little undivided attention. "A pair, they've had a few weeks of the rudimentals, hypnotraining and the usual, but I've decided to waste one of them today." His smile thinned into a feral grimace.

She shrugged. "So? What's amusing about that?"

"Good show!" He shouted encouragement, his voice mingling with cries from the other boxes as the woman on the ground managed to trip her tormentor, and while he was down, scrambled for his club and got to her own knees to return some of the punishment.

"I said, what's amusing about a pair of rank amateurs killing each other?"

The feral smile broadened. "Three things. They're both offworlders, so they really don't understand anything. And they're friends. They won't want to hurt each other."

"Ahhhhhh." Her smile was as sweet and animal as his. "Hence the inductors."

"Yes. We'll be able to monitor as well as control the pain levels." A chuckle. "Bribe me, C'holder, and I'll let you play with the controls a bit."

Her eyes sparkled. "I'll like that. You're usually selfish with those inductors of yours, C'holder."

"The gladiators—" He yawned. She forbore to comment the obvious, that as much as he used inductors on his gladiators, he used them for his own private amusements even more.

She licked her lips again. "Your bribe? You want it now, while we wait—or later?"

"Later. And I'll want a different bribe from you, C'holder."

"Different?" She pouted.

"You'll give me the usual whenever you're bored, C'holder. No, this time—" He cuddled down onto the cushions and gazed down at the arena. "This time, I want that stiff-necked sister of yours at one of my amusements."

"Esme?" Medee sat up, stared at him. "She'd *never*—"

He stretched languidly, a golden panther preening in the sunlight, and caught her gaze with a look that made more than one contracted shiver, despite the heat. "I know. That's what makes it amusing. Your untouchable sister. Provide her, and I'll let you borrow a pair of my inductors whenever you choose, word of a c'holder."

"*And* let me watch—everything?"

He laughed aloud. "Greedy. That's what makes *you* amusing, C'holder. All right." Another languid stretch. "You can watch."

"Done." She nibbled disdainfully at another comfit, spat out the mouthful, and then started bouncing up and down on her cushions, like a child eager to see the circus parade start. "I think they're almost ready."

He nodded. A man was hustling the two amateurs, both limping, off the sand, while three others frantically used long twig brooms to smooth off where the struggle had disturbed the pristine dunness.

Meanwhile, tall transparent screens were rising from the walls rimming the small arena.

"Why—"

"Offworlders, as I said. It'll be even more amusing if they can hear us, know we're here—but can't see us."

"If you say so, Golden." Below, the three sweepers were dashing off the sand. Then, as she remembered, "You said three things, C'holder. What's the third?"

He settled down comfortably, an iced drink in one hand. "No weapons. They'll have to work to kill each other." He sipped, sighed in appreciation. "And it will be kill. If they do manage to damage each other so neither is capable of killing—well, we'll worry about that if it comes. Otherwise, they stay in the arena, with us playing with the inductor controls, until one of them is dead." He took another long sip. "It should be an interesting afternoon."

Some ten minutes later, Medee was complaining bitterly. The two naked men in the arena had simply agreed that they weren't going to do anything to each other.

Singh cut through her complaints. "The inductor controls." He pointed languidly. "Convince them."

"Ahhhh." She settled down in front of the panel, following his bored instructions, planting the monitor on her forehead. "Oh." She had looked back down at the arena. "I recognize the taller one. He had red hair, lovely gleaming red hair; why did you take it off?"

Singh made a face. "I had some plan or other," he muttered. The now ex-redhead had been surprisingly stubborn.

"Pity," she said, but she had already dismissed him from her mind. "He was a pretty thing. I thought of putting in an option, but you'd already collected him. He's a spacer, isn't he?"

"Ex-spacer." He finished the goblet and dropped it carelessly. A contracted scurried to pick it up. "Both of them. Work on him first, the taller one."

Below, the two men were standing, gazing in puzzlement around themselves. They were both completely naked, and totally bald, though with one it was natural; the other had had his hair removed. The taller one was young, in late adolescence or just past it, while the other man had the maturity of a man in his prime, in what would have been called middle age in an earlier era. Both moved with the easy grace of natural athletes, though one was tall and greyhound-lithe, the other compact and neatly muscled, with calm, competent nutmeg eyes and a usually ready smile.

Suddenly the younger man doubled over, screaming in agony, and the other moved and supported him. Their voices carried clearly.

"Rowan, what's wrong?"

"Georg—help me—*hurts*—"

"Tickle the other, but not so strongly, woman. They won't be able to fight if they're doubled over in pain like that."

The man called Georg quivered, but didn't drop his friend. "Why are you doing this to us?" His deep husky shout echoed through the arena.

"You must fight," Golden Singh's voice was unrecognizable though the megaphone of his cupped hands. "You must amuse us. One of you must kill the other."

"Never." Georg again. Rowan was simply slumped, moaning.

"You have no choice. It is one of you—or both. We will keep the inductor on you until you give in. No one can take such pain indefinitely."

"Georg." The youth Rowan was kneeling, hands clamped to his head, swaying back and forth in pain. "Make them stop. I can't stand it!"

"Lower the level, I said," Singh drawled. "He can't fight."

She moved a control, and the young Rowan relaxed, head back, eyes closed.

"We have lessened the inductor. You fight now," Singh called down.

"No. You can't make us." Lower, but still audible to the small audience: "Courage, Rowan. They can't make us hurt each other. The inductor causes pain, but it does no permanent damage."

"They're not hurting you," Rowan snarled.

"Yes, they are, but they can't make me—"

"Spacer," Singh called down again. "You're wrong about the inductor. It can cause permanent damage. Too much usage, too long, and the mind reacts to it. The inductor can be turned off, but you will still feel as if it were turned up full. You live in pain, spacer. Constant pain. For all the rest of your life. Useless as gladiators, of course, so that's when we attach the wires."

Rowan looked up at that, eyes that were once trusting as a child's now bleak. "The wireheads!" He glanced at his friend. "Georg—"

"Courage, Rowan." Louder. "Wireheads, too, are useless as gladiators."

"So are you. At present. Yet wireheads can be useful, properly programmed, as sparring partners. As you may have experienced. The choice is yours. Delay too long, and the inductors will induce burnout, and you will both be wireheads. Amuse us sufficiently, and one of you will live to fight another time."

"Georg—" Even from the distance of the box, they could see Rowan's chin trembling.

"Rowan." His voice was gentle, but the arena was silent and all could hear clearly. "They can't make us, Rowan. If we do their evil, of our own free will, we share the guilt. Sparring in training, that's one thing . . . but *this*— We only have to agree and continue to—"

"I don't want to *die*, Georg. I don't want to live as a wirehead, either, so much pain in my mind I don't even know what they're doing with my body."

"Concentrate on the taller one, C'holder," Singh spoke softly. "Not high all the time; tune it down to a little nagging ache . . . then shoot it up again and down quickly—"

In the arena, Rowan relaxed again, then convulsed as though someone had rammed a hot iron against his back. Georg reached over and wiped the sweat off the high smooth forehead. "Rowan," he said persuasively, "you don't want to share this bloodguilt."

Even from the seats, the aquamarine eyes that went with hair of flaming scarlet were feverishly bright. "I don't want to die, Georg."

"Ahhhh." Medee took her hands away from the controls long enough to clap them gleefully. "A year's standard on the shorter one."

"You think so?" Singh smiled his feral smile. "Two years' standard—on the taller one. Once he forces the other to fight—"

"Nonsense," Medee pouted. "Look at him, he may be shorter but there's twice the muscle on him. He probably has half again the strength of the taller one, and the way he moves, quick and clean, he's a natural, that one."

"It will be a more even fight than you think." He reached over to take the controls from her. "Watch this. As though his feet were dipped in molten lead." Below, Rowan jumped and howled. "They'll fight all right, and you'll see which is the natural. Now—" A sucked-in breath. "—as though his teeth were being pulled out." Another pitiable howl. "He's more desperate—and of weaker fiber. That gives him the advantage."

"Being weaker?" Medee wrinkled her petite nose.

"You've still much to learn, C'holder. Watch."

"Georg—" The man below pleaded.

"You really think living like this is something to fight for, Rowan?"

Above, Golden Singh smiled his dreadful smile and played the controls with the touch of a maestro.

CHAPTER 12

The petite Navigator, whose black was a foil for hair like a curtain of the mistiest of blushing dawns, paced up and down, lip caught between amethyst teeth.

The newest apprentice-recruit stood watching her, hero worship mixed with a boy's first crush making his tawny eyes glow. Finally he dared to break the silence. "They're not so very late, Lady Alizon. They've a far distance to walk, after all."

She whirled, hair a glittering cloud. Almost she opened her mouth to snap, then the tautness smoothed away as she smiled at the boy. First love was so painful, calf-love or not. She sighed deeply. "I know, Lysander. It's just so difficult, the waiting."

His mouth tightened. "They should have let me come."

She tousled his mop of unruly curls. "You have to sleep sometime, Lysander. And what can you do for the Lady Jael," she pointed out, as others had, over and over, "if you're reeling blind from exhaustion?"

His large lower lip protruded. "How much sleep is *she* getting?"

"The important question now is, How much sleep are you getting?" His lip came out even further. "I can't do anything at present for my sister Jael, but I can do something about you, my man."

"I can't sleep, Mistress Alizon," he said on a rising note. "Truly, I can't."

"I have something in the dispensary that will help."

"I don't want—" He backed a step away, hands out as though to barricade himself. "You gave me one of your somethings two days past, and I could scarce drag myself out of the bed when the night had passed. Please, Lady Alizon. I want to help when I'm needed, and if I cannot be awakened—"

She planted a kiss on the forehead wrinkled into a frown, all motherly, though the actual age gap between them was smaller than either guessed. But something of the lost, uprooted look in his eyes appealed to her, so she showed him the gentle caring side only her closest friends were privileged to see. "All right, Lysander, I'll allow you your way—this time. Yet the time drags so slowly. Perhaps you and I can fill it in with a game or so while we await their coming."

"Your kind of game or mine?" He was dressed in Navigator black, unadorned, and a restless movement occasionally revealed that it was not his accustomed garb, that he would have felt at home in clothing far different.

"Flip," she said shrugging, her mellifluous voice a caress to the ears. She unclipped her glittering ident, not realizing that the fate of a world hung in her hands, and caught the rectangular plaque between slim facile fingers. "You may call, Lysander, face or back?"

"Face." He didn't hesitate.

She laughed gently. "A foolish call. Did you know that people are ten times more likely to go for face as back? If you make a habit of gambling, my man, always ask your opponent to make the call. You'll win far more often than you lose."

He laughed, the laughter more mature than his freckled boy's face. "I made the real gamble when I entered here, Lady Alizon."

She froze, the ident glittering in her hand. "But—your lady c'holder approved—"

"Oh, yes. But you made her sign a quit-claim to allow me to enter. She can now no longer protect me; I have only whatever contracts you Navigators have signed. And while they protect you, except in such cases as the Lady Jael—"

She caught his wrist with her free hand. "I thought—Lysander, is there something we don't know?"

Again he laughed and, with an odd role reversal, shook her hand off. "You offworlders are as very babes when it comes to contracts. For now, there is nothing to worry about. But the sooner I am sent to one of these training places of yours, and am away from Rabelais completely, the better." He winked. "Once I am away, it won't matter, because I'm *never* coming back."

"Lysander." Hands on hips, a petite Amazon. "You told us your c'holder had the complete disposing of you."

"She did." He sighed. "You offworlders— You don't understand contracts—"

Alizon snorted. What any other world called contracts she understood all right. But then Rabelais was unique, and the all-compassing, life-molding, incredibly complex documents this world used— She awarded him her sweetest smile. "I wish to understand, Lysander. Though I have a feeling your explanation may be long. So let us choose and begin our game, and while we play, you will make me understand why you feel more at risk than any of the rest of us. Unless it has to do with this affair of the Lady Jael?"

"Oh, no." He shook his head. "Flip, lady. You are right, it may take more than a small while." He shook his head again, muttering "Babes" beneath his breath, but she heard it nonetheless.

Laughing, she flipped the ident, and the glittering rectangle rose and fell. She caught it on her forearm, her hand cupped over it as she stared down as though seeing through the solid lavender skin.

Beneath her hand, the small ident neatly flipped itself over, so that the face side smiled up. Alizon grinned. Let the lad have his choice, there had been little enough simple fun in his young life. What good was psi, anyway, if it couldn't be used to ease things along occasionally?

She raised her hand and showed him, and felt a small inward glow at the broad grin that split the freckled face. "You see, my lady? Not such a fool's call, after all."

"Your luck was certainly in," she replied with a straight face. "And since the choice is yours, what would you like to play?"

"The one I saw you playing with the Navigator Lord Xavier the evening I came in for my testing. I walked by, with the Navigator Lord Housemaster Ling, and I saw you two, sitting opposite each other—I didn't realize then that what you were doing was playing a game, but the expressions on your faces . . . expectancy, discovery, pleasure . . . that's when I knew I'd made the right choice."

"So." She smiled gently, a hand on his arm guiding him into one of a pair of chairs on opposite sides of a small table. "So Estaban and I were a factor in your decision, eh. I'll have to tell him. Sit you down and I'll set up the program, it won't take but a few seconds. It's called Trends, by the by, but how did you know it was a game?"

"I asked. I said I was curious; was that part of a Navigator's work? Housemaster Ling said it was and it was not, that playing such games polished the skills that Navigators must have. So"—a freckled face split into a grin—"you will teach me and I will be more ready when I arrive at the world that is a learning place."

She ruffled his hair again. "Sometimes I forget what it is to be so young and eager."

His face went solemn. "No contracted is ever too young, for whatever work his c'holder commands." He said it without antagonism, a fact of life.

"Well." She settled into her own chair. "You'll make up for it now. Trends is fun."

It didn't take her long to program the holo playing field, though he slowed things down by his exclamations of awe and wonderment as the three-D game board was built up.

"Shall we make all your pieces contracteds?" Alizon wanted to know. "I've set the first game to a world based on Rabelais, and I've always felt it was most satisfying to work my way completely—"

"A contracted?" He snorted. She had already explained some of the rules as she programmed the display. "Lady Alizon, a contracted *never* works his way to anything but more contracted's work!"

Her facile fingers paused on the pressure-sensitive keyboard. "Would you prefer another worldbase? I thought, since you are familiar with your world and I am not, it would compensate a little for my having played the game so often."

"A kindly thought, Lady Alizon. But we had both best start as free-contracteds, or better still, small c'holders. Otherwise—" He shrugged.

"Perhaps you'd best help me program in the ground rules."

"There are c'holders and c'holders, Lady Alizon," he informed. "Even among the powerful ones, there are those who use their power, and those who, like my former c'holder, do not, or at least, only enough to protect herself and her people."

"They don't like the system, but there isn't anything else, so they use it when they feel they must."

He blinked. "I never thought of it quite that way, but yes—" A toothy grin. "Yes, you're right."

"Um-hum. Now, listen, in Trends, you're allowed one major innovation per turn, a major being defined as one that affects at least ten percent of the populace when fully implemented, plus up to three minor innovations. An innovation may not conflict with previous innovations, except when—"

The game was well established when she remembered what else she had meant to ask him. "Lysander, what did you mean, about yourself being in jeopardy here? Surely the rest of us will not be drawn in, should the Lady Jael's trial—or whatever you call it—go askew?"

"Oh, no." He was worrying a bit of lip between his teeth. "It's not that. It's—you insisted that my lady c'holder sign a total quit-claim."

"For your protection. We couldn't have her trying to snatch you back sometime in the future, you know."

"My protec—" His jaw dropped. "I think you mean that."

"We do. I mean, I do."

He snorted, punched in a minor innovation, and she watched the display change with marked lack of attention. "It was the worst-possible thing you could have done. May I suggest, with all due respect—"

"What?"

"That instead of a total quit-claim, you have the c'holder in future make an assignment of trust."

"Explain." Her gaze was on him, but her ears, satyr-pointed, were curved delicately toward the outside door.

"Because if there's a lien outstanding, a quit-claim will allow it to be brought forward, whereas a trust assignment will allow it to be thrown back to the original c'holder, where it can do no damage."

"A lien? But I thought your c'holder—"

"Held a contract for the rest of my life, including all I produce. But—it takes two to make a baby. Now, if an object is produced by two or more contracteds, belonging to two or more c'holders, and that object is by nature indivisible, then it will be assigned to the c'holder whose contracteds had the largest share in its production. But the other c'holder or c'holders have a lien. Usually such are satisfied by balancing out, but sometimes it merely—continues to exist."

She put a hand to her mouth.

Lysander shrugged.

"But you said—you couldn't know who your father was—"

He nodded, punched in a minor innovation. "Truth. I cannot and do not. My mother had been attending her lady at an occasion at her lady sister's. Things got a little—as they tend to get at the Lady C'holder Medee Oriflamme's occasions. Much wine, much . . . playing. My lady did not like such revelry, she attempted to leave. There was a confusion, and she and some of her attendants were separated. My mother was found, several hours later, in the private rooms of the c'holder who tried to interfere with my lady. She was unconscious. She had been beaten. She has never remembered what happened that night. In fact, her memory is faulty for that whole period of time. It—changed her, so my mistress says. The c'holder says he found her there and assumed she was a new contracted sent by his hostess to amuse him. He rearranged a contract to the benefit of my lady, as is customary among c'holders when an involuntary breach of contract occurs. My mother could neither remember nor deny his tale. I think he was angry against my lady, and revenged himself against her woman knowingly. But a contracted had best not make accusations against a powerful c'holder. When my mother began to show, it was obvious she had been more than beaten. My lady arranged for several of her male contracteds to be able to swear that they might possibly be the sires. I was called premature. But it is a flimsy cover, and if the c'holder involved ever thinks to do a little counting, I could find myself under his lien."

"But you'd be his son. Wouldn't that make a difference? Most men—"

He made a sound between a snort and a raspberry. "A c'holder? Some, perhaps. Some scatter their seed through so many contracteds that one more or less—" His mouth twisted, an expression far too old for his years. "If it happens, please arrange a fatal accident for me, Lady Alizon. I know you Navigators neither respect the sanctity of contracts, nor believe in the weighing of souls on the scale of contractual honor. Nor do I. Just be sure it appears to all as an accident. I would not have you pulled down with me—"

"Lysander, we didn't realize—"

He winked, a gamin expression that those who had known his mother before would have recognized. "So? I have lived with it all my life, in a sense. If anything had happened to my lady . . . there's always a jockeying at a c'holder's death, no matter how carefully contracts are assigned. She would have protected all of hers to the best of her ability, but—" He punched in his major innovation and leaned back in his chair, smiling broadly. "Your turn, lady."

She slanted a glance at the display, then stared at it, transfixed, eyes widening. "What have you done!" she said in a hollow voice.

"Won, I think." He was smug. "The balance is mine."

"What," she spoke slowly, as though her lips had difficulty shaping the words, "impelled you to remove my outside influence?"

"I could see how badly it would damage you." He paused. "Is it against the rules then, to use an innovation to cancel an opponent's innovation? You said conflict, but this isn't a conflict, it is—"

"No." She was still staring at the display. "No, you are correct, total removal is not a conflict, according to the rules. But it's seldom used, because in the long run it's as damaging to your own side as your foe's. Innovations impinge on everything, and if they're removed suddenly—" She licked her lips. "Project a few moves, and see what it's done to you."

"I don't see—"

"Because you've not the skill to project yet. Wait. I'll freeze the game, and then carry it on, using the most obvious moves and projections, instead of our input."

He watched, as her fingers stroked the keyboard and the display altered. Then he looked up at her, horrified. "That's terrible."

"Yes. Bloody destruction of both sides. That's why it's an unwritten rule: You can expand an innovation, alter it, turn its direction, but never simply cancel it out." She rubbed her forehead wearily.

"I lost, didn't I?"

"We both did. I can't salvage enough for even a scrub result, and you'll likely end a total wipe-out." She licked her lips. "Lysander—"

His eyes were downcast. "I guess that's what you get for playing with a stupid beginner. I'm sorry for wasting your time and ruining your game, Lady Alizon—"

"No." She laid a hand on his freckled arm, eyes glowing. "No, you did something none of the rest of us would even have thought of. You came with a fresh mind, and you gave us— Lysander, let's regress the game to the beginning. I want you to help me get it as close as possible to what Rabelais is truly like, today, this very second."

"Well, that's what we had."

"Only an approximation. I want it *accurate*. Then—we're going to take the offworlders away."

"Why?"

"Because we're going to use the program to project the ultimate results. Oh, Lysander, we've been such *fools*. So shortsighted. We thought about the loss of the High-T goods only. Never about the psychological results of the loss of the offworlders themselves. The escape route. The knowledge that there is another universe out there. The loss of— Lysander, if there had been no offworlders, what would you have done?"

He blinked. "Stayed with my lady, I suppose. And hoped that she could have transferred me to a like mind when she died."

"Lysander, if the offworlders go, if it looks like the c'holders drove them away, what will the contracteds think?"

Lysander shrugged. "That the c'holders don't care enough for the offworld toys to continue to turn their possessors up sweet. They don't care, you know, if the contracteds have enough to eat or not, if they work from dawn to the next dawn doing something an offworld machine could do in a heartbeat. They never starve, they never work. They don't care—" He stopped, wheels obviously turning within.

"It wouldn't look as if the c'holders feared that too many contracteds might look at the offworlders and begin to think such thoughts as might make the c'holders rest uneasy at night?"

"I don't understand." But his eyes were narrowed in concentration.

"You wouldn't. You can't see that contracting is slavery in all but name. The freedom of Rabelais," she spat out sarcastically.

"If slaves see a way out—however small the possibility of using it —and then see it snatched away. . . . My ancestors ran an Underground Railroad, back on manhome. I never thought that I, too—" Her smile was dazzling.

"I still don't understand. I thought I lost."

"You won. Your people won. Oh, help me set it up, Lysander." Then, still smiling: "The revolution will come, Lysander. People don't change. It was too late for the c'holders when the first ship of the Ingathering landed here so long ago. All they can do now is choose how they'll have it. Slow enough so that they keep at least some of their influence—or nasty and bloody. And the way Jael's trial goes will determine the fate of this oh-so-stratified society of yours. If the offworlders go—bloody revolution within a generation. If we stay—slower and maybe controllable. I don't know. I'll have to run some projections. But I've played this game often enough. I never thought I'd be playing it in life."

"Isn't that what life is, Lady Alizon? A game played for real?"

"Out of the mouths of babes! Oh, Lysander, I hope our paths cross when you're grown. You're going to be something else then, my man."

His lip stuck out. "I'm not so young now—"

She only smiled. "Patience, my man. Not even your c'holders can stop a planet in its orbit, or a boy from growing into a man. And I don't need a projection program to tell me you're going to be quite a man—when the time comes."

But on Rabelais, a man wasn't a man if he was a contracted; he was just lines on a piece of parchment.

CHAPTER 13

Some parts of the sprawling port were better than others. So when, not far from Guildhall, the four Navigators wearily returning heard the piercing screams of mortal terror, they looked at each other in shock.

"This way." Spyro pointed.

His companions started running.

"What if," Estaban Xavier spat out—his hair may have been sil-

ver, but his face and hard muscular body were in their prime—
"what if, this is contractual . . . and we're interfering . . . ?"

"A *trap!*" Spyro skidded to a halt and held out his hands to
stop the others.

"I'll not stand by—" Nikady, the young albino, was still smart-
ing from his recent encounter with Zaqanna.

They turned a corner, and a row of buildings and vessels,
painted a gentle lavender by the ringlight, stood before them. And
a group of people came running toward them, screaming and
shouting.

The runner in the lead spotted them first, screeched "No!" in a
high terrified voice, and literally flung herself to her knees, skid-
ding to a halt. "No, please, no, I've contractual duties, I'll be a
c'breaker, please, no, don't keep me—"

The Navigators flowed around her, facing the gang chasing her.
She buried her face in her palms and broke into angry, noisy sobs.

In an instant, it was one on one. There were four pursuers, four
Navigators. Spyro took the man in the lead, a tall, muscular brute
who didn't bother to challenge but simply swung the chain he was
carrying across the eyes surrounded by a scarlet-and-blue devil-
monkey mask.

Spyro laughed and ducked, his foot coming up in a savate kick
that doubled his opponent over, gasping and helpless. Spyro gave
him a contemptuous shove that sent him to the ground, and
whirled around to see who needed help.

Estaban was rolling with his opponent in the mud, one hand
clutching his foe's wrist, slamming a hand holding a knife against
the ground. He looked in no immediate danger. Nor was the
fourth Navigator, he with the emotion-reading head nimbus; he
was slugging toe to toe with a burly snarling man who was giving
as good as he got, but both men were only using fists.

Nikady, on the other hand, was slender for all his height, and
was matched with a gorilloid muscular man centimeters shorter
but twice as burly. He had gotten the youngster against a wall, and
as Spyro strode over, his fist sank deep into the long body, obviously not the first time, either. Nikady gasped and doubled over,
and his attacker raised a pair of clenched fists to bring them down
on that vulnerable nape.

The blow never landed. With surprising speed, Nikady butted
his head forward, his crown smashing the wind out of his opponent's midsection; and in almost the same movement, he followed

through, using the stiffened spear hand and ridge hand. One, two, without even a gasp, the man went down.

Nikady straightened up and leaned against the wall, albino-pink face for once bloodless white.

"Nice," approved Spyro. He turned. "Anybody else?"

There wasn't. The man Spyro had downed was scuttling away, the man who had been in the fist exchange had turned and was frankly running, and Estaban was astride his opponent, pinning his arms with merciless knees and methodically trying to punch his face through the back of his skull.

"'Nuff." Spyro hauled his companion to his feet. "Leave enough to ask questions of. Nik's is down for the count for hours."

"So's mine." He wiped away a smear of blood and mud from his taut mouth.

The fourth Navigator, Toki of the emonimbus, limped over to where the cause of the dispute had crumpled into a hysterical sobbing heap.

"I say," he said as he squatted, trying to find a face under the mass of tousled fawn-brown hair, "what's wrong? Can we help?"

"Leave me alone, I'm contracted, I tell you," came out, almost drowned in a barrage of fearful sobs.

"Well," said Toki the squatter reasonably, "if you'll tell us where you're contracted to be, we'll help you get there, if we can."

"Wha—" A dirty, tear-smeared face peeped up at him. "You're not—"

"Not those men chasing you." He smiled gently. "If you're contracted to them, we regret interfering, but nobody told us—"

"Contracted to *them*—" Childishly, she swiped her runny nose with the back of her wrist. "You think I'd be contracted to those—those—"

"Portscum," Spyro barked in his hard voice. "I take it such as they had no fear of breaking your contract."

"Please—" Her voice trembled.

"Don't worry." Nikady had joined the group. "We'll take you wherever you're going, Miss—"

"My name's—" It was drowned in a large sniffle. "I was going back to—" More sniffles. "I quarreled—" Huge sniff. "—my escort, I wasn't contracted to *him,* I didn't owe—" Sni-ifffff. "Only he wanted, and I—I said—and he said— *Kaaa-choo!* We quarreled, and he turned around and said—and said—" Another burst of sobbing.

"That you could find your own way back." Spyro straightened up and glared in the presumed direction of the unknown escort. Had he been present, he would doubtless have gotten the edge of Spyro's fists.

She rocked back and forth on her knees, tears still streaming. "Uncontracteds, they'll do *anything*—"

"Why not?" Estaban's voice was at its cynical worst. "They've nothing they can lose, have they?" The dry note in his speech made her look up, watery blue eyes wide and childish.

"Don't you believe in contracts, either?" She drew a shuddery breath and swiped at her nose again. "Are—are you uncontracted, too?"

Winged brows black as ebony rose. "On the contrary, my child, I put my pundonor before my life."

"Pundonor?" She echoed the unfamiliar word, head cocked like a child who sees a closed hand offered and isn't quite sure whether a sweet or castor oil is concealed.

"Honor is the closest translation in your tongue." He was eyeing her shrewdly, the amber eyes under the black brows that contrasted with the silver hair narrowed. "Honor. Though I suspect your people have forgotten that word, too. When one is reduced to putting one's faith in a piece of paper—" His well-cut mouth twisted. "Fear not, child. My word is worth more to me than all your contracts rolled into one. My brother spoke for all of us just now. We'll see you safely home."

She ground a fist into her mouth and whimpered, "I feel so terrible—"

"Shock." Nikady was peeling himself out of his tunic as he spoke. "Here. You need warmth." He knelt beside her and wrapped the synthi around her, not trying to guide her arms into the sleeves, simply draping it around her body, now racked with epileptic tremors.

"Where do you live?" Spyro asked.

"At—" She looked up, got her first good sight of his devil-monkey face, gasped and flinched back, shuddering. "I'm so cold," she whimpered.

Nikady slanted a glance at his brother Navigators. "We're not that far from Guildhall. We could take her there, give her something warm to drink; our sisters could care for her."

Estaban frowned. "Yes, except that she's said she's contracted, and by keeping her at Guildhall, we risk accusations of contract breaking, and such might affect our sister's fate adversely."

"Oh!" Nikady rose to his feet, drawing her wilting body with him. (With no little difficulty, as she was shorter than he by better than a third of a meter.) She stood, or rather drooped, supported by him, quivering, eyes closed, head leaning against his bony length.

"She'll need to be carried, I suspect." Estaban moved to her other side, so the limp, shaking body was held between them.

"But *where?*" Spyro asked.

"Come, child." Estaban swooped and held her like a baby. "You must tell us where you are to go."

With a final, trailing-off whimper, the dangling body went completely limp.

Spyro reached over and shook the head roughly, which only made a tangle of fawn hair bounce. Another, harder shake, and the jaw dropped and a line of drool trickled out of one corner of the opened mouth.

"Fainted," was Spyro's disgusted verdict.

"Poor kid." Nikady brushed back a hank of hair sweat-soaked to the smooth pale forehead.

"Lucky for her we came along when we did." Toki's emotion nimbus had settled to a worried mulberry.

"Yes." Estaban settled his burden more comfortably in his arms. Then, catching the gaze of the others, he went on, "I suggest we've little choice but to take her to Guildhall."

Spyro nodded. "Since we don't know where she belongs, have we any choice at all?"

"And"—as if the other hadn't spoken—"that we send a message to the Center for Contractual Adjustments, reporting that we found an unknown contracted, that she'd been attacked by a gang of uncontracteds and has lost consciousness, and that we'll return her wherever she belongs as soon as she or they can tell us where that is."

"Estaban?" Nikady sounded puzzled.

"On second thought . . ." Estaban started forward, long legs eating the distance in a lithe panther lope. "On second thought, one of us goes to the Center now, immediately, with that message."

"I will," said Toki, nimbus shot with suspicious mud-brown, "if you think it really necessary."

The three trotted to fall into step with Estaban. "He's right, Toki." Spyro was frowning thoughtfully. "This world abounds in pitfalls. Especially now—we cannot be too careful."

"You surely don't think—" Nikady burst out.

Spyro and Estaban exchanged glances. "Best not to take chances," Spyro stated firmly. "Would *you* give them any weapon, let them seize any chance gift of the gods to use against our sister?"

"Right, then." Toki, mud and mulberry now laced with decided olive, reversed his course and began walking briskly back in the direction they had come from. "Tandritanitani, it's a long walk, though."

"Our sister walks farther, each day," Estaban muttered. Again, he and Spyro exchanged glances.

CHAPTER 14

The unknown girl hadn't recovered consciousness by the time they reached Guildhall. The three Navigators explained in a few words what had happened, and soon several of the female Navigators and Guildhall workers were fluttering around the girl, wiping her tear-stained face, patting her hands, and—because the Navigators were mostly High-T—running a mediscan over the limp body arranged on one of the settees in the downstairs living area of the large building.

Alizon reported to the three men, draped exhaustedly over comfortable chairs slightly away from the "sick bay," showing in varying degrees the masculine embarrassment when women go all maternal and fussy. Alizon was as cool as usual. "She's not been physically hurt, I'm sure. It's just exhaustion and shock. She evidently got the scare of her young life. I'd like a word or two with the slime who left her to go alone."

Estaban had been studying his nails. He looked up, golden eyes agleam. "Probably assumed she'd be safe enough. Normally she would have been. They fear contract breaking here like nothing I've seen on any other world."

Spyro pursed his lips. "Medically speaking, what do we do now?"

Alizon shrugged. "You could have answered that yourself, Spyro. Medically speaking, the best thing to do is let her sleep the worst off, undisturbed. Then tomorrow, or the day after if she needs that long, we can organize transport, take her wherever it is she needs to go."

"That's medically speaking." Spyro was thinking aloud. "Maybe what we really ought to do is shoot her full of wake-up juice, find out where she belongs, and deliver her there now, tonight. That's the safe route."

"But—" Young Nikady started a protest, but Estaban's hand on his arm silenced him almost in midsyllable.

"The medical consequences of that could be pretty severe," he said slowly, "don't you agree, Alizon? She might be prevented from doing her contractual duty"—he put the slightest ironic stress on the last three words—"for much longer than the few hours it would take her to recover naturally from her shock and fright."

"Plasmaed if we do and plasmaed if we don't," Spyro muttered.

Estaban shrugged. "I think not. If we do what seems most sensible . . ."

Alizon cocked her head and entered the arena, banners flying. "What seems most sensible to us might not to the locals. I could ask—"

"I know." He flicked her smooth cheek with a careless finger. "But only we know best the ill effects of filling her full of drugs when her bodily reserves are so precarious. I'd say we had no choice but to let her try to recover naturally, at least for the rest of the night."

"What little there is left of it," Spyro commented dourly.

"Unless Toki brings us different word from that center of contractual jiggery-pokery of theirs."

"That's right." Alizon made her surrender, in all pride and honor, banners high. "I'd forgotten you'd sent Toki to report all this. Good thinking, Estaban."

He tapped his own bronzed cheek. "I'm fond of this. I like to keep it in one piece."

It rather settled the argument, and a few minutes later the sleeping (or unconscious) girl was established in a bed on the lowest private floor, with Alizon sitting up in a chair to keep an eye on her. "I've had as much sleep as I want anyway," she lied with honest, clear eyes, "and if she does awake suddenly, she's less likely to take another fright if she finds another woman in the room with her."

The men agreed and, yawning, went to their own beds for some much-needed rest. (Lysander protested, but Spyro simply dragged him along, his burliness making nothing of the boy's still growing muscle. And by the time he got the lad to his own bedroom, he was half asleep and only groaned protestingly when the man tipped him into his bed and pulled the covers over him.)

Estaban lingered, though, his champagne gaze moving from the brown-haired child-woman huddled in a curl on the bed to the petite pastel one-hundred-percent adult feet-up in the rather hard chair. Alizon blew him an airy kiss and made a shooing gesture, finger on lips in the immemorial shush pose. Then he smiled, flash of white teeth in the dark face, blew a kiss in return, and vanished.

Alizon read for a while, then her head began to droop lower and lower. She was unaware when a hand brushed against her neck, pushing an auto-inject ampul against the bare skin, and without realizing it she slid from drowsiness to total unconsciousness, between one even breath and the next.

Leany smiled down at her oblivious victim, and arranged her so that she wouldn't be warned by cramped muscles just how long she'd been sitting unmoving. Two hours, they told her. It should be enough.

She had been well schooled with the offworlder magics, and the woman hadn't felt a thing. Now the next step—

She pulled out the odd necklace she'd been given, pushed the tiny button, put it on, and waited. And blinked. Nothing had happened. She could still look down and see herself clearly. But this room had certain basic furnishings, like all the rest, and there was a mirror in the corner. Leany went and stared at herself—and gasped.

A vague shadow faced her, instead of a buxom young girl.

It had worked after all!

Giggling to herself, she raised an arm. The shadow changed shape slightly. If one looked right at it, there was something there. But in the dimness of the corridors at this late night hour . . . She nodded. Two hours.

She pulled the little screen disguised as a pretty bangle out of her pocket and activated it as she'd been taught.

Twenty-two.

However many Navigators were out of the Guildhall for various reasons, checking out berths, spending the night with local friends, bar crawling, honor-guarding Jael, whatever, they wouldn't be likely to risk *the* Personal out where any casual search would grab it.

So.

Twenty-two Personals to check out.

Starting with Alizon's.

It was on a chain around her neck, and Leany listened, with the small button in her ear, until she was sure it was Alizon's and no other's. Her cheeks were slightly pink as she replaced it back around the delicately molded throat. Personals recorded *everything,* and Alizon hadn't gotten around to editing out the private bits in a while.

One down, twenty-one to go.

She slipped out into a long hall, went down it cautiously, giving a flick around before slithering into each room that the screen told her housed a Personal.

Her search was quick. She listened to each one until she was sure it wasn't the one she sought, then went on.

She jumped each time a sleeper moaned or turned over; whenever she heard a sound she froze, not breathing. But most of the sleepers were simply unmoving lumps under the heavy covers, wrapped-up bundles against the crisp chill of the night.

Once she heard footsteps behind her, and she sagged against the wall, unmoving, her mouth dry, her heart pounding so loud she thought that whoever was coming up behind her must surely hear and wonder. But the footsteps shuffled past, and she saw a back clad in an exotic robe of some sort, bisected by a thick braid of startling green hair. The Navigator went into a small room that was unoccupied (by Personals, according to the screen) and came out seconds later with a tall mug of something that fizzed gently. The Navigator, head bent so she couldn't see his (her?—the robe draped loosely) face, dropped a couple of tablets into the goblet and was already drinking thirstily (Leany could hear the noisy gulps) as he (she?) turned back into a room Leany had already checked out.

She waited until the door closed, and glanced down at the screen. All Personals seemed to have stayed in the same position; this was one she had already plugged in, it seemed to have returned, and there was no Personal in the room the Navigator had visited.

She let out a long sigh. If she'd gotten caught—

Time was running out. Nineteen. Up onto a high floor. Twenty. And twenty-one. And the one in the room she was to go back to, that was the twenty-second. She looked and looked again. Each dot on the screen had a tiny blue glow around it. Checked out. She was done. Finished. Through. No Personal.

She tripped back down the stairs, humming absentmindedly under her breath.

And froze in the doorway.

Two Navigators were standing, talking in low tones in the middle of the hall. Right outside her room. If they decided to enter . . .

She watched, hardly breathing. The low murmur of voices reached her, but not the words. She waited, licking her lips.

"In the morning, then," Toki was reporting to Spyro. "They have precedents for this, like everything else. They said to wait until she could tell us; or, if she remains unconscious, they'll have to search through the records to try to trace her." A snort. "That'll take years, from the look of things. You should see the place. Heaps of parchment, scrolls, paper; would you believe stone tablets and some I think are hardened clay. Room after room after room. I suspect they're sure she'll be able to tell long before they manage to identify her. Or she'll be reported missing." A sudden grin. "So am I. You have to see that place to believe it."

Spyro snorted. "I believe it. All of a piece, this mad world." A shrug. "Good enough, not going to disturb her tonight. Morning's soon enough, I guess." A huge, jaw-cracking yawn. "Back to bed for us both."

Toki nodded. "She's not really hurt, is she?"

"Doubt it. Scared, exhausted, panicked, shock. If anything goes really sour, Alizon'll push the panic button, toot sweet. Trust our girl." Ruefully. "Have to admit, I need the sleep. Not as young as I was."

Toki's nimbus turned a satisfied robin's-egg blue. "Nor I. And I've to pack yet." A sigh. "Tomorrow. Soon enough."

Spyro yawned again. "Forgot. You're shipping out, aren't you. Don't worry, brother. I'll get in your licks as well as my own."

"I'm not worried—about *that,* brother."

"I know." A thwack on the taut thin arm. "You're taking the Gaurdy Loop, aren't you?"

"For my sins."

"I'll see the word gets passed ahead, if I can."

"Thanks, brother."

"You'd do the same for me—"

Talking and yawning, the two men sauntered off down the hall, one turning in a room a few doors down, the other continuing up the stairs.

Leany consulted the screen. Yes. The one had gone into a room she'd already checked out, and—the screen now showed twenty-three blips, one unringed. She literally ran down the hall to the stairs, got to their base just in time to see a door closing one flight up. She hurtled up the stairs, got the door open a crack, watched the newcomer enter a room.

She waited, counting under her breath. A hundred. A hundred again. Finally she went to the door, held her ear against it. Someone moving around, brushing noises, a low-voiced mutter, a clink as something dropped from tired fingers.

She waited, and eventually was rewarded with an unmistakable *fwooomp,* and a sigh.

Again she counted. The man was tired, he should go to sleep quickly. She only had to be patient—

At last she couldn't wait any longer. She eased the door open. He was a heap under the covers. He snored.

Men! She tiptoed over to a long dressing table, heaped with oddments in untidy piles. The Personal was plainly visible, he'd dropped it right on top. She plugged it in, shut her eyes—

Unplugged, nodded, punched in the checked-out code on the screen, and slipped out, speeding back to her own room.

Alizon hadn't stirred, and Leany slithered back into the bed, shut her eyes, and was asleep within seconds. This time she wouldn't need the drug to make her appear unconscious. She was exhausted, mentally and physically. She snuggled into the welcome sleep with a grateful sigh.

Outside the door, one of the shadows hesitated, then clicked off. A Navigator stood there, hands still on the control of a camouflage cloak not dissimilar to the one Leany had been wearing. He put a thoughtful finger to the side of his mouth, cocked an eyebrow—and then went casually back to his own bed.

This was Rabelais. But the offworlders had another name for it. Rope. As in, "Give a man enough rope to hang himself."

Or a woman.

CHAPTER 15

"I *can't!*" "Can't" was never a word pleasant on a c'holder's tongue. The Lady C'holder Medee Oriflamme spat it out as though it burned her mouth.

There were a dozen people in the sybaritic room, all sensuous furs and skin-caressing synthetics, gleaming marble and provocative scents. But only two of the inhabitants counted. Two were c'holders. Contract-holders. The rest were contracteds—furniture, lines on a page. They ducked out of the way as the Lady Medee paced up and down, gauzy draperies molding to her wire-thin but sinuous figure in a manner that made more than one of the males present lick his lips and hope his lady didn't realize—or if she did, she would be amused and not insulted. Contracteds could be gelded for raising their eyes too high.

"If there is anyone who has influence over him, it is you." The other c'holder spoke in soft, dispassionate tones. It was as though she were a muted, blurred copy of her sister. Feature by feature, almost alike oval faces, pointed, cleft chins, tilted light eyes. But Medee glittered, she fizzed, she crackled with energy, overflowed with life and vitality. Esme sat upright, spine stiffly straight, hands primly folded, paler hair without her sister's boisterous waves confined to a single rope falling down her slim back instead of rippling buoyantly around her shoulders.

"No one has influence over Singh," Medee spat. "No one. And no one can stop him from taking what he wants. No one ever has, and no one ever will."

Esme stared down at her slender, well-kept fingers, the fingers that only a supreme effort of will held still instead of trembling. She wasn't about to inform her sister that *she* had stopped Singh, at least in regards herself. By deliberately showing him only the sort of woman he wouldn't cross the room for. She had protected herself from him by never arousing his shallow, transient interest. (Well, there had been the single occasion, a narrow escape, a lesson hard learned.) Except for that once, he had never realized that the soft quiet shy ghostwoman who drifted through the fringes of his life would be worth the snapping of his fingers for, and she intended to keep it that way. He tended to want all the harder what he thought might be denied him, so she was always very careful. Very, very careful. Clothes deliberately sexless. Hair held neatly back. There were ways a woman signaled a man, and she knew them, had known she had to be under conscious control around her fellow c'holders since she was a child.

It made a girl grow into a woman very fast. But that wasn't the problem now.

"Nonetheless, he must be convinced to stop this madness. Medee, sister, think for once. What he intends doing will affect us all. If the Navigators interdict this world, and the ships stop coming—"

Medee only laughed. "What real difference can it make?"

"In the short run, our lifetimes, perhaps nothing," Esme admitted.

Medee laughed again. "Then what does it matter?"

"Have you ever heard of an offworld science called histometrics, sister?"

"Offworld stupidity." Serpent-swift, her hand darted out to pluck a sweetcake from a nearby table. A fly that had been sampling its icing buzzed angrily away. Esme said nothing. She did not allow food to be left out, and her kitchen was kept meticulously free of insects, by netting, constant vigilance, and cleanliness and neatness. But Medee was greedy and impatient. Her contracteds knew to keep food available at all times and in all rooms.

"Not stupidity. It's a method of predicting how people in the mass will react, how a society will turn. I watched them use their programs, on their computers, to predict what will happen to our world." Medee licked her lips of aquamarine icing and snorted. "Our society is stratified and rigid, sister. Such societies break before they change."

"Change?" Medee licked aquamarine from her fingers and addressed the air—or her contracteds. "I liked that. Have it available from now on, but with nuts on the frosting." To her sister, with a happy giggle: "Our life is perfect, why should it change?"

Esme looked down at her slim fingers. "All things change, and our world too, in time. But now—we have sampled the forbidden fruit, sister. The offworlders have come, too many of our people are aware that there are other ways, other worlds. Change is coming, C'holder. Perhaps not in our lifetimes, but it will come. And what we do now determines whether that change will be peaceable or ugly."

"Nonsense." She paused in front of one of the many mirrors lining the room, placed a curl just a fraction lower on one painted cheek.

"Is it? If the offworlders go, it will look as if the c'holders drove them away, as if they feared something to do with them. As if—sister—" She put out a hand, her gesture, from long habit, submissive and restrained for all its pleading. "—numbers cannot lie. There have been too many parallels in history to our situation. Show someone a sweet, let him hope, let him yearn—and then snatch it away. If the offworlders go, the revolution will come, perhaps as soon as the day after. And it will be ugly, bloody, savage."

"You're mad." Medee stopped her pacing to stare at her sister. "What do you mean by revolution, anyway? I've never heard the word."

Esme's eyes dropped again, as though staring down at her hands, clasped again in her lap in that characteristic pose. "Bloody change, sister. Very bloody. If you cannot tear up a contract, people may think, you can end it by tearing up its holder."

Medee spat, barely missing a contracted, who knew better than to flinch away. "You've been talking to Karolly again, him and those offworld friends of his." She spat again. "Bad enough when it was merely some of the men from the ships . . . but now—a between-c'holders memorandum, when he could have had her under standard life-contract—that *woman*—that offworlder—"

Esme suppressed a smile. Jealousy? From her gorgeous sister who could have any man on Rabelais for the crooking of a finger? Any man but Karolly, it seemed. Had she, Esme, visited the older c'holder too often? There was nothing between them, had never been, except a similarity of interests, like mind meeting like. She was glad for him, unselfishly, that he'd found his happiness. Perhaps if he had been so lucky, then she—

It was true that her arguments had been gotten from Karolly and his friends, c'holders and offworlders.

"She amuses him in her differences from an ordinary Rabelaisian contracted, I suspect," Esme offered. "Her value is her differentness, and when that wears off . . . in fact, I find her discourse amusing myself. She has visited many different worlds and speaks of them most glibly."

"Lies." Medee pouted.

"I have asked Karolly for a first option on her, for when he tires of her prattle, and he has agreed." It was a lie, but she knew Karolly would see the wisdom of implementing it as soon as possible.

"A contracted is a contracted." Medee's lip still stuck out, like a sulking child's. "This solemnity of yours bores me, sister." A sly smile that Esme couldn't see. "If you are so perturbed about this foolishness, why don't you speak to Lord C'holder Singh yourself?"

It took an effort to suppress her shudder. "Because I know it would be a waste of breath, sister."

Medee slinked up to her sister. Two birds with one stone. "Only because you have avoided him in the past," she purred. "He is insulted, he feels you . . . disapprove of his activities."

Esme chose her words carefully. "I haven't the right to approve or disapprove of another c'holder's conduct, sister. Yet it is truth that many of C'holder Singh's activities are not such as I myself would care to join in."

"Even when you wish to be on his good side?" She tweaked the long hank of dun-brown hair with hurting playfulness. Esme's lids fluttered to hide the response: he has no good side! "Suppose I could tell you of an amusement of his which I know he would be most pleased for you to share, one that would not offend your sensibilities."

"I doubt that, sister."

"He has spoken to me often of his wish that we both share his happinesses." Esme shuddered. "And you have already expressed an interest in this adjudication concerning the offworld woman, the Navigator. I know C'holder Singh plans to attend, and so do I. If you were there, too, to speak sweetly in his ear at the right moment—" Her eyes glittered with unholy amusement.

"I—will consider it."

"He takes me much for granted, sister. A word from you, an encouragement would have the flavor of novelty, and might sway him." Behind her sister's back, her teeth flashed in a sly grin. The beginning wedge. So easy. Singh had not specified what kind of amusement, and he'd be the first to admit that he considered the adjudication of the woman he wanted, the woman he meant to tame slowly and deliciously, as an amusement of a high order. "He respects you, you know. Your intelligence, your perspicacity. Are a few hours in his presence, in a crowded room, too high a price to pay?"

Esme bit her lip. Medee practically hugged herself. For one of

Singh's regular amusements, she would have had to trick or kidnap her sister. For this—why, Esme had practically begged to be allowed to martyr herself. For that was how she thought of it. Delicious! Singh would love it, love watching her watching the trial. She would have to tell him all, he would congratulate her. . . .

Back in her own, much sparer rooms, Esme looked from face to face of her contracteds. "Well?" All knew that she would make, in the end, her own decision, but also that she wanted their opinions, honestly and freely expressed.

"Don't do it, mistress." A tall guard was the first to speak, firmly and unhesitatingly. A swordstroke had scarred him, blinded one eye. He loved his sweet and no longer childish mistress with a fervor that burned within, but he knew he could never speak. Not that she would punish him for daring, but he knew (that knowledge a heavy burden) that she wouldn't believe, would take it as gratitude, respect, yearning toward her own power as a c'holder.

"Why not, Jakanaan?"

"I don't trust her. I don't trust him. And—" He shrugged. "All the apologies in the world can't mend some things, once they are broken."

She smiled, and once again he felt his heart jump. Such a lovely, wistful smile. "And will you not protect me, Jakanaan?"

"With my life, lady. Yet if that is not enough—"

"I would not have such a cost, Jakanaan. It will not be necessary."

"You aren't going." Esme's tirewoman, Nialla, spoke so eagerly that it was obvious where her own feelings lay.

"I . . . don't know. I must discuss it with Karolly, I think." Another smile, that smile only these intimates were privileged to enjoy. "Though his mind is muchly on other things, for now."

Nialla nodded. Once she had been a laughing sprite without a care in the world, then a drooping, hurt child whose lip trembled at every sound. But she had recovered eventually, to become the quiet woman she now was. Yet once she had told her mistress (who had smiled, after, knowing the recovery was complete) that any time she could be spared from her duties, the C'holder Karolly Zarkos would not have to order. But he had never asked, either, and she had understood, and accepted. For all his fine mind and breadth of understanding, he was a man of his milieu, and would never trust himself to a contracted, would never believe a contracted could make such an offer from sheer disinterested liking (not unleavened with a hint of pity), and so would not allow himself the possibility of being hurt. Nialla clucked softly, remembering. "I hope she is lovely. The C'holder Zarkos deserves only the best."

Esme cocked an eyebrow. "She is young, and holds his interest. I would not call her lovely, but I would be more than pleased if she would accept me as Karolly's friend." A sigh. "Not that she's likely to." With a twinkle. "She has gills."

"What?!?" from all in the room.

"Gills. The organs fish have. So she can go underwater and stay there as long as she wants." Everybody in the room continued to look amazed and stunned. Even if the river that flowed by the city hadn't been choked with garbage, it was swift and treacherous in spring, and barely deep enough for wading the rest of the year. "Karolly says that she claims that swimming—what she calls playing about in the water—is the most delightful sport there is, and anyone who can't swim is missing the best that life can offer."

"Well, I haven't gills," Nialla commented, her fingers busy mending an embroidered overcloak.

"We drift away from the subject." Esme was thinking aloud. "Do I attend this adjudication, as the guest of C'holder Golden Singh, or alone, or not at all?" She looked from face to face. One by one, they shook their heads.

"Unanimous, is it?" Shamefaced or grim, they all nodded.

"Has it occurred to any of you, that now that my sister has openly invited me, if I do not go, and she tells Singh, as likely she will . . . he will think I have refused from fear of him. As I would have. I have already expressed interest in this hearing; what other reason would I have for not attending? So, I am afraid, and from wondering why I am afraid, he will conclude that it is he I am afraid of. He may not use it often, but he has intelligence and to spare. So, he wonders exactly what it is about him I fear, he thinks about me, he thinks of himself and me. . . ." She looked from face to face again. "Safer, I believe, to go, and make it clear that my interest is in the adjudication, and only in the adjudication."

"And if he takes your lack of interest in him as a personal insult?" Jakanaan pointed out.

"A narrow tightrope—because that is the risk I must take." Her eyes were troubled.

CHAPTER 16

Golden Singh returned late one evening to his favorite villa on the outskirts of the city of Pantagruel, intending to have a few hours' sleep, the sleep he always enjoyed after a busy day, the sleep of the light of heart.

One of his contracteds met him just inside the entrance arcade and stuttered out a message.

Singh didn't allow him to finish before striding past, barking "No!" and adding orders for his comfort as he passed.

The noise started less than half an hour later.

Bang! Bang! BOOM! Crash-CRAAA-ack! The distant, inexorable thud of drums, and an intermittent, raucous blare of trumpets that would have roused a corpse, much less a man.

Singh shook his head, and growled an order. His bodyguard, who was actually a gestalt of echo-clones, a dozen bodies with but a single personality, cocked his head as one of his echoes led a squad of ordinary contracteds to investigate.

Within a minute, he could inform his c'holder, "The noise comes from outside the grounds of your contracted villa, in the street left open for all c'holders of class C or better to enjoy. The noise is produced by the C'holder Karolly Zarkos, and he says to inform you that he already sent you a message that he wishes to speak to you immediately, and he merely intends to amuse himself to wile away the time until you are ready."

Boom SQUACCCCK! Boom, boom, BOOMITY, boom! Distance and thick walls muffled the sound; outside it must be literally deafening. Singh propped himself up on his elbows. "How long—"

"Until you speak to him, he says," the bodyguard informed.

"Nonsense." Singh nestled down among the sensuous sheets. "Bring me something to stuff in my ears. I'll not speak to C'holder Zarkos until it pleases me." He lay back, smiling in the darkness lit only by attar- and civet-scented candles. "But you may inform C'holder Zarkos that if any of my contracteds fails to perform their duties because of the distraction of his racket, I'll have him before an adjudicator on the charge of c'breaking."

"Yes, lord. Lord—" He hesitated, and then: "He told me a further message. Would you hear it now?"

Singh rolled over, yawned. "Since I have no intention of talking to him, I just might as well hear what he has on what he calls his mind. Let's have the message, then."

The guard stood stiffly, and Singh knew that his echo, standing near Karolly Zarkos, somewhere outside his grounds, was repeating his own statement.

"I greet you, C'holder Singh." The formal phrases made it clear the guard was simply relaying what his echo-clone was hearing. "I anticipated both your refusal and threat. The choice is, as always, yours, Brother C'holder. You may speak to me now, and enjoy your sleep undisturbed. Or I shall play with some interesting toys an offworlder friend of mine supplied me with. I shan't set a foot on your contracted-for property, but I doubt you'll sleep the rest of the night. As for interfering with the contractual duties of your contracteds, I here and now proclaim my intent to supply you with sufficient contracteds of my own to fulfill all necessary contractual duties involved. It is you who will suffer, and you alone, C'holder. In fact, I rather hope you refuse. I've been aching to try out these gadgets called fireworks. I understand the sight is spectacular, and the sound earth-shaking. I'll give you a count of fifty to start making up your mind, and then I'll start setting them off."

"Ach." Singh had had run-ins with Karolly Zarkos before. And though he'd considered himself the winner—he was *always* the winner!—somehow he had this suspicion that Karolly might not agree with him. Luckily for all concerned, their paths hadn't crossed all that often, their interests being too dissimilar. "I'm awake now. Will this talk you're so keen on take long?"

"Not long." The echo faithfully relayed Zarkos' words. "Why not come out and join me? We can see what my friends are so enthused about. I hate to waste the things, and they might amuse you."

Singh sat up and scowled. "I'd rather sleep. Let's take as little time as possible. I'll meet you on the grounds. The guards will escort you in." He was stalking toward the door, naked (since he always slept naked) as he spoke. Then, to the guard captain: "Don't repeat this. Pick a safe spot in the gardens. Let him inside with a reasonable number of his escort, and muster enough of my guards to outnumber them."

The guard captain crossed his forearms and placed his hands on opposite shoulders and bowed in acknowledgment. "Yes, lord.

The white marble folly is about halfway between your current positions and is easily defensible."

"Good enough." As Singh passed through the curtained archway to his sleeping quarters, two more echo-clones and a round dozen contracteds fell in before and behind him.

By the time he got to the 'denia maze that surrounded the marble folly, his guard had doubled and doubled again.

The ring was high, and gave the meticulously landscaped gardens a glow of ghostly beauty. The lush scent of the pale-white 'denias lingered on the air and competed with the bright spiciness of gingermegs and the sharp tang of the pinnas and cinnacloves.

C'holder Karolly Zarkos was sitting in an open litter, his face turned expectantly, a sardonic expression clear in the light of the torches held by his escort. "Greetings, C'holder." His voice was harsh and cynical. "I knew you'd see reason. This talk won't take much of your time, after all."

"I hope not." Without looking, Singh sat himself down. Though nothing had been there when he started to sit, he wasn't disappointed: a contracted hurriedly thrust a small garden seat, exquisitely carved with the legend of Danaa and the shower of gold, under him. "Well, C'holder." He sprawled comfortably, long naked legs idly splayed, fingers linked and supporting his neck, a picture of insouciant insolence. "You wished to speak with me, and here I am. So—speak."

"You have influence with the Adjudicator Lyhunt."

Singh stiffened almost imperceptibly. "No more than any other c'holder interested in seeing the sanctity of contracts upheld."

"I phrased that clumsily." Karolly Zarkos smiled, an expression that had reminded more than one offworlder of an ancient poem whose repeated refrain was "Beware the truce of the bear." "Of course, like all c'holders and contracteds, you would do all in your power to uphold the sanctity of contracts. I meant to say, you have some influence about Pantagruel in general, and with the adjudicators' courts, likewise, as your words are well known to contain no little leavening of wisdom. And, of course, as you supply contractual labor to them on occasion, you have, perhaps, more opportunity than another might to expound those words in the course of contractual duties." The smile broadened slightly, as the bear showed fangs. "I also believe you have some contractual dealings with the free-contractor Zaqanna, he who has brought a charge of suborning to c'breaking, which is to be held before Adjudicator Lyhunt quite soon."

"And what is *your* interest in this case—aside from seeing the sanctity of contracts upheld?"

The bear-smile twisted into an expression of incredible cynicism. "Oh, above all, C'holder, let us uphold the sanctity of contracts at all costs." His voice deepened, became an almost bear-growl. "So, for the sake of all contracts, I tell you this case must not be brought before the adjudicator. Or, if it is, the Navigator must be adjudged guiltless of all intent of c'breaking, and apologized to, and allowed to go her way, freely."

"What!" Singh erupted out of his chair, and contracteds scattered out of his way.

"You heard." Zarkos' voice was hard. "The woman goes free, Singh. Win her if you can by open methods, that is the privilege of any man, c'holder or not. But don't risk all of us because you desire this one woman out of so many."

Singh shrugged and dropped back into his chair. "Desire her? I? She's an attractive wench, what man could deny it, and I'd not be disappointed were I lucky enough to get her under contract, but admiration is not—"

Karolly Zarkos made a chopping gesture. "We can't risk interdiction, Singh. And the Navigators can do it, and will, if they lose one of their own, whether such loss is acceptable under our society or not. And if our world is interdicted—"

Singh laughed. "So, I have heard this argument before. No more offworld magics. So what! I have plenty of contracteds, my contracts are solid, I can eat my own estate's food and not long for offworld exotics. I have all I care about; I'll not miss the offworld imports."

"Even such as your guard." Karolly flicked a hand at the tall band of echo-clones, who had been an import.

"I have them." Singh shrugged again. "I don't need two sets."

"Singh—" He hesitated, obviously not his usual custom. Then he sighed and unhooked one of the necklets from around his bull-thick throat, and held it toward the other c'holder. "See this?" It was a triangular plaque of hammered gold, set with multicolored jewels that glimmered even in the dim torchlight, and made proportionate to the largeness of the man who wore it.

"A pretty bauble." Singh shot it a bored glance and looked away again. "Local, one of your contracteds, perhaps. Not an import. So what has it to do with the question?"

"Its shape." He slid it off the heavy chain and set it on the arm of his litter, balancing it carefully, almost not breathing as he took his hand away. "You see, how precariously it sits."

Singh started to snap a finger at it, and Karolly placed his big hand between; even the wind from the fingers moving almost knocked it over.

"Wait." Karolly draped the massive chain over the arm, looping it, and then placed the triangle inside the loop, the chain now supporting it. "You see how much more stable it is now, with the chain holding it upright. This triangle is *us,* Singh. And the chain is the offworlders and their magics. Little as you regard them, they make life easier for all. Dried food. Machines. Medicines. Clothes. Amusements. Hope. The offworlders hold our society stable, Singh, and if they are taken away—if hope is taken away—" He jerked off the chain suddenly, and the little golden triangle sailed to the marble chip walkway below. Karolly stared down at it soberly. "Men can endure much if they think there is no better. But if they see better is possible, and the hope of it, even the sight of it, is taken away—"

Singh casually rose, made a gesture, and one of the guards scooped up the trinket and, obeying the impatient movement of his fingers, handed it to his master. Singh flipped it up and down in his palm, laughing. "Our society. Do you really believe we will all wither and die if the offworlders go, Zarkos?"

"I think we may learn the hard way that nothing endures forever, even contracts," Karolly replied soberly.

"Nonsense," Singh snickered. "*If* the offworlders go, it will be the memory of them and their toys that withers and dies, and all will be as it was in our grandfathers' time, and perhaps the better for it."

Karolly Zarkos stared at him, then leaned back in the padded seat, sighing. "*I* will not wither and die, Singh. If this adjudication goes not as it should, I will retire permanently to my estate in the Gargantuas. There my contracteds are all loyal to me, all that we need can be raised on the estate, and the mountains about are high, the entrance to my valley narrow and easily defensible. My friends will be welcome to join me there, but—"

"Shut yourself away from life." Singh strolled over to the litter, still jouncing the triangle in his hand. "I call that dying, in truth."

Zarkos shrugged. "It is better than dying in truth. Let this world of ours be interdicted by the offworlders, and the dying will come. Not tomorrow, perhaps not even next year, but it will come."

Singh pursed his mouth. "Death is not a subject that interests me greatly." He dropped the dangle into the other's lap.

"It wouldn't." Karolly threaded the triangle back on its chain and fastened the chain about his neck.

"But amusements, now—" Singh said slowly, a sly note rippling through his voice that caused the other to stiffen and eye him warily.

"One woman is very much like another," Karolly said slowly. "You've a world to choose from, C'holder. You may have any and all you wish. But the woman who is a Navigator must be allowed to go her own way."

Singh smiled, his finger brushing down Karolly's bearded cheek, his voice poisonously sweet. "One woman is very much like another, eh. So you say, so you have said. If I give up my hopes for the Navigator woman, who may not turn out to be a c'breaker, after all, I may have replacements?"

Still suspicious. "As many as even you could desire."

"But I only want one—at a time, C'holder. An offworlder for an offworlder. *You* have an offworlder woman by contract, so I hear. She must be something out of the ordinary, to have ensnared such a—fastidious one as yourself for so long. A bargain, C'holder. Assign me your rights over the offworlder who has so enthralled you, and I will be too busy even to think about the other one."

There was a silence broken only by the sounds of breathing and the gay tinkle of water dancing through the nearby rock garden.

Singh's smile broadened. "Well, Zarkos?"

For the first time in this interview, Karolly was not in control of himself. "Assign you—" He repeated, voice hollow. "Assign *you*—"

Singh waited, his smile that of a cobra facing a bird.

"Never!" Low but firm.

"But one woman is very much like another, eh, C'holder?" Singh's voice lilted. "And if *you* are not willing to give up this one, the matter cannot be so important to you, after all."

Karolly stared up at him, his deep-set eyes shadowed, as if the bearish face were a skull. Softly he said, "I know you, Singh. I wouldn't wish my greatest enemy a day under your contract, much less a woman I admire. You—" He swallowed. "If it must be one or the other, it will not be *mine*." He glanced at the golden-skinned man, as unnaturally beautiful on the outside—thanks to gene manipulation—as he was inhumanly ugly on the inside. "So be it. Have you noticed one oddity about a triangle, Singh? Any point may be the top—or on the bottom."

Singh reached down, his strong fingers caught the flat gold dangle—and squeezed. "But it always remains a triangle," he informed silkily, adding, as his fingers released the bauble, "It pleases you to talk in riddles you think I cannot understand. The more fool, you."

Karolly balanced the twisted piece of jewel-encrusted gold against his palm. "I've never underestimated your intelligence, Singh, those obscene 'amusements' of yours prove that if nothing else. But I do know how your obstinacy and self-love and confidence in your own powers blind you to whatever you do not wish to see." He joggled the triangle slightly. "*Is* it still a triangle, Singh?"

Singh reached out, mouth wry, and straightened the dangle somewhat, though it would never be what it had been. "It is as much a triangle as matters"—honey dripping from his tones—"and will remain so as long as matters—to me."

"And you will not admit that—" Karolly sighed and shrugged. "I waste breath. I thought I would, but I had to try. Fare-thee-well, Singh. I trust you will be proved correct, and that the triangle will remain a triangle, with the right point up—as long as it matters."

"Sure you won't change your mind about the offworlder, Zarkos?"

"You want a new playtoy." He slipped the chain over the bear-like head with the unbearlike baldness that left its upper half smooth and hard, and flung chain and triangle at the other's feet. "You may have this of mine—but nothing more." A gesture, and his litter was raised by the alert contracteds. His voice floated back. "Perhaps it is for the best. Never was anything worthwhile achieved without . . . hardship."

Singh's mocking laughter followed him out of the scented garden.

CHAPTER 17

The Gilded Cage ran on a dawn-to-dawn basis, but the late afternoon was the slowest time. Zaqanna checked the main room, saw that there were only a few small groups scattered about, well cared for by a pair of pouting barmaids and his cunning second-in-command, and retired to the small room he used as an office cum safe-for-special-items cum place to relax, when and if he could.

He knew he ought to check the upstairs rooms, and the special rooms for c'holders a transmatter away. And he would. Soon. He drew the curtain closed, slumped into a chair, flexing his tired ankles beneath the gilded sandal straps.

Leany was in the room, pouting at her image in a special High-T device he had gotten sometime back off a spacer. (How he had obtained it didn't bear close inspection—even on Rabelais.) It was an interesting gadget. It looked like a simple mirror, though the image it gave was much more precise than polished silver or bronze. But below the screen was a bank of controls, and by playing on them the image could be altered. It had taken Zaqanna and his girls a long time to find the patterns they knew, and they still discovered new ones occasionally. The image could be altered in a number of ways. Simple matters like a different hair color. More complex ones like a mouth widened, made more generous. Eyes slanted, wrinkles removed.

Zaqanna looked at what Leany had done and frowned. Somehow she had changed her round-cheeked, sensuous prettiness to a svelter, more sophisticated image. High cheekbones now thrust commandingly through taut skin below eyes that rested in faintly darkened hollows. The mouth tried for spare, disciplined beauty. The hair was short—and tiger-striped.

"You can't carry it off," he said bluntly. "Even if we could find and get under contract a spacer who could make the changes."

Her mouth pouted even more tightly, and the expression on the image looked strikingly incongruous. "Can they do that even, on other worlds?"

He shrugged, unbuckled a sandal to rub at the reddened mark

the wide strap had left. "So I've heard." For the first time, he realized that there were other figures in the room. Perched on a footstool, legs curled under, eyes rapt on Leany, was the newest addition to the Gilded Cage. Zaqanna noted the enthralled expression and smiled to himself. Perhaps temporary could be extended to permanent. If the lad's c'holder disliked mar and scar—how much longer before the ankle healed and he would go back?—then perhaps something could be arranged, some offworlder trick that would make the lad look and—after the contract was reassigned, of course—be fixed. His clients (most of them) disliked mar or scar likewise. The lad had already proved himself industrious and willing, in small ways. Good enough. Zaqanna would never have signed a temp contract, chores for food and a place to sleep, if he hadn't had thoughts of getting more out of it. And he would. Yes, indeed. Offworlder tricks—

His eyes moved to the third figure in the room, long, sprawled in a chair, likewise unmoving. "Well, Ryker," he prodded, his plans for the boy flashing through his mind in a second, so there was almost no pause between Leany's question and Zaqanna's comment. "Isn't that the truth? That the offworlders change their faces as I change my tunic?"

"Some." He didn't move.

"Can change—or do change?" He had learned this truth about the offworlder long since. He answered only what was asked, no more, no less.

"Both."

"Could I be changed?" Leany made a slight adjustment to the "mirror" and the imaged chin became just slightly more pointed.

"Oh, no," the boy exclaimed, in horrified tones. "You mustn't change, Mistress Leany! You're perfect as you are!" Zaqanna nodded to himself in satisfaction, as Leany giggled and the long straight elegant nose lengthened even more and began to hook down like a witch's.

"The boy's correct. Your current face is quite—appropriate." Ryker said it in his usual impassive monotone, but Zaqanna found himself blinking. It was so seldom the gaunt alien volunteered a word.

"You think so?" he asked, taking the words at face value.

"Your customers think so, and that's what matters, isn't it."

"Oh." He slanted a glance at Leany, now licking her lips, the mirror back to true image as she practiced various seductive expressions. "Yes, that's what counts." She heard and a smug preening expression showed in the reflection, and his mouth hardened. Time for another lesson, eh? But not in front of the boy. Let him keep a few illusions—for now. He put on a broad smile, thumped the youngster on his bony shoulder, and said, voice rollicking with joviality, "And what are you doing sitting here, may I ask? Aren't there tables to clean, floors to sweep? Don't you believe in earning your keep?"

"Oh, yes, sir." The boy zoomed off the chair as though he'd been touched with an offworld electrojolter. "It's just—" His eyes slanted down toward his bandaged ankle and came up, wide and clear. "I'll get to sweeping, right now, sir." He turned to go.

Zaqanna's hand reached out, caught his shoulder. "You will *not*. That ankle'll never heal if you're on it till it hurts. Tell Guilius I said to find you a sit-down job. Washing dishes. Or peeling the taties if the new load's in." A smile. "Away with you, then."

"Yes, sir! Thank you, sir!" And he was off, at a fast limp.

The smile faded, the voice turned cold. "Take a lesson from him, 'tracted. You're pretty, but don't let it make you lazy. I can find better girls on the Exchange any day, younger, juicier. You *work* to keep your place here, or else—"

"Oh, C'holder." She whirled, threw herself at him, knocking him back into his chair. She flung her arms around him, planting wet kisses all over his face. "I'd do anything for you, even if you weren't my c'holder, don't you *know* that?"

"Of course." He patted her back. "But I'm tired right now." He was as sincere as she was. "Run along and get your beauty sleep."

Her lip came out in a pout. "You'll visit me later?"

He *was* tired. "Yes." Also bored with her. She was so . . . predictable. But for now, while her youth and looks held, she was useful. And as a Judas goat, weeping crocodile tears, she had no equals. Not that he'd tell her that.

When she had gone, hurried on with a spank on the rump that was almost a punishment, he turned to Ryker. "Well?"

The man didn't move. Except for his chest rising and falling, he might have been dead—or a turned-off mechanical.

"What did you find out?" Zaqanna asked sharply.

"Did you expect them to tell an outsider anything?" Ryker replied.

"You're an offworlder, one of their own kind. They might have confided—or let something slip."

"They're very worried. I don't believe their worry is feigned.

One of them ships out today. He was biting his lips so hard I'm surprised he didn't choke to death on his own blood. And I've never seen colors like that on an emonimbus before. Body signs don't lie. He'd not be acting like that if he thought she had even a fair chance."

"No suspicion of Leany?" A mutter: "The fewer involved the better, but I wish we hadn't—he hadn't insisted . . ."

"With the dye out of her hair and no makeup?"

Zaqanna snorted. "She looked different all right."

"I saw them escorting her to the Lady C'holder Oriflamme's. She was chattering away, blithe as could be. And they were hovering and protective. No. None of them rumbled her. I'd've known."

But one Navigator had "overslept" and not been available to return the little contracted to "her" c'holder.

Zaqanna smacked one fist into the other palm impatiently. "If only the lord c'holder hadn't desired the Navigator—"

Ryker, not having been asked a direct question, said nothing, and Zaqanna began a restless pacing up and down. "I know what Leany said, but I'll not feel safe until that Personal is found and destroyed. Or—is your equipment ready, just in case?"

Ryker simply continued to half-sit, half-lie in his chair, eyes staring into nothingness. He didn't bother to answer rhetorical questions, either—or questions he had already answered. Zaqanna clenched his fist—and dropped it. There was simply no way to get a hold on this man. Except . . . "You want some early?"

"No."

"Why not? Just this once? I may need you later on."

"Need away. The contract was plain. Times specified."

Zaqanna's lip curled. Leany would have recognized the expression and muffled whimpers beneath a ground-in fist, desperate lest she attract his attention. But his voice was bland, almost coaxing. "But I signed the contract, too. I am willing to sign a rider, to just this once—"

"No. Once is the beginning of the end, and you know it, dunghiller. No. Now and always—except at the time."

Zaqanna knew when he was licked. "I but thought to benefit us both."

"Did you." In anyone else, that dryer-than-dry tone would have denoted wry amusement.

"And—the other errand?"

Anyone else would have said, You still wish? After what the

woman reported? Ryker only answered the question. "Yes. I found them. One is willing."

"Only one?" A mutter. "I don't like depending on uncontracteds."

Silence.

Zaqanna sighed. "Where do I meet him?"

"At the Blushing Flower. Tonight."

"And his fee? The usual? Passage off?"

"No. He has passage off."

A frown. "Well, what then?"

"Simple enough to state. His sister was contracted away from him. He wants her located and returned to his protection."

Zaqanna spat a curse.

Ryker studied dust motes dancing in the dimness.

Zaqanna sighed again, propped a foot on a stool to rebuckle his sandal. "Tonight, at the Blushing Flower, then." Straightening his shoulders, he prepared to go about his business. He was not aware of eyes like steel-gray mirrors—or the jaws of a trap—following his exit.

CHAPTER 18

Reis had finally made up his mind.

Well, not made up his mind . . . exactly. But he'd heard enough to know what he'd better do. He had to get that Personal back to the Navigator—and fast!

Otherwise—

It wasn't just the woman anymore. Much as he disliked her. (Or told himself he disliked her. He had his male pride, after all.) It wasn't just a single woman, albeit what a woman. It was all of them, all the offworlders who had had some protection from this upside-down slavery-is-freedom world of Rabelais, or thought they had, in those idiotic port contracts they all signed. If they could take her—a Navigator—they could take anyone. Not now and then some fool who'd broken their rules-that-weren't-rules. Any of them. Anytime.

That was the word around the port. No matter what happened now, it was going to hurt this world, though the effects would take a long time to be seen. Communication was slow, carried catch-as-catch-can on the FTL ships themselves. The little bad word was already spreading. And if they took her, if it was a *big* bad word that began to spread— The large liners would react slowest, because it would have to go all the way up to regional offices, and routes would have to be altered. The independents like himself, that would be quicker.

It wasn't as if Rabelais boasted any cargo that couldn't be duplicated on a dozen similarly primitive worlds. Exotic foods, native medicines—okay to fill spaces in a hold with. It was more that Rabelais was a convenient stopover, a lot of hyperlines twined near its sun. But other worlds were convenient, too. Not as convenient, maybe—but a whole lot safer. Rabelais' loss—their gain.

If the Navigator was shanghaied into slavery . . .

Not that he cared about Rabelais. Let it suffer, let its rulers suffer. After he got Rowan out, of course.

And if somebody bowed the Navigator's proud head a trifle—he caught his lip between his teeth, didn't even realize he'd bitten until he tasted the salt tang of his own blood. She really had gotten to him. Deep. Rejection could do that. One-way attraction. It was why he'd held on to the Personal as long as he had. Let *her* suffer. Let her—

He reached into his pocket, stroked his lucky piece, felt the slick hardness of the small Personal beside it.

It wasn't going to be easy, giving it back after all this time. He couldn't even chicken out and say he'd just found it. He always had been a rotten liar, and knew it.

He'd just—

"Hel-lo, spacer," a husky voice crooned. "Lonely?"

He blinked and looked down—and jumped. He knew her, all right, though he didn't think she recognized him, except as a sometime customer for drinks. At the Gilded Cage. But he'd studied her, how he'd studied her. Zaqanna's Judas goat. For an instant he saw nothing but a flood tide of pure crimson fury. Then he relaxed. This was Rabelais, with its vaunted freedom that was nothing but a series of cages. He didn't have to revenge himself on this pathetic betrayer. Zaqanna and Rabelais would do that for him. "You under contract?" He asked the question that all the offworlders knew to ask immediately.

"I'm not under contractual duty right now." She licked her lower lip, made full and lush by paint and even fuller now for the pout on it. She was wearing more than her usual costume at the

Gilded Cage—but not much more. Little was left to the imagination of the beholder. And of her profession no doubt whatsoever.

Even if he'd had a weakness for brassy-yellow hair and over-blown voluptuousness, the part he knew she'd played in Rowan's betrayal would have left him nothing toward her but disgust and anger. Nonetheless, she might be worth some information. Except that the last thing he wanted was for her to know what he was about right now. "I've business myself, right now. Perhaps this evening?"

She turned a shoulder, flung him a saucy, practiced seductive gaze over its rounded whiteness. "Perhaps. If I"—a languid movement of her full hips—"haven't found I have some business myself . . . elsewhere."

He knew the moves of this game, and flicked a finger under her soft white chin, ignoring the many people who were passing in the busy aisle between two rows of ships, empty landing spaces, and storage buildings. He made his voice husky. "I could make it worth your while."

Her hot eyes ate his body, and he knew he had nothing to worry about. Broad shoulders, packed muscle tapering to sturdy hips. He didn't think she'd have any complaints.

From the look in her eyes, she didn't think so, either. "Where shall we meet, when you're through with your business?"

"It *is* business," he asserted, with perfect truth. He had a whole series of errands to run. He had been busy with the ship lately, or in the city proper making efforts to locate Rowan, and he'd let a lot of little details slide. He rather expected they'd take most of the day. He didn't want her dragging along with him; he didn't want her around when he returned the Personal, and he certainly didn't want her waiting at his ship, and maybe finding out what he'd rather she didn't know. He shrugged, and went on, "My last call will be with the port contractor; I have to negotiate a rider with him." He grinned. "Who knows how long it'll take. If I remember right, there's a small eatery, the Bruised Pomegranate, nearby that accepts port-chits. If you'd be willing to meet me there, as near after sundown as I can make it . . ."

She minced a step away, and slanted him a languorous gaze over that round white shoulder she used so effectively. "I might be there, spacer . . . and I might not." If Zaqanna hadn't other duties for her, she meant, or if she hadn't hooked another victim. He had a shrewd suspicion that pumping spacers was her duty at the moment. Bad luck he'd run into her, he'd have to get out of it as best he—

"What the Wheel!" he exclaimed, eyes widening and fixed on something happening beyond her.

She whirled, so she faced straight what had startled him, and stamped her foot. "Not again!"

He watched, jaw literally dropping. Two lines of sturdy enforcers had appeared, seemingly out of nowhere, about twenty paces apart. They were almost arm to arm, and they began walking toward each other, herding all the people unlucky enough to be caught between the two lines into a confused mass.

"What's happening?" He wasn't aware he'd spoken aloud until she answered.

"Some contracted-for goods were taken without contractual authorization from a warehouse. The enforcers have been searching for them since day before yesterday."

"Oh!" It was the first he'd heard of any missing goods.

"So they say." She flicked him a knowing smirk from between darkened eyelashes. It was a "what-I-could-tell-if-I-would" glance.

"Oh!" He watched, jaw still sagging, as the enforcers winnowed through their catch. Free-contractors were being released almost immediately, with the most perfunctory of searches and profuse apologies. (Had a c'holder, with litter and guards, been passing, the trap would not have been sprung.) Contracteds got a little more thorough search, but were being released fairly quickly, especially if they claimed contractual duties. The rest—

Essentially, the offworlders.

Reis watched, eyes aghast. They were getting thorough searches, and not polite ones. Stripped to the skin, their bodies probed. One woman protested, and she was rapidly accused of hindering-a-contracted-in-his-contractual-duty, the whole rattled off like a single word. When she shouted she hadn't meant to hinder, she simply objected to being harassed for no reason, she was dragged away.

Reis turned to Leany. He didn't know the woman, her uniform was from one of the major liners, those giant, self-contained ships that stopped on Rabelais as short a time as possible, to restock, to give their passengers a chance to stretch their legs. Despite the fact that those liners had all the luxuries known to modern technology, their passengers still seemed to need a change of scene occasionally. "What will happen to her?"

Leany shrugged. "Nothing. A more thorough search, I suppose.

I doubt they'd bother to have her up in front of an adjudicator for hindering."

"*More*—thorough—" He stared as the unfortunates within the trap were subjected to as exhaustive a body search as was possible without High-T scans.

Leany shrugged, again, bored. A woman should know what to expect.

Reis was shocked at how quickly it had been done. The searched ones, minus most of their possessions—though there were loud promises to return same as soon as they had been proved not under contract—were already being set free. He shuddered. If he'd been caught—

He gasped as if somebody had kicked him in the solar plexus. Searches! Were they just searching the odd offworlder? Or was this an excuse to search offworlders—*and* Guildhall? What a fool he'd been! Guildhall! The first—and last—place they'd look! His ship was probably safe—they couldn't search every inch of every ship in port, and he knew some clever hidey-holes . . . but Guildhall?

Idiot! Even to think of returning it to Guildhall!

An enforcer brushed past him, shot him a hard look. Reis muttered an automatic apology, and then looked down at Leany. "This has delayed me. I must hurry. If you could join me later at the Bruised Pomegranate . . ." His hand went to his pocket, crackled port-chits suggestively.

She made a face, lips pursed, and ran fingers up his brawny arm.

He had to get back to the ship, hide the Personal—or be safe and put it down the disinter . . .

Safe—

If he lost his ship, and no more ships came to Rabelais . . .

He shuddered inwardly. It wasn't just Jael any more. It was every spacer on Rabelais.

Even he himself.

CHAPTER 19

The Blushing Flower was not dissimilar to the Gilded Cage, the main difference being that its clientele was entirely local, thus it didn't need to look "native." Two doormen naked but for their weapons stood at attention, and from within wafted sounds of music and light laughter and provocatively sensuous scents.

Zaqanna stood about a dozen paces away, eyes scanning the shadows near the curtained doorway, the latter embroidered with an abstract pattern in soft flesh tones, which somehow subtly suggested curving perfumed limbs and satiated lassitude. "Turn and walk away," came a voice from the deepest shadows. "I'll follow."

Zaqanna shook his head slightly, moved up to the guards, spoke to one of them, went inside, laughed and joked with his fellow barkeep, got the special wine that was his ostensible reason for coming, promised a different but equally prized vintage in exchange, looked over a new girl but refused the offer to try her out, and generally spent about the same amount of time he always did, had he been coming as one of several errands, and not a "busman's holiday."

When he came out, he strolled briskly along, a man with naught but business on his mind. "Curse you!" came the voice from the shadows.

"Follow," was all Zaqanna replied.

The city was old, built and overbuilt and built again. Higher floors were actually wider than the ground floor, so that they almost met in the center of the street in many places. Even in the daytime many of the streets were dim, filled with obscure niches and hideaways. Any denizen of the jungle knows the best places to lair, and Zaqanna had been walking only a few minutes when he turned sideways suddenly and slipped into a little blind pocket that was surrounded by unwindowed walls of high-rising stone buildings. He turned to face his follower. "Here," he informed. "It's safe. If you get caught, it's no use accusing me; no one will believe you."

The other, still holding to the shadows so his face was a vague blur, snorted. "Your world, cock. Think I don't know that. The important thing is, can you do it?"

"Do what? Can you do what I want? That's what's important."

"No, it isn't. Didn't the zombie tell you what I'll have? I want my sister back."

"A woman?" He snickered. "What's a woman?"

"Important to me and mine. I warn you, cock. I'll find this Personal for you if it's there to be found. But I won't hand it over until my sister's safe with me. And I mean *safe*."

Zaqanna shrugged. "She's under contract, you say. C'holders are usually willing to do favors for each other. My patron is powerful. It can surely be arranged."

The other shifted impatiently. "It had better be, cock. I'm dry-sick of this world of yours. I can't go back without my sister. And if I can't go back—maybe I'll feed Our Lady of the Dolorous Shallows a sacrifice." He chortled. "I don't think you'd like that, cock. Two sacrifices, so it won't matter what your world does with contract-breakers."

Zaqanna didn't believe him. (Ryker would have recognized a man at the end of his tether speaking simple truth.) But it shouldn't be too hard to trace down an offworlder woman. A man, perhaps, too many men got caught in the gears of Rabelais. But women were scarcer. The ships were more careful of them.

"I'll find her if she's still in the city to find. And I'll get her back, though the arrangements may take some time."

"You find her. You release her. And if she's been taken out of the city, you find her and have her brought back."

"All right." Words without contracts were worthless. "You know what you're to do."

"Yes. When do you want delivery?"

"I visit the Main Contract Exchange every two or three days. Tomorrow after the noon break. Or two days after that, at the same time."

"All right. Tomorrow, with any luck. You go first, cock. I'll wait a few minutes. Unless you'd rather we be seen together."

Zaqanna didn't bother to answer that. He was whistling cheerfully when he left.

CHAPTER 20

It was close to dusk, one sun down and the other spreading a dying splash across the sky, by the time Reis had gotten back to his precious *Scalded Cat*. He hadn't been stupid enough obviously to rush back, he had accomplished all his errands but the visit to the port contractor, though sweat was trickling down his spine and his back crawled from the constant anticipation of the fall of a heavy hand on it. At least, he had had time to think out the answer to one of his current problems.

He honestly wasn't going to be able to make his appointment with Leany. Yet he didn't dare arouse the slightest suspicion. There was only one member of the crew who hadn't been on board and introduced when Jael made her visit, and Reis didn't think any of the others had bothered to mention it to him, even casually. All he had to do was send Prax—after "accidentally" encountering him in one of the ship's corridors—and he didn't think the girl would be disappointed.

Setting it up was simple. A frown, a mention of his dilemma—can't be in two places at the same time, don't like to let the woman down, may have another opportunity later—

Prax was amiable. Prax was always amiable. The man was, oddly, since he was a civvy, not a bred spacer, one of his best crew members. He was competent, soft-spoken, the oil on troubled waters. Yet as long as he'd been aboard, Reis couldn't say he knew or understood him.

At least he hadn't accepted another berth, as two other members of the crew already had. Though if the *Scalded Cat* remained grounded for much longer . . .

No matter. Leany wouldn't be disappointed. Prax, except for his artificial arms, was as gorgeous a specimen of sheer masculinity as Reis had ever encountered. And the prosthetic arms were almost artist's creations in themselves, translucent synthi with moving jewel glows and shining chrome ever rearranging themselves within, and held a unique attraction of their own. From comments let drop by the female crew members, Leany would have nothing to complain of in the most important area, either.

Prax, as Reis had anticipated, merely shrugged acquiescently. The freighter-master hurriedly showered—his excuse for the brief detour to his ship, and not such an excuse, either—and trotted out, whistling. *That* should take care of the Personal, all right!

The two men split close to the Bruised Pomegranate, and Reis hurried on his way, satisfied that he'd fixed everything just so. He wouldn't have been half so smug if he'd known that young Liu had spent a very cheerful, masculine half hour discussing his very male fantasies involving the striking Jael with Prax, who thus knew all about the Navigator's visit to the *Scalded Cat*.

Leany was momentarily openly disappointed that Reis had been "unavoidably" detained, but she knew her trade well. Soon she was laughing and flirting with Prax, telling all and sundry, in words and body language, that there was no one else on the entire world of Rabelais that she'd rather be spending time with.

Prax had given her one shrewd up-and-down assessment, and shuddered inwardly. But if his captain wanted this woman turned up sweet . . .

He laughed and flirted back, and all and sundry would have thought that there was no one else on the world of Rabelais that he'd rather be with, either.

The Bruised Pomegranate made it easier than it might otherwise have been. The café used two different chefs each shift, so that the offworlders could choose from a selection of exotic cuisines—basically the simplest kind of foods that showed up consistently on world after world, with a sprinkling of various imported oddities—plus a menu of pure native fare.

They made a play of selecting for each other, Prax explaining the various offworld delicacies and helping her to narrow her choices, and she doing the same for him on the native offerings, though the ship had been grounded long enough that he was at least familiar with most of the common foods.

By no sign whatsoever did he let slip that he was praying his full-range Immos would protect him.

In fact, he wasn't. It was the risk one took, traveling, and he was so accustomed to it he rarely even thought about it.

It was during the dessert, an assortment of native sweets for her, and a single imported bittertingle for him, that he caught her chin in his hard artificial fingers and said slowly, "Pity I no longer light-sculpt. I believe you would be quite an inspiration."

She giggled and fluttered, taking it for a compliment.

He didn't tell that, had he created such a piece, he would have called it something like "Betrayal."

"Oh!" she exclaimed, looking over his shoulder and forming her soft lips into a disappointed pout.

"Is anything the matter?"

"Just—someone I know. Maybe he won't see—"

He couldn't have missed seeing. Yet he would have passed by, except she put out a dimpled hand and stopped him. "It's my evening *off*, Free-contractor," she said, in a hard voice.

The man with her hand on his arm simply stopped, his odd flat silver-gray eyes flicking over the pair at the table, bored and incurious.

Prax, recognizing a fellow offworlder, rose and bowed with the formality of his own home world, stretching out a hand. "I'm Engineer First Praxiteles, off the freighter *Scalded Cat*. Pleased to meet you. Any friend of the Lady Leany's is a friend of mine."

Leany giggled; it was a nasty sound. "Ryker doesn't have friends, he free-contracts with my c'holder." A downward twist of full lips. "He takes Elysium—full strength."

"Wha—" Involuntarily, Prax took a step back.

"Controlled," Ryker informed in his usual impassive monotone.

Prax had a glass near his left hand. He picked it up and downed a hearty swig. "I would have said that was impossible."

Ryker made a small movement of one shoulder; it might have been a shrug. He could care less what Prax or anybody else thought.

"What's it—" Prax started, then stopped. He'd heard tales—which spacer hadn't—of full-strength Elysium. He didn't believe half of them. And, partly due to home-world manners and partly to the shell he had put around himself since the accident that had stolen both hands and art, he didn't want to seem to be prying now.

". . . really like?" Ryker had heard it many times before. "Try it yourself and see."

Prax sank back into his elaborately enameled chair. "I don't think it could be worth it." Elysium addicted with one dose.

"It is." The drawn mouth twitched. "If you can control it."

"No, thanks." Prax shook his head. Though there had been a time when he had been tempted to commit suicide, in the nastiest way possible. But he'd lived through that particular trough of utter depression, and learned to accept. Now he stared at the gaunt man who claimed to control an Elysium addiction.

Leany didn't like attention being off her for any length of time. Now she pouted. "Zaqanna didn't send you after me, did he, Ryker?"

He just looked at her. Zaqanna doesn't send *me* on errands, that look might have implied. Though he did, sometimes. If Ryker chose to oblige.

"Well," she prodded, licking her lips until they glistened. *"Did* he?" Not because she thought he had, just to keep the attention of her companion, who was staring at Ryker, nothing but a vacuum-head when all was said, as if he were some strange and intriguing new specimen.

"No. I'm just . . . killing time."

Prax sucked in air and nodded, almost imperceptibly. *That* was it. Time. Time between doses. If you could take the deprival.

Ryker nodded in turn, as if he, too, recognized the odd affinity between the two men. "Perceptive," he said.

Another deep breath. "If you're ever on Rodin, my name is Praxiteles. My work is displayed in the galleries in both Danaid and La Belle Heaulmiere."

Again the two men had communicated more than words. Prax had extended one of the highest compliments he was capable of, and Ryker knew it. Not that it mattered, to *him*. And Prax knew *that*. Nonetheless, a mixture of admiration and pity had impelled his speech.

Ryker didn't even shrug. But after a second he said, eyes still uninterested and speech still monotone, "If I am ever on the planet Rodin, I will look in the galleries of the cities Danaid and La Belle Heaulmiere for the works of the sculptor Praxiteles."

Prax nodded. Cripple recognizing cripple, he thought. Though his had not been of his own choosing. He slanted a glance at Ryker, tall and gaunt, still standing beside the table, his whole attitude, Why not? I've nothing better to do. In a flash of insight: But it *was* my choosing. As was his. He frowned. Perhaps— And then shook his head. No. When one has known perfection, how can one bear anything less. . . .

He couldn't help staring at Ryker. Because Elysium was said to give totisensory illusions of paradise. Which was why it addicted. Users simply couldn't bear to return to mundane reality. But this man had conquered. Controlled his longing. Lived his drab hours until the next taste of perfection.

Eyes of gray shallow as unpolished steel. Praxiteles, once the pampered pet of a world renowned for its artistic geniuses, who were expected to produce to the highest standards, had finally met someone who had fallen farther than he had. He didn't realize it—yet—but an odd healing had begun. Only begun, for now. But someday—

Leany would have gotten far more out of happy-go-lucky Liu. But Liu had been on the ship during Jael's visit, had actually met and spoken with her. Reis would never have sent him into the lioness's den.

Prax was used to keeping his counsel on his own affairs. He had no difficulty restraining what he knew of his master's business. At first.

Leany, as Zaqanna well knew, was adept at small talk. Once Ryker had meandered on his way . . .

Prax had never had any intention of letting this chance-met woman breach his privacy, or bringing her back to the room that held the evidence of the part of himself he held secret—he fondly thought—from the world. And he'd heard enough to realize that the Gilded Cage was little more than a gilded trap.

But there were plenty of places where they could wander freely, dance to music both native and alien, eat strange foods, see unique-to-this-world sights. He could play tourist as well as any other.

And talk . . .

CHAPTER 21

The Guildhall had once been roughly in the center of the then newly established port. But the port jammed up against the city walls, and had to grow in the other three directions. Now Guildhall was almost to one side, comparatively close to the walled city. Originally it had been built by an offworld machine that sucked in air, broke down the molecules to their individual atoms, and spewed out a foamed synthetic that had a startling structural strength. But that had been centuries ago. Bits and buildings had been added, the early ones again of the synthetic, the later ones of native materials.

Then the synthetic itself began to fail, and walls had been reinforced and covered with whatever materials available.

Now the Guildhall was not a single building, but a complex inside a thick-walled courtyard, some structures small and simple, others larger, and the main building quite huge. Parts of it, even now, still showed a dulled synthetic, bits of rainbow made solid and shot with gold and silver gleams. Parts were facaded with brick or stone, adobe or the woven dried plant fiber used so ubiquitously on Rabelais. Endless graffiti adorned all the walls—names, portraits, comments. The Guild symbol, a hand with a pointing finger wrapped in a coil of wire, was relief-carved almost two meters high over both the outer gate and the main door.

It was neither the outer gate nor the main door Jeroa was aiming for. Nor did he intend climbing the wall. Anybody who penetrated any part of the compound would be spotted in seconds, thanks to High-T scans. The same went for the underground drainage system, city-wide, added to and updated countless times over the centuries. *He* would have adjusted his scans to check out the labyrinth under his feet, and he didn't doubt that the Navigators had, too.

Not under, and not through—all that left was over.

It's just like moon-sailing, he thought, as he glided in slow lazy loops over the sleeping port. At first he'd been afraid that his launch—from the highest port of a large liner, with a friendly crew member watching him off with a reminiscent smile, odd payment for an enjoyable day—hadn't been high enough, that he'd spiral to earth far from his goal. Then old habits took over, and it was the white foaming waves below him, not the heterogenous port. A waggle of the organi-synthetic wings, made by himself and transparent to most scans, and he'd felt the first slight lift of an updraft. For precious minutes he'd just glided, an Icarus unafraid of the gentle ringlight, back in a happier time when his greatest problem was sweetfish or decapus for dinner. Sweet loops through air kissed with salt . . .

"Tam," he shouted challenge to the winds, "catch me, Tam!"

And remembered.

Tam.

Not the waves, not the home shallows. A world called Rabelais, where the price of freedom was eternal slavery.

He cocked a wing and spiraled lower, a keen-eyed—thanks to High-T longsights—bird of prey. There. The huge Guildhall compound was unmistakable, its own lights and the gauzy ring giving it a ghostly essence.

The intruder arrowed in, his spiral gradually centering on the main building, several stories high. Now if there was just a level spot to land somewhere on the roof. . . .

He spilled clumsily, one leg crumpled painfully beneath, the spines of the wings bending and gouging him sharply all over his body. He went limp, waited. No sirens or other evidence of detection went off, though they could be waiting for him when he went into the building proper.

He unstrapped the wings, inspecting them closely. Not that he'd be able to launch from here, but he might be able to retrieve them somehow, later. Lucky no spines broke, he'd've been transfixed, but he'd been pretty sure his skill would save him that, despite the quality—or lack thereof—of the homemade wings.

He grimly assessed the scatter of other buildings from his aerie. If the main building proved a washout, he would have to risk trying another, or all of them, though they were mainly storage or native servants' quarters. . . . Sufficient unto the tide is the evil thereof, he thought wryly.

At least he had some help. Around his waist was a TRT that made the one Leany had used days earlier the child's toy it was on another world. Even if they had shielded the all-important Personal, this screen would pick it up. He studied the display screen carefully and nodded. Only the main building.

Carefully reconnoitering the rim, he spotted an opening about a story below. Fly-feet attached to his shoes gave him suction, and he went carefully down.

And in. Open window, empty room.

He consulted the searcher again. Plenty of Navigators about, plenty of Personal tags with their smaller blips. Trouble was, the building was multi-level and the screen wasn't. Best he should climb to the top floor and work his way down.

He cracked the door to the small room, slitted an eye out . . . coast clear. He soft-footed it to the stairwell, dark and shadowy.

The top floor was obviously used for storage. He checked out each room methodically, the searcher at full range and then close up, to be certain he wasn't missing anything.

Nothing. Nobody. No sharp challenge breaking the soft night stillness.

The next floor down was also storage; the next held sleepers. He tightened the fool-the-eye nervously. It wouldn't protect from a determined search, but in the night dimness and with a sleepy glance—

He started at one end of the hall, entered a room with a double blip. Holding his breath, he edged toward the table, where the small Personal lay with a pile of other oddments. Gentle snores made a soothing background melody as he hurriedly plugged in the Personal and sensed enough to be sure that it was not the Lady Navigator Jael's.

He had equally good—or bad—luck in the next three rooms he tried. Either there was a sleeper and Personal, which checked out to be the wrong one, or no one at all, and no Personal.

Then his luck ran out completely.

He was bending over a sleeper who evidently preferred wearing the Personal even in bed when he felt a sharp edge kiss his throat and an amused voice said, "Make a move but what I say, thief, and it'll be your last."

The edge against his throat meant business. He froze obediently.

A hand gave him a thorough up-and-down pat. He felt his pockets being searched, then heard a low buzz that said the hand examination was being amplified with a scan of some sort.

"Well," came a second voice from the darkness, cool as new-drawn dolfin's milk—and totally unsurprised.

"You were right on orbit, Alizon," said the first speaker. "And you can join us; I've bagged our fox."

Alizon sat up, pale hair spilling behind her like a rippling tidal pool, her eyes blank holes in a skull-carved countenance. "Thanks, Spyro. I'm glad I didn't give you that psychic goose for nothing." Jeroa felt a prickling sensation, as though intangible fingers walked over and *through* him. "He's clean," the psychic informed.

"Good. I have him tight." A hesitation. "I somehow doubt it was your virtue he was interested in, sister."

She slept without night clothing, even in the cold weather, and the young thief's breath hissed in as he stared at that shimmering body.

"Well." She was judicial. "Perhaps that *too*." Jeroa felt a slap, though her hands were both plainly visible; it was hard enough to be the warning she meant it to be, but not so overpowering that he was thrown back and got his throat cut by the knife. "Give me some privacy and a moment to get dressed, brother. Then I'll join you. Two heads are always . . ." It was their in-joke. Navigators were two-headed when they linked with their computer symbiotes.

"You heard the sister." The blade went in, very softly, pressing and denting the vulnerable flesh, but not cutting—yet. "I want you to rise, slowly, keeping your hands where I can see them. Understand." It wasn't a question.

"Yes." Jeroa, caught in his thievery, clenched his fists but obeyed, rising slowly from his bent-over position. The knife followed him up.

"I think I've gotten you clean, and the sister's given you a psychic going-over, but just in case—" The other hand came to hold his neck still for the knife, while the thumb pressed in painfully. Jeroa held very still. One jerk, one movement, and his jugular would spill life's blood, and both he and his captor knew it. He concentrated on breathing without moving any other muscle in his body.

"Now"—his captor sounded almost disappointed—"out the door, scum, and we'll wait for the sister to join us. Then the three of us will have a little talk." The last sentence reeked of menace.

Jeroa obeyed, the tension in him revealed by the nervous tic of the muscles in his taut arms, the thudding of his heart so loud he thought the other two must be flinching from the sound.

Alizon was rather less than the promised minute, but more than decent in a stretchy shipsuit, with an overtunic that came below midthigh, her long mane confined in a band at the nape and swinging freely below, a rope a man could hang himself with.

"The room next to mine is empty," she informed in a low voice. "I don't think we need wake anyone else up, do you?"

The hand and knife held Jeroa still. "No," replied the other Navigator. "Either she or I can break you with our bare hands, thief. Remember that—and go into the room."

He didn't bother to inform them that he'd been trained in unarmed self-defense, long ago on a world that seemed impossibly far away. Sooner or later the man behind would relax, take the knife away . . .

But not until after he'd been stripped to the skin and humiliatingly searched. And until the woman faced him, a little spitter held in one competent hand. He glared at her, naked, furious, but trapped for fair and knowing it.

The man called Spyro came to stand beside her, his face a devil-monkey mask that made Jeroa jerk and then thrust out a defiant chin. "What do you think, Alizon?"

"I'm waiting for him to tell us." She was short and petite, but even in the half-dark—they had only bothered to switch on one eternaglow—her almost colorless eyes were as hard as two-phase shipsteel.

"You had it right." He tried a bluff. "I'm a thief. I was looking for something I could steal, trade for food. I'm hungry."

The last was true. Uncontracteds ate garbage—if they were lucky.

"I thought contracteds were at least fed," Spyro started, but Alizon interrupted.

"Look again, Spyro. They've brought GA to this world—but not much. And listen. He's offworld. Like us."

"Yes." A feral smile that made the crimson-and-blue fold into an even more terrifying mask. "I suspected as much. He has too much High-T on him, he uses it too well."

Jeroa tensed for a spring, and the spitter shifted. "I'll take your right leg off at the knee." Alizon might have been informing him she intended to change her green overtunic for a gold one. "Incredibly painful, a crushed kneecap, so I understand. And on this world, you're unlikely to be able to get a replacement cloned. Now, thief, why don't you settle yourself comfortably in that chair"—her free hand pointed—"and we'll have a nice long talk."

"Unnecessary." Spyro gave a short hard bark. "I think we both know why he's here."

"I thought so at first—but he's one of *us*, not one of *them*."

"Bought." Infinite contempt in the single word.

"Nye." He reacted to the sneer, "I wanted—" He swallowed the rest.

"Yes?" The harsh voice was suddenly *very* sweet.

He clamped his lips tightly closed.

The gazes of the two Navigators met, and a message flashed between them. "Hans could get it out of him, and fairly quickly," Alizon said pensively.

Spyro shrugged. "Who cares what they bribed him with. The problem is, what do we do with him now?"

Two pairs of eyes assessed him. The once pampered son of a family who owned fishing and farming rights to thousands of hectares of shallows was weighed and found—

"Useless." Alizon was incisive. "Nothing but an embarrassment."

"Right." Spyro didn't even bother to nod. "Waste him."

I tried, Tam!

The click of her thumbnail sliding into position was very loud.

CHAPTER 22

Several hours after they had met, Prax was watching the dawn carving the sky with lavender fingers, while Leany sat on a soft foliaged hummock, brushing her hair with a bejeweled brush, and humming softly under her breath.

They were in a ruin that had once been a building of some sort and was now merely the remains of walls covered with growth, so that the sweet crisp scent of life hovered around. Prax knew how to get back to the port, it was a solid walk, but a not unpleasant ride on the small levo he had commandeered from the *Scalded Cat*'s cargo hold.

He watched the slow changes in the sky, mind perhaps on more than his eyes were seeing, while the woman preened and arranged her appearance, adjusting and altering, using the small mirror he had gotten for her from the large open-air bazaar they'd visited.

"Praxiteles." Her voice was low, soft, sweet.

"Yes, Lady Leany?" His was smooth, courteous as always.

"Will you be berthed at this port for much longer, do you believe?" Will I be seeing you again? implied.

He answered honestly. "I cannot know that, Lady Leany. I am an engineer, not a shareholder in my vessel. And your world—" He was not criticizing, simply stating the facts as he saw them. "—for a world that proclaims loudly that it has no laws whatsoever, seems to take far more time than those that do, in what I can only call red tape."

"Red tape?" She made a moue at herself in the mirror, licked her full crimson lips and then applied something that made them glisten even more.

"Formalities." He stretched, the unique artificial arms reaching toward the sky, so that the dawn shone through them and tinged them lavender. "Customs. Whatever. Acts that must be gone through, balances that must be achieved, so that our cargo may be unloaded and new cargo loaded. How much longer it may take . . ." He shrugged.

"And have you many duties while in port?" She carefully pulled down a lovelock, wet her fingers and smoothed it just so.

He didn't smile. "Many, I'm afraid. As do you. But with luck, we can again arrange that our uncommitted time coincides—"

She smiled prettily at his back. "I'd like that, Praxiteles. Ahhh, your master, he is one of the powerful offworld c'holders, is he not? He has contracts on much cargo, many ships—I ask only because I would you were free more often, and it would be easier if—"

"In the first place"—he stared up at the ever-changing sky— "he's not my master; he doesn't hold me with something like those contracts of yours. I signed on his vessel, yes, but only so long as *I* choose. I could walk away in any port, change vessels—"

False eagerness. "Then why don't you stay *here*."

He swallowed a smile. "Even if I wished to give up star-roving, Leany, I'm afraid there are too many worlds I would prefer to yours. Don't take it personally, my dear, every man to his own taste. I'm afraid I was bred on a High-T world, and if I ever settle down again, it would be on another High-T world."

She pouted. "High-T. You offworlders are always talking about High-T. But what's important is *people*."

This time the smile was clear in his shrewd eyes, but she was busy again with her primping. "Yes, my dear, of course. But I'm afraid we High-T types take certain amenities for granted, and miss them when we're without them too long. You spoke of the master of my vessel a while back, worrying that his problems might affect me. They don't, except that the longer he takes arranging his affairs, the longer I am aground instead of voyaging. I'm an engineer, I do it well, but most of my duties are aloft, not planetside. I've finished all but the most cursory of checks to ensure all goes as expected." A wry smile. "Nonetheless, I do *not* haul cargo around, or worry that the holds are filled or the port officials satisfied."

He had used port-chits to contract a headband for her, a gaudy thing dripping with sequins and feathers. Now she placed it against her hair, trying it higher and lower, tilted and straight, for effect. "An engineer? And what does an engineer do, please, kind sir?" She turned to give him a playful pursing of her full lips. "When he's not playing escort to an ignorant native who knows nothing of such offworld affairs, that is."

He half-turned, lounging against a broken stone wall, so that the scent of cinnamon and wilted gardenia rose from the crushed yellow leaves. "I keep the ship running, in effect. It is propelled through real-space by sixteen—" He stopped, and smiled. "I make

certain that all within the ship works properly; no, not all. All that
is concerned with the ship's movements, or with the living space
within the ship, that is. Others guide it, or monitor instruments, or
decide where we're going, or—"

She frowned, tilting her face prettily.

He chucked her under that round chin. "A ship is a complex
system, and there are many different duties aboard her. Mine are
important, but there are others similarly important."

"You make it so simple, I think I understand. Many different
duties. Yes. You do not navigate, I think. I know what the Navigators do, they are like caravan guides, who say what route the
ship is to go, though they may not choose the destination."

"Yes." He nodded. "Navigators are special. It takes much
training and rare talent, to become a Navigator."

"Do you have a Navigator aboard your ship at present?"

"No, as a matter of fact, we do not. He did not wish to continue to wait while the master arranged his business. But it is of
little moment. There is a Guildhall here, many other Navigators.
When the time comes for us to go, one of them will be chosen."

She rose, came over to where he stood, cuddled against his
breadth, purring like a contented cat. "Will it matter to you, who
is chosen?"

He shrugged. "No."

"After all, you will have to live with him or her, in rather small
quarters—"

"And with the rest of the crew, both male and female." He put
an arm around her shoulders and sighed. The dawn was already
fading.

"Have you met many of the Navigators?" she persisted. "Do
you think you'll like whichever is chosen?"

"I have encountered some of the Navigators here in the course
of my duties. It matters little if I like or dislike, as long as the
Navigator does the job properly, that's all that's important."

She dropped a kiss on his nearest shoulder. "If the Navigator is
a pretty woman, you'll not be so—so casual."

He chuckled. "You sound jealous. Don't be. Navigators are—
special. They are Navigators first, and men or women second."

"*No*body is a man or woman second," she retorted.

"Navigators are. They have to be. Their duties demand the utmost from them, they've nothing to spare for—for the ordinary
parts of living. That's why they tend to be so wild, some of them,
when onplanet."

She "walked" playful fingers up his arm. "And if your Navigator is a woman? I saw one recently, a woman so striking she'd induce a stone statue to rise and follow her. If *she* were to become your Navigator—"

"Leany." He put both hands on her shoulders and turned her to face him fully. "I have no knowledge of which Navigator is most likely to accept the berth aboard my vessel when the time comes. He who was our Navigator has already shipped out. And the others—it may even be one who has not yet arrived. It is between the master and the Navigators themselves. I believe he intends to wait to choose until his cargo is essentially complete, which it is not yet at present. When that time comes, I will do all in my power to make the Navigator's stay aboard our vessel as smooth and untroubled as I possibly can. My life, and the life of all others aboard, depends on the Navigator's skill, and that skill must have an easy mind to operate properly. Whatever I or the others can do or refrain from doing to keep that mind easy—" He smiled. "What a trivial thing to be having words about. We're both tired. Time I took you back and left you to get some much-needed rest."

She dared persist. "Then your master isn't interested in the lovely lady Navigator?"

He snorted. "You don't understand priorities. He's interested in his cargo. When he's ready to leave, he'll go to Guildhall to check the postings. But, from the look of things, that won't be anytime soon." He chucked her chin again. "You've no need to be jealous, my pet."

She made a face. "I didn't mean to act like a silly green-eyed witch, Praxiteles. I just didn't realize how a master worked getting a Navigator, how—how impersonal it is, that's all." A flutter of darkened lashes. "You—you're different, Praxiteles. I've never felt like this before."

Rembrandt protect me, he thought, rolling mental eyes skyward. But he said all the right things. And was very, *very* thoughtful as he guided the tiny levo back to the ship and stowed it in the proper hold.

CHAPTER 23

"No!" It was the Navigator woman, her finger sliding away from the fatal contact.

"No?" Spyro faced her, face wrinkled into the most hideous expression Jeroa had seen on it yet. "Why not!"

She almost seemed to be searching for a reason for that impulsive denial. "I—can we afford it?"

"He's uncontracted. You worried about *law* . . . here?"

"Not law. But—won't they wonder why he doesn't come back? Think, brother. If he doesn't come back, they'll think we killed him to hide something. And what could we be hiding but what he's obviously been sent here to find."

He spat out a curse, his face, under its tattooing, horribly contorted.

She smiled slowly, sweetly—and Jeroa, who had faced the wrath of the devil-faced Spyro with only a single involuntary jerk, found himself shuddering.

"I think we ought to let him finish his search," she said, still smiling that knowing smile.

"You . . . what!" Jeroa felt his own jaw dropping.

"I think we ought to let him continue his search," Alizon repeated, with relish. "I think we even ought to help. After all, we don't want anyone else startled out of sleep and zeroing him unnecessarily, do we? It's a privilege"—pastel eyes lit with tiny flames fixed on Jeroa—"that I might yet reserve for myself. If necessary."

For an instant Jeroa bit down on his lip. He felt like a child in the presence of two adults, as if great events were swirling around him, but he was only interested in a promised sweetie.

Then he remembered that the sweetie was his sister. His shoulders straightened, and he gave Alizon a clear eye-to-eye gaze. (But not quickly enough to catch the flash of sympathy when he thought of his sister, almost instantly veiled.) "And if I find what I'm looking for?" he asked boldly.

Spyro snorted. "You think you can find what we've been splitting our tripes hunting the past days, thief?"

"I have—" His gaze flicked over to the small searcher.

"That playtoy. We have better. It's gone, you wormbrain, and—" A breath to regain control. "Let's put it this way, thief. If you don't find it, I'm going to spend a considerable amount of time making you very, very sorry, before I deliver you to the"—his lip curled—"*man* who sent you, and let him make you very, very, *very* sorry for failing him."

Jeroa shrugged. If he didn't find it, there was nothing—nothing!—he could do for Tam. There had been nothing all along, but at least he'd been searching, telling himself that once he found her he would manage somehow to rescue her. It had taken this slim chance, this single *real* chance to drive home to him how helpless he really was. If he blew this one—and he knew he had.

Again he missed the swiftly controlled gleam of sympathy in pastel eyes.

Yet his very real despair had done its work. "If you do find it," Alizon said softly, sharing unwillingly his bitterness and sudden death of hope, "we'll take care of you. And—the Guild has some influence here even yet. Perhaps we can do something about what drove you to this."

Hope flared, and he looked up at her . . . then, shoulders hunching together, rejected her offer. "You'd say anything," he muttered.

"Word of a Navigator." Very soft—very firm.

"ALIZON!" Spyro practically exploded.

"No, brother, it's said, and I hold to it." But her eyes remained fixed on the coltish young man trembling in the sights of her spitter.

"But *why?*"

"Because." To Jeroa, "Well?"

He took a deep breath, and grew up. "Thank you. I doubt you can help, but I appreciate your willingness to try." A wry smile. "Especially under the circumstances."

"Alizon," Spyro spat, "you're a fool!" Then, between teeth red as fresh-spilled blood, "Your word only holds if he finds it—"

"Spyro." Her free hand rested on his wrist. (A psychic quickly learns *never* to reveal unasked-for secrets.) "We *need* it. And—maybe he'll be lucky. I've just given him the best reason in the world to dig."

Spyro snarled. Jeroa recognized green jealousy, mixed with anger and disgust. "If he doesn't find it, he's *mine.*"

Angry now— "Spyro!"

The next hours were nightmare. Jeroa was marched back to the top of Guildhall, this time with a searcher that made his, as they'd said, a child's toy. But he kept consulting his—just in case. The more sophisticated machine might, for whatever reason, have been programmed not to respond to the tag coded for one particular Personal.

He started his search again. At least they had given him his clothes back, though Spyro had gone over them with a fine scan, and made sure they were only clothes. The rest of the pitiable remnants of his personal belongings he had not gotten back.

Room by room, floor by floor. Not just using the searchers, but with eyes and fingers, wall by wall, drawer by drawer, shelf by shelf, even the floor. On his hands and knees, fingers reinforcing sight.

With Spyro's roiling male fury ever at his back, though nothing was said except comments like "There's space behind that trim above the door, check it," or "Sorry to disturb you, Achmed, but we're making another search for the Personal of our sister, Jael."

The men and women awakened usually grumbled, but scrambled out of beds to allow them to be probed, and allowed their rooms to be ransacked without a murmur, even offering to help. Spyro merely shook his head, saying something like "Thanks, but we've got it down to a method and another pair of hands would only throw us off."

The hours inched away. Room by room, with a thoroughness he could never have accomplished surreptitiously. Room by room by—

Neptune's depths, what an assortment of personal oddities Navigators accumulated. (Not that they were all Navigators. Native servants, apprentices, even spacers offered a room in the Hall for one reason or another.)

Rooms, walls, people blurred together in his mind. A few totally-bizarres stood out.

A packet of plain dirt, wrapped in blue foil with a pink ribbon tied in a perky bow.

A shriveled hand, with a plain gold ring on the forefinger.

A collection of weapons that would have done an armsmaster proud, their owner a slim lithe sprite who couldn't have been more than fourteen standards.

A deathmask of hammered gold, with sapphires for eyes.

A—

Even time blurred, but all ordeals must eventually come to an end. He staggered out of the basement, and Spyro goaded him up the narrow outside stairs. "Now the outbuildings and the grounds." He might have been just up from a sound sleep instead of spending hours at the nerve-deadening task of guarding his prisoner.

Jeroa clamped his lips together on a moan. "Now the outbuildings and the grounds," he bit out. It *couldn't* take as long as the main building.

It didn't. Barely.

Guildhall was clean. He even went over the outer walls, centimeter by centimeter.

Spyro kept his word. Alizon bit out one angry protest, then left, realizing that her words and presence were only goading him on.

Jeroa was grateful. At least she wasn't witness to his humiliation.

Not that, once Spyro had laid his weapons carefully out of reach, Jeroa didn't try to give a good account of himself.

But if Jeroa had had training in unarmed combat, in skills of self-defense, Spyro had had more. And tales to the contrary, a good big man can always take a good smaller man. Actually, Jeroa was by several centimeters the taller. But Spyro was much bigger, in bone and muscle, and all of it driven by fury. He outweighed Jeroa by over ten kilos, and every gram of it counted.

It wasn't long before Jeroa was simply trying to defend himself from the worst of the avalanche, and then he was incapable even of that.

He was dumped at the front entrance of the Gilded Cage like a piece of unwanted garbage, and he lay, for a long while, before he managed to get one swollen eye open enough to realize that it was now late afternoon, almost dusk, and the scavengers were starting to zero in on the blood, both dried and still oozing.

He didn't lay helpless long, somebody spotted him, and he was half-dragged, half-carried inside. He didn't know much until there was the sting of raw native spirits in his mouth—Zaqanna had no intention of wasting good stuff on him—and a ball of molten lava hit his protesting stomach.

"Well?!?"

Jeroa struggled to open swollen eyes, and couldn't. He sensed presences, closenesses, was vaguely aware that the noise level was low enough that they weren't in the main part of the bar.

He worked his broken mouth. "Caught . . . me. . . ."

"Obviously. And you told them who sent you."

"Dint 'ave . . . to. Guezzd."

"You fool! I'm going to—"

"No!" Even the uncontracteds had heard about Zaqanna's ingenious "punishments." His mind whirled, groped for a protection—and found a bluff. "No . . . contrack . . ."

"Uncontracted." It was a gloating sneer. "I can do anything I want to you." A splat, as Zaqanna spat. "I'll let you heal some first. Whoever worked on you must have enjoyed himself. At least it shows the only thing you're good for. I have clients—"

"CONTRACK!" It was an effort to form even so simple a word. " 'Ave *contrack!*"

Zaqanna froze. "You have no contracts!"

"Wrong." He lied without a qualm. "Girl. Likes me." It was becoming easier to produce the words, he was learning how to use swollen lips to fake the letters they couldn't form properly. Slitted eyes made a creditable masculine leer. "Wrong 'bout all I good for."

Zaqanna smacked his fist into the other palm. It never occurred to him that Jeroa lied. But— He smiled, a feral display of even yellowed teeth. "So, you have a contract, do you? But you'll never be able to fulfill it, like that. Which of the Navigators did this to you? I'll tie them up as c'breakers—"

"Contrack for when heal. Girl Nav'tor." Why he protected them he didn't know. Except for a glimpse of softness, just for a second, on the woman Alizon's face.

"I don't believe you!"

"Don't. Takes all ki's. Other Nav'tors angry, but they free agen's 'mong 'selves."

Another splat, this time expressing frustration. Then an oddly impassive male voice spoke. "How far did you get before they caught you?"

"Ryker?" Zaqanna sounded almost shocked.

Jeroa could almost hear the shrug in the sudden silence.

"Whoever I try to recruit will need to know." It wasn't an explanation of curiosity, just a statement of simple fact.

"They could move it."

"One would expect them to," the expressionless voice replied. "Therefore the searched places should be examined first."

"Of course." One eye came unstuck enough for Jeroa to see Zaqanna nodding. "Well, uncontracted, where *did* you search?"

He snorted and spat blood. "Everywhere."

"What!" Impatiently, "Clean up his mouth, Leany, I want to be able to understand more than half of what he says."

"He's all mucky, let him clean himself," said a querulous sulking voice.

A *thuck* from behind him, like wet meat smacking against a wall, and there was a piercing scream of pain. Then a face bent over him, and a cool cloth worked on his swollen mouth, cleaning the dried blood away. Part of the wetness dribbled down his cheek, and he got one eye opened further, saw an angry round female face, a red patch on one cheek and tears streaking the paint.

"Some of my clients *prefer* criers," Zaqanna said softly.

Hate and fear struggled in round blue eyes. But Jeroa knew too much about her to feel sorry for her.

In a few more minutes, he was drinking thirstily, not sitting up, but propped up on pillows and a rebellious softness.

"Now," ordered Zaqanna.

He looked around. He was in a smallish room, and there were three people with him: Zaqanna, the offworlder who had recruited him, and, almost out of his range of vision, the brassy-yellow-haired woman, who was helping hold him up. (None of them knew about the youngster crouched in a shadow just beyond the door, ears straining.)

"Mother Sea protect me, I'm exhausted." He shut his eyes, almost wanting to fall into the beckoning, spinning oblivion.

Zaqanna slapped him, and the pain in his broken lips almost sent him completely under. "I said, I want to know exactly how far you got!"

"Tol' you," he mumbled. "All the way."

"They caught you after you finished?" Disbelief.

"Naw. In middle. Made me finish. Wanted Pers'nal. Thought I might fin' som'pin' they missed. Then . . ." His voice trailed off.

"He's lying."

"Easy to check."

"Is it?"

"Simple probe. Still fresh in his mind. Just take a few minutes."

"No!" He tried to struggle up. He had remembered The Word about Ryker.

"Down." Hands held his shoulders, then the gaunt zombie face was looming over him.

"Another of those who sees it as mind-rape." Still no emotion in that empty voice, not even boredom. "Don't worry, I've seen it all before."

"Dry you!" But a man who's been worked over by an expert, after over half a day of exhausting effort, can't put up much of a fight, and within a minute he was strapped into a chair, and Ryker was competently attaching various electrodes to his head and body.

And a few minutes after that, Ryker was reporting, "He's told the truth. They caught him before he'd gotten started good, and made him finish the job."

"They must want it bad." Zaqanna sounded thoughtful.

"Wouldn't you, in their shoes?" Leany spat spitefully.

"Um-um. Ryker, no chance they fiddled with his mind?"

"So I couldn't detect it?" In any other voice, incredulity would have been boiling through that statement. "No. He's clean. It's all fresh, not a hairline crack anywhere. It happened just as he said. They caught him, they forced him to search, he found nothing, and one of them worked him over and dumped him here."

Zaqanna glared down at him. "Better pray to whatever powers you offworlders believe in, that your *lady* Navigator doesn't tire of you soon."

"She won't." He was sure. Word of a Navigator.

Ryker knew the truth of *that,* but since he hadn't been asked or for his own reasons, he said nothing.

"Get out! You're bleeding on my furniture." Zaqanna's angry bellow covered the small sounds of the boy slipping away, eyes smug and suppressing a satisfied grin.

Jeroa was unclipped by competent hands, staggered to his feet. Just for a second his gaze was caught and held by oddly shallow eyes of silvery gray. Then the incongruous affinity was gone, and he turned to leave. There was still Tam to worry about.

Tomorrow was another day.

Still, he would have given a pretty to know what went on in the office after he had left.

"Well, that's that. But just to be sure—can you do it?"

"Now?"

"Yes."

"Yes."

CHAPTER 24

Seven people of wide-ranging power sat in a room, negotiating the fate of a world. The table they sat at was round, ceramic, brilliantly enameled in native motifs. No one participant sat at the head or foot, for there was none, symbolically proclaiming that all were equal here. It wasn't true, but each held a different sort of power in his or her own field. One whose pale face was illuminated by a nearby flickering taper wore Navigator black.

"I believe I have made our position plain," she said. "While the Master of this Hall yet lives, this world will not be put under official interdict. Nonetheless, word will be passed. Navigators will leave, in the course of their duties, and none will come to replace them. And as the supply of Navigators available locally dwindles, the independents will stop coming—"

"Yes," said the woman next to the Navigator, tall and svelte and hard as a whip, "we can't afford to be stranded here any length of time. If anything happens to our Navigators—we're not like the big liners who can afford a spare—lose our Navigator and we need another, and fast. If none were locally available . . . look at that miserable devil Reis. Run afoul of local custom and like to lose his ship any day now. If this world comes under even unofficial interdict, the independents will shun it."

Beside her, a gorgeous Greek god of a man patiently built a high tower using small multi-hued shapes of stiff material. "It will take us longer, but the big lines will shift routes, also. We carry extra Navigators because we need them. The heavier the ship—beg pardon, Captain, for mentioning what you already know—the trickier the maneuvering where the hypers twine. So, we'll adjust likewise. This world has always been of borderline usefulness. None of the small but precious cargo we'd pick up on other worlds. Its position is convenient, but there are others almost as convenient. And the risk of losing crew, or worse, *passengers* . . ."

A burly, harsh-featured man sitting across from the liner captain looked up at that. "I believe it has been firmly established, Captain, that the two passengers your sister ship complained of losing both stayed behind voluntarily."

The captain snorted. "Volun—? A silly child running away in a pet without a thought for the consequences. And her no less silly brother, thinking *he* could do something about it."

The harsh-featured native pursed his lips, then his mouth twitched as he spoke again. "You'd have extreme difficulty, Captain, forcing her back aboard."

The captain added a heliotrope octagon to his structure. "You don't have to tell me what I already know. You and your cursed contracts. And I refuse to beg pardon for saying what I think of them."

A slender young woman with the serene face of a Botticelli angel laid a soothing hand on the angry man's wrist. "You're safe enough expressing your opinion here, Captain. But you misunderstand. It is not our customs, or our contracts, which bind the offworlder here, but her own decision." She smiled, and he was suddenly lapped in warmth and peace. "She has much will, for one so young, and reason enough for staying. You might"—again that beguiling smile—"bend your efforts to persuading that foolish brother to continue his way with you."

He frowned. "You speak as though you know them both."

"No." She shook her head, denying. "Yet I know—enough. She'd not thank you for tearing her away—now." The harsh-featured man stirred restlessly. "In truth"—she patted the captain's hand again, before withdrawing slightly—"she'd scratch your eyes out and flee back here by any means available."

"Enough." The hard woman representing the independent spacers stirred. "We're not concerned with the fate of one or another private individuals here—"

The harsh-featured native smiled grimly. "Are you not?" he murmured, his gaze catching that of the Madonna-faced woman. "Are you not?" A smile and a knowing look again passed between them, causing the liner captain to scowl and chew hard on his classic lip.

"We're concerned about a trend that's developing." The hard woman who was an independent captain scowled at the natives. "We're losing people, all of us, losing them ugly. And this with the Navigator—"

"I know," said a wispy, not-young man who had kept silent previously. "Navigators are special." He slanted a glance at the two c'holders. "We're not unaware of that, Free-contractor. But the sanctity of contracts—"

"If I hear that phrase one more time . . ." the liner captain growled. "We all know this is a setup. The question is, what are you going to do about it?" His gaze went from one to the other of the natives.

"C'holders . . ." The not-young man deferred to the other two.

The Madonna-faced woman sighed. "Adjuster," she murmured, "we must make them understand—"

"I understand." It was the seventh member of the conference, a bland androgynous figure who could have been any age, features totally unremarkable except for deep-set shrewdly glinting eyes. "But then, I have lived and traded here quite a while." He turned to the two captains. "Look, you two, you've heard it often enough, but you don't understand it. They have no laws here. Which means, since Nature abhors a vacuum, that they must have something. Something very strong, or there'd be total anarchy."

The independent captain sniffed and muttered, "What do you call what they have now?"

"Workable," the androgynous merchant answered unhesitatingly. "Because they have contracts, and respect them. Obey them, as you or I would obey laws or custom or ethics or religion or whatever else greases the gears of our various societies. Now the adjuster"—he nodded toward the wispy, not-young native—"and his cohorts, they have some latitude, of broad interpretation. But they can't go against what is actually written in the contracts, and you must have read some of the local documents, and must realize—"

"All I understand—" The independent captain was blunt. "—is that crew and passengers have been disappearing here in greater and greater numbers." The harsh-featured native looked up, and then back down to his fingers, neatly clasped on the table. "Some, I admit, are staying of their own will—or so we're assured. But some—the Navigator Lady Jael would never wish to stay, she has Navigator's Syndrome, in an acute form. She would never stay long voluntarily on any world, no matter how attractive."

"You are all four adamant." It was the Madonna-faced c'holder. "If the Navigator is condemned, you offworlders will withdraw." Her questioning gaze went from one to another.

"Unofficially until the old one dies." The Navigator nodded firmly. "Officially thereafter."

"As soon as possible," the independent spacer affirmed.

"As soon as routes can be altered," the liner captain added.

"It will take those of us who have set down roots longer," said the merchant. "I myself have goods on order, contracts yet to be fulfilled. Yet I nor none of my colleagues will risk being marooned here permanently. Once the links to other worlds have been broken . . ." He sighed. "I will regret leaving. No other world could suit me quite as yours does." He slanted a sad smile toward the natives. "No other world could accept—" Another sigh. "Yet if the Navigators and then the vessels withdraw, I will have no choice. This world is tolerable only as long as I'm protected from the most stringent—without an enclave of High-T culture, I fear—"

"Exactly what we do." The harsh-featured c'holder had an incongruously pleasant tenor voice. "True anarchy. Even bloody revolution."

The woman c'holder stretched out a hand. "You speak for all your associates?"

"I'm afraid so, lady." The merchant was firm. "I regret. Some will linger longer, others have only been looking for an excuse to take their profits and leave." His mouth twitched. "Your society is not easy for an outsider to adapt to, lady. I apologize, but it is truth."

"Even though—" The harsh-featured man with the tenor voice spoke mildly, as though commenting on the weather. "—even though you *know,* your sociometric equations make it clear that the withdrawal of you offworlders will cause an upheaval, almost certainly a bloody readjustment, on this world you profess to appreciate."

The four offworlders shifted uncomfortably. The merchant spoke slowly but firmly. "It is a bloody, painful operation to hack off a gangrenous limb, but necessary, unless the patient is to die."

"Better cripple than dead, eh," the harsh-featured c'holder smiled grimly.

"My apologies." The merchant nodded. "But truth is truth."

"You're all agreed." The burly c'holder looked from one to another. "If the Navigator is not set free, this world goes under interdict."

The Navigator nodded. "So I have already said. Unofficial, as long as the old one remains Master, but that will still close you down fairly quickly. And once the old one dies—" A shrug. "It will make little difference by then whether the interdict will be official or not. If we cannot save our sister, we will see her avenged."

The Madonna-faced c'holder flinched back. "You *want* bloody revolution here."

"Lady." The Navigator was firm. "I wish no sorrow on innocents. But a people, so it is said, choose their society. Yours is cruel, and would be the better for changing. And if there is blood spilled in the changing, that is because you yourselves have made it necessary."

"A slower changing—" The male c'holder started, but was interrupted by the Navigator's fierceness.

"Slow or quick, if our sister is lost, it matters little. Except that I would not have other worlds follow in your footsteps."

The Madonna-faced woman put a trembling hand to her mouth. "You want us to serve as a horrible example."

"If you steal away our sister—*yes!*" Her hand curled around the ID swinging at her throat. Then, slowly: "Listen you, you who live safely on your world with all the might of your world solidly behind you. We move, we go from world to world, and some worlds welcome and cherish us—and some do not. Envy behind the smiles, malice, greed, cruelty, who can say? Worlds are all different. Sometimes our only safety—yes, I hope you serve as a perfectly *vile* example." She paused, tossed back the mane of straight pale pink hair. "If you do not wish this horror—and it will come if we go, we have proved that to you—then you will see to it that our sister is freed, returned to us unharmed, able to make her own way freely from this planet."

"We have *tried,*" the male c'holder frowned.

The adjuster leaned forward. "Lady," he addressed the Navigator, "would it be sufficient if your sister were condemned and yet returned to you?"

"Can you be sure of doing that?" She was wary.

"If the free-contractor were to be convinced to accept equal value for the Navigator's person, then the Office of Contract Adjusting and Interpretation"—he rolled the title out in full—"would be willing, as the Navigator is a stranger to our ways, to forgo the punishment such a condemnation would ordinarily earn—"

Alizon the Navigator caught her underlip. "Then I suppose—"

But the male c'holder was shaking his head. "We know who stands behind the free-contractor Zaqanna—"

"Yes," the adjuster nodded, "and this is a time for truth. We know who wishes to hold for his own the Navigator woman. We also know how fickle his attention has always been. A few days, a week, and he will be searching for a new toy, and the woman can be quietly optioned back. Zaqanna the free-contractor will be satisfied with other contracts, and the woman can be returned to her own people, none the worse—"

"None the worse!" Alizon rose to her feet, hands clenching the table so tightly that her knuckles stood out like rounded ivory dice. "None the *worse?* You can't be serious!"

He spread out his hands. "It is not as if she's a woman who has never known a man—"

Alizon was literally trembling in her rage. "I *see!* Because a woman has been hurt, abused, and humiliated in the past, therefore further hurt, abuse, and humiliation will make no difference. You—" Her fingernails made a scratching keen on the table as she visibly restrained herself from going for the adjuster's eyes.

"I don't understand." He was honestly confused. He thought he had come up with the perfect compromise. As a contract adjuster, his life was made up of such compromises; he accepted them, thought them a form of high art.

"No"—between pastel teeth—"you don't, do you. And until someone figures out a way to force a man, rape a man, make a man feel he is the lowest form of filth because he responds to his body's natural urgings, you will never understand. All right. Accept this, then. Our sister is not to be *touched.* She is to suffer no further abuse, past what she has already undergone. She is to be held guiltless, freed, apologized to—"

"Navigator." The liner captain rose, put an arm around her trembling shoulders. "Leave yourself room to parley."

"No!" She shook off the arm. "No." She glared at the adjuster, who shivered, at the sudden feel that death had brushed by him on immaterial wings. It had, for a fraction of a second, but she had excellent control of her powers. "Besides, I have heard too many tales of these c'holders and their games. Once in his clutches, who knows how it will end. Mutilation? Death? No, not one second, do you hear me! Our sister goes free, or this world suffers and suffers and *suffers.*"

The conference continued for hours after that, but the lines had been drawn, and proved firm. When the offworlders finally marched out, the three natives gazed at each other unhappily.

"C'holders," the adjuster appealed, "what can we do?"

"I don't know." Esme Oriflamme stared down at her hands and shuddered. She realized too well the fate of a woman Golden Singh's eye lighted on. Even if she could nerve herself up to offer her own person in place of the Navigator, it would do no good. Singh was fickle. He would tire of her, as he tired of all the others, and—would still want the Navigator. She swallowed, feeling more helpless than she had in a whole life of feeling helpless when it came to opposing the whims and cruelties of her fellow c'holders. "Karolly?"

The harsh-featured man stared at the knocked-down tower of shapes the liner captain had been playing with. "I *could* strangle him," he offered. "At least that way, only me and mine would suffer."

"Karolly!"

"If I thought it would help"—the adjuster sighed—"I'd've offered to do it myself. At least"—a wry smile toward Karolly—"I have no dependents at present, there's only my single person at risk. But stop and think, c'holders. If Singh dies, for any reason, what would happen?"

"A great deal of confusion, as contracts are readjusted." Karolly was thoughtful.

"Singh has friends, associates perhaps would be a better word. He has long shared options and liens with those of like mind. Zaqanna the free-contractor has gone too far to back out now, without the support of a c'holder to stiffen his spine. If Singh is removed, Zaqanna will simply have another of his ilk, slavering at the thought of outdoing his rival, within the hour." He sighed, nodded. "One might be able to retrieve the Navigator, once Singh's interest waned. Were she to go to someone else . . ." He spread out his hands helplessly.

"Then what can we do?" Esme whispered it.

"Nothing," Karolly growled. "Except make preparations for disaster." Unlike Esme, he had never hesitated to use his power when he felt it necessary. He had never felt so impotent as he did now, and it was not a sensation he relished.

"If Singh—" Esme started.

Karolly smashed a sledgehammer-sized fist against the table, so loud and sudden the other two jumped. "Singh has been waiting a long time to win over me in some matter; he sees this as it. The tragedy is, he cannot be made to see what a disaster it would be for our whole world."

"Karolly—"

"I will protect myself and mine. Esme, you will begin to make arrangements to retire with me to my mountain fastness in the Gargantuas. You may bring with you any and all you wish safety for. And—" To the adjuster. "There will be room and to spare for others of a like mind to ourselves. You may pass the word, you are welcome, and those of your colleagues—"

"And—that's all we can do?"

"Well"—his mouth twisted—"we can try what those offworlders are always talking about. We can pray."

CHAPTER 25

"*What* did you just say?" The words were spat out.

Zaqanna paled, eyes wide and frightened. "I can't—I don't—my tongue slipped—"

For once Golden Singh was not languid, his body had soared from its comfortable lounge and seemed, despite that he and Zaqanna were close to a height, to tower over the startled bartender. "The trial is tomorrow. And you are going to say—"

Zaqanna bit his lip. "I accuse the—I used the contracted Leany to entice the Navigator Jael into a charge of c'breaking. . . ." His voice guttered away into a horrified silence. He gasped, then, slowly, "I accuse the Navigator Jael—of—of—I used—"

"What is the matter with you!"

"I don't know. I can't control—" He ran a hand through his hair.

Singh's amber eyes slitted. "Is anyone else involved in this with you?" he rapped out.

"The C'holder Golden Si—" He stopped, because a muscular golden-skinned hand wrapped around his throat and squeezed him silent. "Wait," he managed to choke out, "I . . . know. . . ."

The hand loosened but didn't drop away. Death stared at him out of eyes of molten gold. For once, the haughty c'holder had been galvanized into action on his own behalf. "Explain."

"The psycher . . ." It was a husky whisper. Then louder, as he swallowed and moistened the bruised throat. "When—when he was adjusting my mind. He—he must have made a mistake, done something out of order somehow. He'll have to fix it, that's all—"

His life was held in two strong, merciless gold hands. The adjudication would and could go on without him, but if he died, there would be a delay, as statements to cover his testimony would be taken from other witnesses, and to properly adjust his contracts, liens, and options.

Singh had never been known for his patience.

The golden hand dropped away completely, and the c'holder shrugged. "Worm. You become clumsier by the moon. Can you do nothing right? You have the rest of the night to get it fixed."

He stood, head bowed and rubbing his throat. "Yes, Lord C'holder."

They were in Singh's favorite of Zaqanna's opulent Arena rooms, sybaritically furnished with sensuous furs and synthetics in a barbaric clash of colors and musk-scented candles. And, as always, when the c'holder stepped back, the woman on the lounge curled herself sinuously around his leg and began stroking the long muscle, purring throatily. "Why are you still standing here?" Singh snarled.

"Yes, lord!" He whirled so fast that his cloak snapped the woman in the face, scratching her eye painfully. She didn't break the rhythm of her caressing or stop rubbing her cheek against the long leg and purring.

Zaqanna transmattered back to the Gilded Cage proper in a maelstrom of anger and fear. If Ryker had disappeared as he sometimes did—

He hadn't. He was easy to find.

Too easy.

He was in Zaqanna's study, lying, muscles limp and eyes open, on the simple lounge. Zaqanna took one look and turned gray under his bronze.

Ryker's skin glowed phosphorescently, and tiny glittering motes danced over his open lips.

"Elysium!" Zaqanna snarled. His fists clenched, then he slammed into the bar proper and grabbed his assistant, a sly-eyed middle-aged man named Guilius, who seconded him in evil as in everything else. Pulling him into the privacy of the storeroom behind the bar, he quickly explained what had happened, and what was going to happen if he couldn't get it fixed by the time of the adjudication. Ryker was under the Elysium—at that point, it didn't occur to Zaqanna to wonder why the man had broken his fanatically kept schedule—and Guilius had at least watched him work his equipment. He might be able to find out what had gone wrong. (Zaqanna had no faith in a vacuumhead. He had been slyly encouraging Guilius to learn all he could. Ryker, with a cynical glint in his eyes, had complied, even to the extent of training Guilius in the working of some of the simpler equipment.)

Guilius checked Zaqanna out with one of the probes, then pursed his lips. "I can't tell exactly what he's done, but I can see the effect. You'll speak truth about the Navigator, if asked. And a probe—" He shrugged.

"Will condemn me in a heartbeat." He glared through the wall to his study, where the oblivious Ryker still lay. "Can you fix it?"

Guilius caught his lip between his teeth. If he undercontracted Zaqanna, he just might—then he dismissed that ambition as unattainable. Zaqanna read *all* the clauses before signing contracts. He had deputized Guilius to act for him often before. If he went down, Guilius would go down deeper. His only hope was to do whatever Zaqanna ordered—to the letter.

"I can't fix you well enough to pass a probe." He was honest. "I could blank some of it out, but the blanking—" Another shrug. "It would be obvious you'd been meddled with. He"—a nod toward Ryker's sanctum—"could do it, and leave no evidence. I cannot. But"—as Zaqanna started to protest—"I can give you control of your tongue back. That's easier. As long as you're not probed, it doesn't matter if my meddling shows under probing. I'll just give you a slowdown before you speak of those matters. It won't be noticeable, really, it'll be just enough so that you, rather than that reflex he planted, does the talking. Most of the time it won't even need to be triggered. And when it is, you'll just appear as someone nervous, testifying with caution." Then, because he couldn't help himself: "But *why* did he do it?"

"You're sure it isn't just a—a mistake?" Zaqanna punched his clenched fist into his other palm.

"No. Impossible. Too complex, what he did. He's too skilled to make a mistake, and what he did had to be deliberate, especially doing it so you weren't likely to find out. This was no error, no slip of the mind. He meant to do it. But as for why—"

"I'm going to find out." Too calm. "You set the machine up, so I won't say what would betray me, betray us all." Suddenly the calm was gone, his voice thick with menace. "I thought he was just too eager for his Elysium, that he just made a careless mistake."

"Too soon for his dust." Guilius shook his bald head, watching the glowing colors and moving lines on the screen, fingers brushing across the contact field. "If he's vacuumed now—"

Zaqanna's face was as fierce as the most primitive cannibal.

"There are ways." He strode out, cloak swirling behind him. Guilius shook his head and concentrated on his setup, wondering if he had, after all, done the right thing.

"Well!" The voice came from the doorway as Zaqanna loomed over the oblivious Ryker. He whirled and went pale as he realized that, for the first time in his memory, the c'holder had bestirred himself in person, instead of ordering his wants or sending a contracted. Behind him the crimson z'par curled around his muscular legs.

Zaqanna knew when to shift blame—and fast. "He did it deliberately." He pointed to the recumbent man. "I can have it fixed, at least so I can testify. The mental part was only a precaution, after all. I—we—will be safe enough. But I intend to find out *why* he did it."

"Ask him." A single step into the room, and Zaqanna couldn't prevent an involuntary flinch back.

"He's under dust. I'll have to bring him out." Unable to help himself: "You'll enjoy that."

"Good." A smile that would have made lead turn molten and run. "Do it."

It wasn't pretty. Adrenaline would counter the drug, somewhat. But the body had to be threatened, instinct had to be aroused, though the mind was completely screened off. Even the most brutish methods wouldn't reach the isolated senses, but if the body's own reflexes could be triggered, adrenaline would flow, and the drug's hold loosen slightly.

Zaqanna had a knife, a whip, his skill and practice, even his bare hands.

He chose the whip. The third time the heavy metal-plaited tip slashed down, hard enough to make the limp body buck, the eyes widened and focused vaguely. Zaqanna smiled grimly, and lashed down again, watching red flow from a long gaping slit. "Hello, Ryker." He was hardly aware that the c'holder had come up behind him.

Ryker lay, only the narrowing pupils revealing that he was at least coming out of the drug's grip. Only partially, as the glazed grayness proclaimed. Zaqanna shifted to the knife in his other hand, slicing its microscalpel sharpness down the bony chest, patchily revealed by the whip tears, letting more blood flow freely.

"Why, Ryker?"

Ryker started laughing, soundless jerking choking laughter.

"You'll undo it," Zaqanna promised. "You'll beg to be allowed to undo it."

Ryker relaxed back, closed those glowing gray eyes. "Can't."

Singh took the whip out of Zaqanna's hand, but the barman stopped him with a firm hand on his wrist. "What do you mean, can't?"

A smile of singular sweetness. "Drug. Once I broke the cycle—mindwork like trying to paint a straight line. Can't do it unless you're sober, have a steady hand. Same with mind adjusting. Can't do it if you're not sober, if your mind trembles. Like mine. Reality, fantasy, all mixed up. Drug's taken over now." The smile got broader. "Always knew it would, someday—" He opened the no longer shallow gray eyes. They glowed, with the drug dancing mockingly in their depths. He propped himself on one elbow, somehow, in his helplessness, a figure of threat incarnate. "Worth it, drag you two into the pit with me. Both of you, because you'll take him with you, dunghiller. I'm going to die, but I'll die happy. But you—" The glowing gray inhuman eyes gazed at Singh. "—they'll *destroy* you, C'holder. Take all your contracts, options, everything away from you. Strip you buck-naked, leave you nothing. Not even yourself. They'll put *you* under contracts, do what they want to you. How do you think you'll go, C'holder? The arena, where you condemned so many others? Under the whip? Will you grovel and beg? I wonder. Will you kiss feet, as you've forced so many to kiss yours? You will, I think. You're a coward, my fine lord c'holder. Without your contracts, you'll be shown for the whimpering cringing spineless skulk you are. You'll crawl—"

"*Nemesis!*"

Zaqanna had barely time to throw himself out of the way of the arrow of destruction, arms flung up to protect his face. But it wasn't the bartender the c'holder had sicced his animal on. There was a gurgling scream smothered under the triumphant battle cry of the swooping z'par, a sound as of wet cloth tearing, and a dreadful, bubbling gurgle.

Then nothing but breathing and the soft snarls of animal satisfaction.

A kick on the rump brought Zaqanna out of his defensive huddle.

"It's dead, worm. And I shall come along and be certain that you will be able to speak properly."

Or else, and Zaqanna knew it. But he had no choice. He rose and followed the tall c'holder out of his office, not knowing that there had been a witness to the whole, that a small body was crouched behind the desk, eyes wide and hand clamped to mouth. Zaqanna was too intent on what was to come, hoping desperately that Guilius could fulfill what he'd said he could.

Or else.

He risked one glance back as he went through the doorway. Ryker's body lay sprawled, half on, half off the lounge. It and the room would have to be cleaned, great gouts of blood were spattered about. There was no doubt the offworlder was dead, both the body's limpness and the torn throat proclaimed it, besides the blood. The animal had done little damage, actually, the whip cuts looked worse than the wound in the throat. But it was the throat that had spurted out the life's blood.

Zaqanna shuddered. Ryker was dead, all right, as he must have known he would be after such a betrayal—as he and Guilius would be if they couldn't satisfy the c'holder. But why had he done it?

And why had he died smiling?

CHAPTER 26

Jeroa walked about three steps into the room—and froze, eyes blinking in pure amazement. It was like—like— His head jerked around, his body trembled in uncontrollable epileptic tremors, eyes watering in the sudden rush of emotion.

He was standing on a slightly irregular sandspit, feet actually sinking into the brushed-beige surface. Around him murmured the blue-green waters of the shallows, above him arched the indigo sky broken only by the swooping gillgulls, their faint hard cries echoing in his ears. A slight sea breeze ruffled his skin, bringing with it the sharp mint and bitter iodine scent of the ubiquitous sealand-weed, the fresh salt tang of the shallows water itself, and the distant plops as the trained dolfins harried the sea herds to their chosen pastures.

He took a deep breath and almost sobbed aloud. Home!

"Do you like it? It's mostly illusion, but he tried very hard to make it just as I described."

He whirled. She had come in almost at his heels, but the shock of what he had seen had deafened him for ordinary sounds.

He stared at her blankly, then gave her a leisurely assessment, from the gleaming piles of her braided hair to the jeweled sandals that revealed painted toenails and vulnerable white skin.

"Jeroa"—her voice was sharp—"it isn't like that!"

"Isn't it?" He looked her up and down again. Then, bitterly, "You look like a rich man's pretty toy, Tam. If the family could see you now—"

"Customs are different here. I dress like this because I want to please him, and this pleases him most. Don't worry, Jerr."

"How can I not, Tam. Even if the family never finds out, how can I go away and leave you—trapped—like this?"

"Trapped, Jeroa?" She laughed, a merry child's trill. "It is not I who am trapped, I assure you."

He understood her well enough. His mouth twisted down. "Oh, you're pleased with yourself, you think you have this—this *man* well wrapped in your net. But, oh Tam, you're so young, so young and—" He couldn't say innocent. Not now. "All right, you're safe enough—for right now. But when you get older, Tam, older and not so pretty—then what? Will you get sold again, Tam, wind up in one of the those places by the port? Oh, *Tam*—"

She patted his hand, this girl who had been a child when they landed. Who had committed a child's foolishness—and paid for it. "They don't have marriage here, Jerr. But they do have an equivalent, a contract. You don't have to worry about me—ever. Today, tomorrow, next year, when I'm old. You don't understand."

He shrugged and went and placed his hand against a sandtree that looked so real it was a shock when he touched smoothness and not hairy scales. "I understand. You're grateful to this man who bought you, rescued you from, well—"

"Well"—her smile was sunshine over sparkling water—"that, too. Gratitude. But mostly, I love him, Jerr. I want to spend the rest of my life with him. I'm his wife in all but the word, and that only because they don't use that here." She placed a soft, perfumed hand on his trembling arm. "Jerr, I'm happy. Be happy with me."

"Oh, sure," he snarled and jerked away from that soft hand. "You're a *slave*—'in all but name'—to some primitive dryhead who probably can't count above twelve without taking off his shoes—if he wears shoes. And I'm to leave you here to 'be happy,' and just toddle off my merry way, knowing you'll never be able to come home, never see the estates or the family again, never—"

"Jeroa!" Her sharp voice stopped him in mid-career. "If I'd married the Duclos heir and gone to live in Beta Continent shallows, how often would I have seen the family?"

"Seldom isn't never."

"I didn't love Honore Duclos. I love Karolly."

"That's absurd."

"Is it? You weren't so eager to join our family to the Garcias that you were willing to give up this Grand Tour."

"More fool I. Look where it's landed us."

"It's landed *me* happy."

"Happy? Sure, sis. Happy and proud. So happy and proud you never sent a word to let me know where you were, to let me know you were safe. They dragged you off when I wasn't even there and—"

"Sent you word?" The plucked, painted brows rose. "I thought you were gone. The schedule was tight; I never imagined you'd jumped ship—"

"*Gone?*" He caught both dimpled shoulders and shook. "Left you alone and helpless on this ball of dry mud? Did you really think that, Tam?"

She smiled. "No. I just thought you wouldn't have realized until after the ship had taken off and it was too late—"

His jaw dropped and his hands fell away from her. "You did it deliberately!"

She shifted nervously, those childish shoulders hunching in a gesture that was half shrug, half flinching from an imagined blow. "I don't know, honestly, Jerr. I just knew—I never intended to finish this tour and go back. This world or another, I didn't much care. I wasn't going back!"

"You hated Duclos *that* much?" In the last five minutes he'd learned more about the no-longer-a-child who was his sister than in the whole fifteen years of her life.

"No, I never hated Honore, he's rather nice, actually. Really he is. But—" She licked her lips. "—but I just couldn't see letting Father arrange all the rest of my life. I might have learned to love Honore, if I'd had the free chance, but all I could see was having every single decision made for me, now and forevermore. Father up to my marriage to Honore, and Honore after. So—I was ready to take the risk. And now there's Karolly, and there'll never be anyone else." She smiled, her old dimple appeared, and for the first time he saw his little sister under the paint and elaborate clothes.

"You were lucky."

"I know. Luckier than I'd dreamed. I wouldn't have done it if I'd realized exactly—" Another dimple appeared momentarily. "I guess you can take the girl out of the shallows, but you can't take the shallows out of the girl."

He understood. Oddly, being weed rancheros and owning the shallows rights for over a quarter of a submerged continent made for a similar we-are-gods attitude as the c'holders. Not that shallowsers were anywhere as servile as contracteds. No, shallows folk were independent cusses, even the smallest of the tenant rancheros. Yet being a rightser made for a—a nothing-*bad*-can-happen-to-me-really instinct. It hadn't betrayed Tamilee—lucky Tamilee!—though he'd thought it had. It had betrayed him, but at least it had taught him a hard lesson he'd not forget ever again.

"Tam"—he held her so he could fix the gaze from her painted eyes—"are you sure?"

"Yes, Jerr."

"And you truly want me to leave you here?"

"Yes. Tell the family I'm married and happy, that my husband is the equivalent of a shallows rightser here, that he loves me deeply and will care for me as solicitously as they could wish. All of which is true." She put a hand on his arm. "Jerr. You can meet Karolly yourself, you've but to say the word. But—you're angry, I can tell, and prepared not to like him. And you don't want to have to report that to the family, do you? Better to say that you know nothing but good about him."

"The nothing part's true enough," he mumbled.

It took her a while longer to satisfy him totally and send him away. He wouldn't have any trouble getting another berth on a ship from the line they'd arrived on, he still had the rest of his ticket; he'd clung to that if nothing else. And—he didn't bother to tell her this, either—he didn't have to worry about how he'd live until lift-off came. Word of a Navigator. And—as this meeting proved—Navigators kept their word. All of it.

After he finally left, she stood quietly in the room designed with love by the man who loved her, head bowed, face blank as she lost herself in thought.

So deep in contemplation was she, that the slight sounds of a door opening, muffled thuds of approach, didn't disturb her. Only when the arm came around her waist, and a pleasant tenor voice spoke, did she jerk and blink. "Was it so very difficult, love?" Karolly said.

"A little." She stretched up to brush his cheek with her lips. "I didn't lie. But I had to choose my truths carefully."

"Don't ever do it with me."

She snuggled against the long length of hard male body. "I told him we might make the Grand Tour ourselves someday and meet the parents."

"And so we might." He gathered her closer.

She giggled. "Only after we've produced a generous assortment of heirs."

He understood. They'd discussed the matter often and honestly. Rabelais was a world of freedom, where parents could treat their children as clauses in a contract or with love, pamper them as potential heirs or ignore them. He assessed himself as caring parents might see him. A c'holder—but that was the minimum they would expect, power equivalent to theirs—and then the bad points: better than twice her age, not her race, ugly in countenance, and— He slanted a glance at the arm that wasn't holding her, the arm balanced on the crutch he was leaning heavily on, because of the empty pant leg dangling, as it had for so long, beside the one thick muscular leg he had left.

She said, as she'd said so often before, "You're a man, my man, and I love you. As you are. If you were only a tenant, poor and wearing ugly ragged clothes, that wouldn't matter, either." On her world, she meant. She still didn't understand what being a contracted meant on his. He did; it was his world, but he also had the breadth of understanding—mostly—to allow for her background, her differing point of view.

Just as he had been ready, for sheer pity of her youth and ignorance, to have her—once under contract to him—sent back to her ship, safe and untouched. It was she who had pleaded with him to give them both a chance. She who had given him the most priceless gift of all, the bone-deep knowledge that the woman he had come to love had come to him freely, of her own choice, stayed with him voluntarily, with the way back always open.

It was the bane of the gods on earth that they could never know whether one came to them because of genuine affection or fear of their power. He knew. And she knew. Because he had been willing to let her go, to send her safely after her brother on the next available ship. Even now, he would let her go, any instant, today, tomorrow, whenever, at a word, though it tore the heart out of him.

But he was safe, she'd never say that word. And she was safe. As long as he lived, and after. He'd seen to that.

Now he had the brother to worry about, too. But not, he fervently hoped, for long.

Speaking of heirs. . . . One of them said.

CHAPTER 27

Zaqanna was on a rampage. Few men wouldn't have been affected by a close brush with the valley of the shadow, the bourn no man returns from, but Zaqanna reacted characteristically. The next victim who crossed his path—

They all knew, of course, but not all could get out of his way quickly enough.

Leany was the unlucky one, this time. She hadn't found the Personal, she hadn't gotten anything from any of the spacers, and she was in the wrong place at the worst possible time. Her final piece of bad luck was that she'd been sent back to the storeroom for an obscure drink one of the customers had insisted on just as Zaqanna, temper a volcano ready to erupt, turned back from seeing Singh through the transmatter and spotted her.

The next few minutes were very bad. Worse was to come. Temper still unassuaged, Zaqanna glared at her and decided to give her to Singh, saying, with a sneering snarl, that in Singh's present mood, it would be a waste—but *he* didn't care, as long as Singh was kept sweet. (For him, anyway.)

Leany knew Singh too well, and she screeched and began to struggle in dead earnest. Zaqanna only laughed and began to drag her, kicking and screaming, toward the transmatter. He was holding her with one hand while reaching for the transmatter plate with the other when she spotted the boy, face grimly pale, sidling out of Zaqanna's private room.

Leany didn't know what had just happened in that room, only that Singh had stomped out, face a mixture of avid glee and unappeased anger, and Zaqanna had stumbled out after, face blankly stunned, then hardening into that direful expression his minions knew only too well.

And she, Leany, was to be the sacrifice this time.

Unless—

A casual hanger-on she'd seen about, a temporary contracted offering his services at unskilled labor in return for scraps—hadn't there been a tale of an accident, of a contractor angry and kicking the lad out because he now limped—

A stranger, and better him than her!

Lysander saw her and gasped, transfixed by the threat in the round, desperate eyes. And something in his face or movement triggered an obscure memory, and— "Zaqanna!" He wanted a victim? He'd have better than he thought!

"Teach you a lesson." His hand was heading toward the transmatter plate, but her bucking was making it hard to make the proper contact. "Or waste you, I care little, so he's—"

"SPY!" She screeched it. Lysander, in the doorway, broke out of his trance and ran.

Zaqanna whirled at the footsteps, saw the running boy, and without waiting to be sure of the truth of the accusation, pounded after him, dropping his burden without a second thought.

Leany fell heavily and then sat up, nursing her bruised hip, lips twisting as she watched the swift chase through the crowded storeroom.

In the open, Zaqanna's adult legs, half again as long as the boy's, would have closed the gap to his quarry within seconds. But in the broken field running that was all the stacked bales and barrels and kegs allowed, the boy's agility and ability to take narrower corridors kept him well in front.

Until he trapped himself in a blind corridor.

"Aha!" Zaqanna's chortle echoed through the storeroom.

In seconds, he was back, dragging the thrashing, grimly flailing boy with him.

"Well," he demanded of Leany, slapping at Lysander with his free hand to protect himself from the boy's frantic struggle.

"I saw him—at Guildhall!"

"And you said nothing till now!" Even though his hands were fully occupied, she shrank back against the coarsely woven wrapping of the large bale she had been flung against.

"I didn't know—" she whimpered. "It was only a glimpse, it wasn't until just now, when I saw him in a similar light—" Lysander managed to twist around like a young eel and sink his teeth into the flesh of Zaqanna's side, and the man howled his anguish.

"If it wasn't him, why did he run!" she finished triumphantly.

Zaqanna tore the boy off and hurled him to the floor, where one arm hit a box with a crack that told of dislocation if not breakage. Before the boy could recover the breath slammed out of him, the man had driven his metal-soled sandal into his midriff, and he doubled up, choking and convulsing.

In those seconds of helplessness, Zaqanna had his belt off and hauled both arms behind the boy's back, strapping them together heedless of the keen of agony as something grated ominously in the damaged arm.

"Now!" Zaqanna panted in triumph, as he used the boy's own loinclout to bind his ankles together. He started automatically to drag the writhing body into his own private room, remembered at the last second what was already inside, and hastily about-faced to a smaller storeroom that was crowded but usable. "Come." He jerked his head at Leany, and she followed unwillingly, the promise of more punishment if she didn't plain in his flashing eyes.

"Stay!" he snarled, dumping the boy with bound ankles doubled under him and the damaged arm at a painful angle. To Leany, he made a simple threat, "If both of you aren't here when I get back—"

It was enough to hold her, and make her hold the boy—as long as, despite his desperation, he was helpless.

Zaqanna was back in a couple of minutes, an offworld eternalite in one hand and one of the smallest of Ryker's gadgets in the other.

"All right." He smiled grimly as he attached the small telltale to the boy's side, where it almost disappeared in the valley between two outthrusting ribs. "Leany, you saw this boy at the Guildhall—"

He had recovered enough breath to be able to protest. "That's a lie!"

"Then why'd you run?" Zaqanna snapped.

"Any contracted knows enough to run when a contractor's angry."

Zaqanna had missed the damaged arm in the turmoil of the moment, but the angle it lay at now made it obvious. He jerked ungently at it, and Lysander howled.

"Would you care"—Zaqanna's voice was silky—"to tell me again how your c'holder kicked you out because your gimpy ankle offended him? How he told you to fend for yourself until you could again fulfill your contractual duties for him?"

Lysander said, with desperate fervor and the wide eyes of a naive child, "I told you, he doesn't care for any mar or scar about him, his delicate sensibilities—" Zaqanna jerked the bad arm again, and he gasped and convulsed.

Zaqanna glared at the ankle, where a strip of cloth had been wrapped to back up the lad's tale. Both of them were remembering the wild chase through the storeroom. Zaqanna's lip curled; he didn't even bother to unwrap the cloth and inspect the ankle they both knew would be whole and undamaged.

"I should have realized"—Zaqanna was grim—"what a thin story it was. Spy!"

"No!" Lysander was all wide-eyed innocence, a child caught in something far beyond childish knowledge. He licked his lips, all naivete yet conscious of a whiff of guilt. "The truth is, I—I ran away. Just for a little, you understand." A shy smile seeking reassurance. "Not really breaking, you see. Just for a little, until everybody forgot—I was scheduled for a punishment, you see, I'd been naughty. And I thought if—if I just wasn't there for a while, they'd all think—I'd been put in the cellar again, and—and everybody'd think somebody else had—"

"Liar!" An animal snarl, then Zaqanna was suddenly genial, a very bad sign. "Care to try another tale?"

"I'm not a spy!"

"No?"

"Nobody sent me to spy!"

"No!" That was surprised. The lad had spoken pure truth on that, and Zaqanna hesitated, then, "And you're not contracted to Guildhall, either, I suppose?"

"No!"

Zaqanna, staring at the telltale, frowned. "They don't hold a free-contract on you?"

Desperately, "No!"

"They didn't send you?"

"No!"

"They don't know you're here, do they?" *Very* jovial. Like a serpent somnolent on oversized prey.

"No—how can they know, when they don't know anything about me, nothing at all!"

Zaqanna tapped his fingers impatiently on one knee. Then, reverting to pure menace. "I'm tired of games. Open your mouth."

"No—umppph!" But the large capsule went down in seconds anyway. Leany crept close to watch the dull look spread over the fierce hazel eyes.

"What did you give him?"

"A truth-teller."

"Why not use it from the beginning?"

"Because it only makes the taker answer all questions asked with truth. I had to know the right questions to ask."

"Oh." She gazed down at the slumping boy, but there was only thoughtful shrewdness in her eyes, not pity.

"There's something funny about his contract with Guildhall. I have to find out—"

It took a while, because the questions had to be carefully phrased, and Lysander answered with literal truthfulness, but eventually Zaqanna looked up at Leany and smiled. "So. He came here against explicit orders. That makes it easier. And—Singh, of all people, can claim a prior lien on him. That makes it *very* simple."

Lysander stirred and moaned. He was coming out of it, but the combination of drug and shock from the pain made him groggy.

Zaqanna's smile broadened. He forced another capsule into the slack young mouth. "And they don't have the Personal, it must have been lost in the streets after all. Well. Singh can have the both of them."

"Both?"

"This little would-be spy, now." Lysander blinked, knowledge and horror blooming in the young hazel eyes. "And the Navigator woman—later." Zaqanna gloated.

"You needn't worry about disturbing my other clients." Zaqanna smiled kindly down at the helpless boy. "All my better rooms are soundproofed."

"No—Guildhall—"

"You ran away from them, boy." Zaqanna was enjoying himself, knowing how pleased Singh would be with a new, untouched —almost, he'd have to put a temporary fix on whatever was the matter with that arm—victim. "And you've admitted Singh has a lien he can exercise. Don't worry." His own not-so-latent sadism cooed. "I'll see your contractual rights are upheld. He won't lay a finger on you until the Office of Contractual Adjustment is properly notified and acknowledges. Why, that gives you—several hours to . . . anticipate." He chuckled, hauling the boy to his bound feet as if he were a sack of meal, and a not too heavy one at that. "The Lord C'holder Singh always says that anticipation sharpens the . . . experience. And being contracted to Lord Singh is an experience you'll not soon forget."

"If you survive," Leany tittered nastily. *She* was safe—for now.

Zaqanna sighed his relief. "The anticipation of this new toy will keep Singh happy, until he can actually start—and after, a little contract juggling, and the boy can disappear—quietly. If Guildhall protests, they can be given their choice of likely options." A happy snicker. "But not this little spy. He'll be beyond their reach."

CHAPTER 28

The courtroom assigned for Jael's hearing was tightly packed. Many of the spectators (mostly spacers) were forced to leave; but Reis had had the foresight to provide himself with a late afternoon appointment with an adjuster whose offices were in the same building—he was allowed to stay.

Zaqanna took the stand first. He testified that the debt-contracted had been industrious, humble, obedient before the visit of the female Navigator; after, she had been sullen, surly, lazy.

The holo recording was shown.

Several of the Navigators testified. But since none of them had known Jael for any length of time, their testimony did little except establish that some Navigators are very, very law-abiding—and some a little cracked.

The heat from the packed mass of bodies grew intense; Reis could almost taste the sweat in the air.

Jael defended herself passionately. She hadn't been so drunk she couldn't remember what she had said. She would never, ever risk local punishment. She had Navigator's Syndrome in its acutest, wanderlust form. She demanded to be psyched to prove the recording was faulty.

The magistrate had been well bribed, an almost needless precaution. "No need of psych with a recording available," he ruled, wiping trails of sweat off his forehead with the full sleeve of his sunshine-yellow robe.

"The recording's wrong, wrong," Jael raged. "If only I hadn't lost my Personal . . ."

Reis recognized his cue. "Your Navigator's Personal," he said loudly. "Could you have left your Personal on my ship, Navigator?"

She turned and swayed, almost fainting in her relief.

"What is this?" the magistrate bellowed. "Clear that intruder out of my courtroom!"

"I have evidence," Reis's voice rose to a lion's bellow. "I should be called as a witness!"

"Nonsense, the list of witnesses has been called."

"I have evidence, I tell you. Let me speak, or there will be grounds for an appeal to the chief arbitrator."

The magistrate hesitated, glanced at the first row of spectators, where a golden-skinned c'holder had frozen in the act of patting the hunting z'par curled at his feet; and at Zaqanna, who shook his head slightly but firmly: *No!* An appeal to the CA could delay a hearing for months; in those months he could make a fortune off the woman. And if the appeal looked as if it would succeed, there were always kidnappers, bandits for hire—he would wring his hands convincingly and wail about his "loss."

But the magistrate had his own worries. He had been too greedy. Too many of his cases had been appealed, with holes in them you could ram a starship through. Far too many of the appeals had been successful. The really powerful ones, the c'holders, were willing to turn a blind eye to discreet corruption, as long as they got a generous share of the proceeds. But too much and too blatant, and people began to mutter, and faith in the sanctity of contracts to tremble. The magistrate had already gotten one not-so-subtle warning; there would be no second. Just an anonymous corpse shoved down a disinter shaft or buried under a pile of rubble.

"You claim you have pertinent evidence." The magistrate pointed his tri-colored rod of office at Reis.

"I think so. I can't be sure."

"Be sure." The magistrate smiled thinly. "If this is merely a ploy to delay punishment, I'll have your ears and your tongue for your insolence."

Reis held up the tiny Personal so she could see it. She nodded; her lips formed the word, Mine!

Hoping she wasn't the grudge-holding type, that it actually was hers and would contain the needed evidence, he stepped into the narrow aisle and forward. "I must speak; I have evidence."

On the dais beside the magistrate's throne, an enforcer asked, "Will you swear by the eternal sanctity of contracts, or will you accept Truth?"

Reis hesitated. The machine called Truth would instantly betray any outright lie; but evasions might or might not pass, and omissions were quite safe. You couldn't lie under Truth, so there was no penalty. But the penalty for *any* falsification while under oath— a form of contract breaking—was horrendous. Zaqanna had testified under oath; he had better risk Truth.

It was only after he had settled in the special chair on the spotlighted dais that he wondered, with a thrill of fear, if the Truth machine on this slimily corrupt world had been tampered with. Behind him was the screen he alone in all the court couldn't see.

"Now, offworlder." The magistrate was still furious. "Identify yourself, tell your connection with this case, and present your evidence—if you actually have any—as quickly as possible. You've wasted too much of our time already."

He settled himself comfortably in the too-yielding chair, tried not to think of its probes and the screen behind him. "My name is Hannibal Reis. I'm master and majority owner of the starfreighter *Scalded Cat,* presently docked at Berth 223 Alpha-Gamma Quadrant at the port." He paused, but neither Jael nor Zaqanna questioned his qualifications.

"On the morning of local date Francis fifth, Navigator Double-A Jael visited me at my vessel—purely business," he added hurriedly, over the snickers. The enforcer didn't challenge, so evidently the machine agreed he hadn't stretched truth too far.

"If I said"—Reis couldn't help grinning—"that my *feelings* for Navigator Jael were purely business, that screen'd rip right off the wall. I'm a man, and she's a flaming attractive woman. But we only spoke briefly, business as I said, and then she left."

"What business?" Zaqanna snapped.

"She is a Navigator presently without a berth; I am a master presently without a Navigator. Unfortunately, as I told her then, I also have an incomplete cargo. While I hope to complete it soon—" (And that is true enough. I *must* complete it soon!) "—I cannot afford to pay Double-A Navigator fees for her to sit on the ground and wait for me to fill my holds, and I told her so. The Navigator asked me to check with her if the situation changed, and left."

"Condemned through her own mouth again," Zaqanna sneered. "Trying to flee justice, she admits her own guilt."

"The guilty may flee, true," Reis retorted. "But the innocent merely continue to go about their business. The business of a Navigator is to navigate. Naturally the Navigator would come to me to ask about a possible berth."

"A Double-A on a paltry freighter?" Zaqanna was infuriated by this kink in his carefully laid plans.

"When that's all that's available, yes." Jael spoke for herself for the first time. "I told the master I would be interested in a port-to-port contract only—"

"A port-to-port contract only." Reis picked it up. "I'm doing the testifying, remember, Navigator." He smiled down at her. "She said, a port-to-port, with the understanding that when we reached a world where she could obtain a more suitable berth, she'd terminate. No master likes to sign on any crew member, but especially a Navigator, on a port-to-port, but any world where she was likely to find another berth, I would be as likely to find another Navigator. But"—he shrugged—"as long as my holds are half empty . . . We reached no agreement, though we did discuss possible terms. I showed the Navigator a bit about my ship, and she left. I have testified about all this to establish that the Navigator was aboard my ship, and when. To my knowledge, she has been aboard my ship at no other time, either before or since."

"Will you get on with your testimony," the magistrate growled.

"I am. Sometime after the Navigator's visit," Reis continued, "I found, aboard my ship, a Navigator's Personal. It could have been the lady Navigator's, or my former Navigator's accidentally left behind when he accepted another berth and shipped out. Either way, I meant to drop it off at the Guildhall, when I was in the area . . . but I've been pretty busy lately . . . and the Guildhall area has been rather unhealthy for offworlders. . . . Of course, if I'd *known* the lady Navigator needed it . . ." (The trickiest point. He hadn't *known* she needed it, hadn't even been one hundred percent sure it was hers, had deliberately kept himself "pretty busy" . . .) He held his breath, but the enforcer didn't challenge.

"I find it"—the magistrate was suspicious—"an amazing coincidence that you are here with this 'evidence' so providentially for the lady, when you didn't '*know*' it would be needed."

"But I never said I knew nothing of the Navigator's troubles. We star-farers are a small community, we know much of each other. I knew the lady was accused of a grievous crime, and since I had business today with the port contract supervisor, whose office is on the floor above this one, and since, as I have already stated, I have both personal and professional interest in the Navigator, why, here I am."

The magistrate ground his teeth. Zaqanna leaped to his feet.

"You can't admit that Personal as evidence." His voice was almost a scream. "He's had days to tamper with it!"

"If it has been tampered with, it will be obvious. The Guild seal will be broken," asserted the Guildmaster, after a nudge from Nikady the albino, who had been examining the Personal.

After that, the verdict was forgone. The unaltered tape reported words and tone and broad emotions faithfully. It could not show a glint in the eye, a flicker of expression that made a mock of pious sentiments.

Jael, a triumphant fury, demanded that both she and Zaqanna be psyched on the spot.

But Zaqanna had wriggled out of tighter spots than this, and the magistrate was eager to earn his bribe. Doubt a Navigator's Personal, that so many lives depended on? Never! The fault must lie in Zaqanna's machine. Zaqanna eagerly concurred that it had never given trouble before, but it *was* old. . . .

So Zaqanna got off with a fine—large but payable. His offense was mitigated, the venal magistrate declared, by a well-meaning if ignorant faith in an obviously faulty recorder. Regrettable that no one thought to check the machine out. . . .

The young albino frothed, but the magistrate was bland. It is the duty, the inescapable duty of every loyal contract-upholder to report any suspicion of contract breaking. Unfortunate that the case was based on machine error. . . .

The Guildmaster got no more satisfaction.

The Navigators did win one point. One of the older ones drawled that as part of the fine they wanted the debt-contracted involved.

The magistrate was eager to content everybody.

The girl couldn't testify, and therefore hadn't been allowed in the courtroom, but she was being held nearby. Zaqanna would swear out an assignment-of-contract on her *immediately* (a warning glare) and she would be formally handed over to the Guildmaster before he left the building.

"Thank you." Jael whispered to the Navigator who had thought to rescue Leany from whatever deviltry Zaqanna would doubtless have inflicted on her.

"My pleasure," he whispered back, winking to emphasize the double meaning.

She saw the glint in his champagne-colored eyes and misinterpreted it completely, as he had intended she should. Pundonor is a hard, strict discipline, and there is almost no sin more venial

than betrayal of hospitality. Leany might yet look back on her life
with Zaqanna with futile yearning.

The Navigators crowded around the magistrate's throne to witness the ornate assignment-of-contract. Jael wriggled through
them to the chief enforcer. She held up her left wrist, the bracelet
still on it. "If you would, Sir Enforcer."

He didn't even glance at the magistrate for a confirming order.
"Immediately, lady."

When it was finally off, he rubbed at her wrist gently—and unnecessarily. It was as close as he could come to an apology for the
torment the manacle had caused.

"And may I go now?" Her mouth was twisted. "Free of this
place I would be."

"You are free, lady," he said formally. "You may go wherever
you will." And because she was, despite her ordeal, still very attractive, he added, very softly, "Wherever you will, lady. You've
but to speak the word."

The choice was hers, completely hers; the offer made, all he
had to offer, in tribute to courage and resolution. And he had been
sympathetic to her, within the boundaries of his duty. She smiled
gently into the ugly face with the kind worried eyes bent over her,
and laid her other hand over his. "Perhaps later, when I am somewhat recovered. For now, for now, I *must* go."

CHAPTER 29

Zaqanna, hurrying toward Jael, heard the exchange, soft as it was.
To fury at the thwarting of his scheme, smart at his loss, worry
about what his frustrated would-be client would do, was added
pure, green jealousy. He had always been justly proud of his male
abilities, taken for granted being able to recruit new stock by simple seduction. Yet this woman had rejected *him*, first by careless
choice, but then under duress. Now this mere brainless contracted
sword seemed like to succeed, where he had not. . . .

But it wasn't safe *now*. . . .

He turned to go, plots seething beneath his impassive exterior.
Bandits . . . kidnappers . . . hidden rooms, equipped with cer-

tain offworld tools, or simpler, older items . . . clients . . . pleased clients . . . and himself . . .

He was gloating over the inner picture of a pleading, kneeling, desperate Jael when he saw the golden c'holder, still sitting in his front-row seat, eyes fixed on some distant prospect, idly smiling while his hand rhythmically stroked the z'par's spiny fronds.

Sheer fear stabbed through him; he turned hot and cold and hot again. Bandits . . . kidnappers . . . secret rooms . . . Screams of torment could be torn as easily from a male throat as a female one. He had to show the c'holder it was only a momentary setback, that he would get what he wanted!

He turned, lunged toward her, grabbed her arm, which felt oddly cold through the thick black synthetic. "I want to talk to you."

She pulled away, but his desperate grip was too tight. "We've nothing to say to each other. Let me by!"

"No. Not until I've said what I—"

"Let me *by!*" She pulled again, and he caught her other wrist. The enforcer moved to interfere, but with a snarl, Zaqanna shoved the larger man away.

"Tavern-master." The enforcer's tone was a warning.

"Only a few words," Zaqanna snapped. "Stay out of this— *'tracted!*"

They were crowded together in the narrow aisle between bench and the low railing that separated the spectators' section. The enforcer moved just slightly back, his face studiously blank, his whole attitude that of giving a man enough rope.

She tried to pull away from Zaqanna again, but there simply wasn't space. "I won't listen—let me *go!*" Her voice was fierce, but not loud enough to cut through the excited buzz around the throne. Her body twisted away from him, her face distorted by contempt, hatred, revulsion.

It all fused in him, lust, fear, fury. He grabbed her other wrist, pulled her close, so that they were breathing common air.

"You *will* listen." His eyes hot, his mouth feral. "You have won—" A hint of sanity reminded him that this room was being automatically recorded, and he could *not* afford an open threat. He forced a smile, but his hungry eyes revealed the truth. "You have won," he repeated, his eyes adding, *for now,* "and I hold no grudges." Very loud, for the record. She was writhing in his grip, straining, eyes blind with—hatred? "Listen to me," he snarled, "I meant every word I said before. . . ."

"Let me go, *let me go—*"

"Whatever is between us in the contractual—"

"The *walls!* Let me go!"

"I have the greatest admiration—"

She was sobbing aloud. "The walls, the walls—"

"—for you personally—"

"PLEASE!"

"—at any time—"

"AIYAHHHHHHHHH!"

She thrust desperately at him, and he staggered, clutching at her in an attempt to keep his balance; at the same time, the enforcer, out of patience, jerked at him to separate them; and over he went, dragging her down with and beneath him.

The z'par had been trained to attack fear, struggling, and, most especially, *screaming.* With a joyous keen that cut through every other sound in the large room, he flowed toward the three in the narrow corner.

"NEMESIS! NO!"

The enforcer had been knocked to his knees when the other two went down. The z'par's keen and its master's shout jerked his head around, in time to see the animal, spurs and fangs full extended and glistening, sailing over the waist-high railing at him.

The imported energy pistol had been assigned him only when he reached his present rank; the sword had been a part of his arm since he could barely toddle. Reflexively, he drew, aimed the point in the center of the dripping fangs. The animal's own momentum forced it almost down the length of the whippet-lean body.

The z'par's death howl was almost drowned out by the chorus of spectators' screams and shouts of warning. The court was thrown into confusion.

All three in the corner were spattered with a thin greenish fluid that burned like acid; and the writhing threshing dying body landed on top of the two on the floor.

"NEMESIS!!!" The golden c'holder took the rail in one leap, to gather up the limp body of his alter ego and walk blindly away, tears streaming down his cheeks.

Jael was buried under Zaqanna, screaming convulsively, writhing, until the enforcer, one eye swollen shut by the animal's fluid, bent down and delivered a precise, measured blow to the point of her jaw, and she went limp and silent, eyes closed, breathing in light, shallow gasps.

"Unfortunate," the magistrate declared, when reasonable order had been restored. Off his throne, he was revealed, despite his flowing robes, as a short, Cassius-lean man. "*Most* regrettable. Strain, no doubt. Never any *real* danger, of course; wild animals not allowed in the quadrangle, in any case, enforcers well trained. She's not hurt. A good night's sleep, and she'll be fine in the morning."

"You'd better hope so." The Guildmaster's voice was grim, his eyes fixed on Zaqanna, who had scrambled to his feet, face pale with fear and pain from burns and a wrenched ankle.

"She was screaming *first*," a savagely angry silver-haired Navigator asserted. "The animal attacked *because* she was screaming, not the other way around."

"It wasn't the tavern-master's fault," the enforcer stated, far too loudly. "He but wished to speak a few words with her, to assure her that he held none of this against her." He looked around, to be sure he had his audience's entire attention, which he did. "He admires her *greatly*. He was but telling her so." His face was blandly innocent.

"He was *holding* her," Nikady the albino accused.

"You will call for a litter," the Guildmaster was saying, "to convey our sister to Guildhall, where she may be properly cared for."

"If she can be." The silver-haired Estaban was still angry. "I couldn't get through to her in time, but I could hear *what* she was screaming. The *walls!*"

All their eyes focused on the trembling Zaqanna. "Navigator's Syndrome," Nikady cursed.

"Triggered by *you*." The Guildmaster's aged voice trembled, as his finger speared the hapless Zaqanna. "Magistrate, a Navigator has been damaged, perhaps permanently. I demand, on pain of expulsion from the Navigators' roster of approved worlds, that this animal be made an example of!"

CHAPTER 30

Hannibal Reis watched the climax of the adjudication with a grim satisfaction. She would be safe—and *he* would be sorry. It didn't get Rowan back for him, or solve his problem with the need for a charter, and/or a cargo—but—

He waited until the unconscious Jael had been carried away by her worried fellow Navigators, and then, biting his lip, went to keep his appointment with the port contractor.

He didn't notice the enforcer with the burnlike redness following him out of the hearing room, but when the man caught up with him after the appointment was over . . .

"Freighter-master Reis, I would discuss a matter of contracting some cargo with you. . . ."

Every instinct of Reis's went instantly on red-alert. Though the enforcer had spoken in a casual businesslike manner, there was a certain taut undertone. . . . The body was alertly upright, but it was more than a guardsman's normal watchfulness. . . . And though the eyes gazed blandly at him, it was as if his attention, indeed, his whole being was spread out, straining to detect something, tendrils probing into every turning and byway, constantly vigilant for . . . what?

Suspiciously. "A freighter-master is always interested in usable cargo—properly contracted-for cargo."

There was nothing sly, nothing to attract attention in the enforcer's easy smile, but it was as if—Reis had his sixth-sense tendrils of apprehension, too—he was nerving himself up to take a deadly, irrevocable step.

"So you said, back in there." He nodded toward the building they had just walked out of. He had a seasoned fighter's face, it would have been ugly without the scars and mars that were the badge of his profession, and the reddened swelling didn't improve matters any. But somehow there was a solidity about him, an aura of trustworthiness. "You said something else, about you offworlders being a small community, where everyone knows something of everyone else's affairs."

Reis nodded. "Yes. And so?"

"It is similar among us, also, to some extent. Knowledge may not be admitted aloud, but it exists, nonetheless. To some among us, the doings of you offworlders—all you offworlders—are of some concern. And so"—a deep breath—"I know where certain cargo you have expressed high interest in is located."

It took him a second to get it, and the greatest effort of will not to break stride, to turn and shake his secret out of this man. "I—see. And you would have a—an agent's percentage, of the value of this—cargo?"

"I would have—" One of the hazel-green eyes was still swollen shut, the other met his for a long breath before glancing casually away. "I would have something of value from you in exchange, yes."

"Where the cargo is of high value, the brokerage fee is likewise of high value."

"Enough of this sparring." The enforcer's tone and pose were still casual—but not that over-elaborate casualness that might have alerted observers to something more significant than two men idly strolling and conversing. "You may betray me, if you choose. You just might get your precious cargo in that way, with no risk to yourself." He pointed upward, as though drawing the offworlder's attention to an intricate frieze on a nearby building. But in the course of following the moving hand, Reis's glance brushed past an open square, in the center of which was a single metal stake, with dangling chains. Reis thought he saw dried blood on the chains . . . and the other items prominently displayed near them. The enforcer smiled gently, though the smile must have hurt his acid-burned skin. "You know what our world is like very well, don't you, Freighter-master. You know the penalties we'd both be risking. But you've known that all along, while you were looking so hard, though you knew that the cargo you searched for was under contract. I'm assuming that you have a way to—to smuggle out that cargo, once you have your hands on it. Smile, Freighter-master, eyes are watching us."

He couldn't smile, his face was too stiff. But he could put on a natural questioning look, and point himself, as though asking a tourist's question. What he said was, "Yes, I can smuggle out the cargo, despite the risk—but can you get me that cargo? And what do you want in exchange?"

"If you can smuggle out one, you can smuggle out two."

"But you—you're contracted!"

"Yes. And—that contract can be reassigned, without my yea or nay. And once that contract is reassigned . . . I am a desperate man, Freighter-master. But in helping you—and I will not lie, our chances of success are—" He shrugged, still smiling. "I am risking no more than I have already lost. And if we succeed, I will have won"—a breath—"everything. And what, Freighter-master, can you contribute to that success? Weapons? A distraction? Manpower? What?"

It was, in the end, a simple plan. Simplest is best, the enforcer insisted. Reis thought it was too simple—and totally insane, but the enforcer insisted it had a reasonable chance of success. "I tell you, you don't understand us," he said, over and over.

They met that night in the Drowning Belly, a tavern several cuts below the Gilded Cage. They didn't enter, but slipped into an alley behind, where Reis was handed some clothing. "Can you change in the dark?"

When he emerged, he was severely inspected by lantern light, certain small adjustments made to his (in his eyes) exotic costume. Finally the enforcer, who had introduced himself as Brine, nodded. "That offworld thing that changes your appearance, what do you call it?"

"A life mask."

Chief Enforcer Brine's eyebrows went up. "It changes your voice, too?"

"Yes. Identification by voice would nullify the disguise. The difference can fool an analyzer as well as the human ear."

"Yet it looks and sounds perfectly natural. You don't look as if you were disguised at all. Marvelous."

"I have a second, for you."

"Unnecessary."

"You won't even know you're wearing it."

The enforcer shrugged. "I will not have to face other enforcers, after, as you will. If we succeed, I won't need it, and if we fail, what difference can it make?"

"I only thought—"

"Let me do the thinking, Freighter-master. Anyway, I'll be—never mind. Keep that cloak well wrapped around you. If we're seen before we get to our destination . . ."

He issued only one more order on that short walk. "Be silent unless you're addressed directly, Freighter-master. And then say only, 'Yes, Lord Whip-master,' or 'No, Lord Whip-master.' Otherwise, silence, and obey all my orders, no matter what, implicitly and immediately. Understand?"

A uniformed enforcer met them. "Friend," Reis's guide hissed.

"You have the thing to make the large fire?" the other asked softly.

"Here." Reis passed it over. "Just push the red button in until you hear a loud click. You'll have five minutes head start. Don't walk, run. And keep running. This produces intense heat. The fire it causes will spread rapidly."

"Don't worry. I will." The face was almost anonymous, between the shadows and a heavy beard.

"Thank you . . . friend," the soon-to-be-ex-enforcer said softly.

"Good luck—and good-bye—Brine," the other replied, before fading cat-footedly into the shadows.

Reis could appreciate the depth of loyalty that impelled the unknown to help his friend. He only underestimated the risk involved by a factor of three.

The enforcer gestured them both on, and Reis was thoroughly confused by the time the other man stopped, said "Now," and pulled down what Reis had thought was a helmet so that it covered his face. It was a mask, the eye-slits cleverly concealed behind a painted devil visage.

"No wonder you didn't want the life mask," Reis exclaimed.

"Here's yours." The other pulled something, and Reis felt pressure around his eyes. "It leaves the lower face completely exposed, that's why you needed your life mask. And here's your prod." Something long and hard was thrust into his hand. "Now remember what I said, keep it moving. And while we're among the men, use it continuously. To the nerve centers as often as possible, like I told you. And for the sake of whatever it is you pray to, don't exclude your crew member. Get everybody. I should be hearing a continuous chorus of gasps and grunts and suppressed moans, unless I'm ordering you to concentrate on someone. You must do this, or anyone we meet will know you're a fake."

"I'll do it."

"Good. Keep busy. Hard, long, and often."

Reis gulped. "I'm ready."

"Right." Brine the enforcer peered cautiously around the corner of a high stone wall. "Not yet, curse their sloth. May they all be contracted—Fian's in place, but he can't argue too long."

"I hear—" Faint but distinct. Shuffle, clump.

"I do, too. I hope that's them. Remember, casual, at the end of the line. Fian'll keep the guard distracted, long enough. I hope. If you have something you pray to, Freighter-master—pray!"

"They're coming." It was a line of a dozen or more yawning men, most bearing burdens of assorted sizes.

"Now," Brine the enforcer hissed. He stepped out, timing it so that an easy walk brought them to the end of the line as it passed through the open gate. Reis saw no less than four armed guards by the gate, arguing with an enforcer. They trotted through the gate and over a moat that bubbled turgidly and stank, thick, stale, and overripe, and into a building that was so dimly lit he felt practically blind. There was a haze of smoke from guttering torches, and his nose twitched at a stench as though the moat were inside as well, an assault of putrid damp mold.

They marched briskly through a maze of corridors, so that Reis knew he was hopelessly lost within minutes. He could thread his way through the thickest asteroid belt, but this man-made labyrinth . . .

Only once were they challenged. "A surprise night march for the lads, eh, Whip-master," a rich voice chortled. The speaker had a round, jovial-looking face under a tilted-up helmet or mask of some sort, but his sleeveless tunic revealed arms so brawny that it was obvious his size was all pure hard muscle. Reis kept his prod moving nervously, but he remembered Brine's instructions. When in doubt, look at the clothing. If they're wearing more than you—obey. Less—prod. This one was wearing a *lot* of different pieces of clothing, though much of it was cut away to display his hard muscularity.

"Been too long since the last little surprise extra." Brine's voice was muffled from behind the mask of terror.

"Three whole days—or is it four?" The unknown's voice rippled with hearty amusement. "You're certainly a glutton for punishment, Whip-master." He jabbed Brine in the ribs so hard that Reis was sure that if it had been him, he would have been flung halfway across the corridor. But Brine never budged. "Get it, Whip-master—a glutton for *punishment*."

"Perhaps"—the muffled voice was cool, but with a deferential undertone—"Lord Programmer, you would care to come along and observe. You could mark out some likely specimens for the next festival."

"Not from this crop. They've too much training for the innocence acts, and not enough for decent gladiatorials. But I might pick a few for animal acts. . . ."

"At your convenience, Lord Programmer."

"Not now. Too soon after—but keep me in mind, Whip-master. Animal acts make splendid examples, you know. If you haven't enough open defiance, you can always goad some hothead into it . . . tsk, I must hurry. He changed his schedule at the last minute again. Wants an individual—" Reis felt Brine stiffen slightly. "—with full ingenuity."

Brine made a deep bow, and a kick warned Reis to at least bob his head. "I'm sure you will excel yourself, Lord Programmer."

A shrug. "I'll do the best I can, but the material's bad. Screaming before she's scarcely touched. He picked her himself, wouldn't you know it, and from a common contracted's mart, to boot. Tsk. Didn't even ask my advice. Be lucky to make her last the night." Lower, to himself. "And why he wanted her hair dyed in stripes . . . well"—a sigh—"no time for shop talk. I just hopped down to the barracks to pick a contrast. Have to make up for the poor quality of the primary somehow . . . you'll be watching out for hopefuls for me, Whip-master?"

A deeper bow. "Always, Lord Programmer."

"Might check out some possibles tomorrow. For now . . . hmmmm . . . wasn't there a jade-haired trained stud in the 'change barracks . . . honorable contracting, Whip-master."

"Honorable contracting, Lord Programmer."

Two corners turned and a long corridor later, Brine said softly, "Whatever you pray to, Freighter-master, pray you never meet that one in his official capacity."

"What does a programmer do?"

"He—programs. Never mind. Just be ready to play your part."

What happened after they unlocked (Reis didn't ask how Brine had gotten a key) the final door, Reis never after wanted to remember. He had thought he would be able to scan a series of bunks and pick out Rowan immediately. He hadn't anticipated—a few of the men were on pallets, with contacts running from their heads to a master panel, but most were floating on air cushions or even water totisensory tanks, their heads hidden in totisensory helmets. Reis took a step closer to the master panel, saw the first of a series of screens portraying what the men were being forced to receive—and doubled over, hands wrapped protectively across his body.

"Don't vomit, whatever you do!" Brine spat out.

Reis managed to get a hand over his mouth, literally hold back the gorge helplessly rising. "Ulmmmmppppph—"

Brine strolled over, stared at the screens with a frown. "Do you have any idea what sort of program your crewman's likely to be getting?"

Reis shook his head helplessly, still trying to control his stomach.

"They're all different, you know. Some are simply to turn the subject into a feral animal, some to train him into an instinctive killer, some to—"

"Turn 'em off!" Reis swallowed acrid burning long enough to exclaim.

"Pick him out, or say he isn't here, and fast. There are five more barracks like this, and a dozen individuals."

"I *can't!*" Even the bodies on the pallets were dimly seen. Rowan's space conditioning would have faded in the weeks planetside, leaving him no darker than a tanned native. Reis tore his gaze away from the screens, but all the bodies blurred together.

Brine must have realized some of the problem. "We'll have them out, then. But it's risky—once they're roused—pick him fast, call him—a slug. Call no one else a slug, anything else but not that. And—hurry!"

Reis nodded, still trying to control the burning solidity rising in his throat—and the real nightmare began. Brine opened the door wide, went back to the panel—and a raucous, drill-vibrato klaxon went off. Brine began shouting over it: "Counting, one, counting, two, last five prod, counting three, counting four, last *ten* prod, move, you slime, five, six . . ."

Nightmare in dark lit by guttering flames, running, prodding, corridors, erupting through wide-open double doors, a mob of naked running men into an arena, a natural amphitheater with rising tiers of seats encircling a flat oval.

"Round, you slime, round and round! I'll tell you when to stop!"

A hand on his arm, an almost voiceless mumble in his ear. "Which one is he?"

He wouldn't have known, anonymous men running in the ringlight, naked or dressed in ragged loincloth or breeches. But one of the men he'd prodded had responded with a spat-out spacer's curse. When he had stared in the face—Rowan. And yet—not Rowan. Rowan changed, altered far more than a few weeks could account for.

There was a crude track around the outer perimeter. He could feel the sharp edges of flint thrusting even through his heavy soles. The men were running on it barefoot.

"He's fourth from the end."

"Good, makes it easier—*faster, you slime!*—when the fire flares, be ready."

It was a good thing he had been warned. The fire must have caught in a series of buildings, shot through several roofs almost simultaneously. One second, there was only the soft pastel ring, the next, crimson shafts of flame, shouts, and an almost tangible wave of heat.

"What the—back to your barracks, slime, until you're called

for. And if any of you isn't in his bunk when I check—go on, *run!*"

Again Rowan was one of the last. Brine's foot lashed out and Rowan went flying onto the flints. "Clumsy—get up, curse you!" But a sly kick knocked him down again. "The rest of you—run! And as for clumsy—prod him until he decides to put on some speed. Get up and join the rest of the slugs!"

Rowan was grimly trying to scramble to his feet, but a neat kick to the side of his jaw dropped him back to the flints, limp.

"Did you have to—"

"No time! Follow me, and fast, and pray that the guards have been drawn away!" He stooped and picked up Rowan and draped him over one broad shoulder as easily as a man putting on a cloak.

Reis followed, obeying unquestioningly, a run, a pause of seconds while Brine unlocked a door with a large key, dashed through it, and relocked it so quickly he almost caught Reis's heels as he came through. They plunged through the seething night, pausing a little later to tear off their disguises and throw on something different, the first ones hidden a piece at a time during their flight, thrust deep into piles of rotting garbage. Rowan was still unconscious, but Brine poured liquor over the three of them, and Rowan was held between them, the three swaying and singing, the picture of three carefree drunks.

On a dreadful journey through an insane, frenzied world.

CHAPTER 31

Disaster came when they were about two thirds of the way to the safety of the *Scalded Cat*. Dawn was forecast by a hazing of the setting ring and a lightening of the night sky. Reis, but not the more knowledgeable Brine, had heaved a sigh of relief. They had gotten this far—

Brine knew better, knew how precarious their position was until they actually managed to hide themselves aboard the ship. When he saw the line of guards marching around a c'holder's litter, he cursed and swiftly swung himself and his two companions to the nearest wall, cramming all three into the smallest space possible, trying to leave room for the wide procession to pass.

He had time only to hiss, "Silence on your life!" before the front rank came abreast of them.

In his half-conscious state, even Rowan must have tasted the tension from the other two, because he stirred and whimpered, then cowered against the wall, eyes not even opening, instinct alone spurring him to quivering, animal stillness.

Reis turned his head to the wall at a signal from Brine, and all three froze, emulating the famous three monkeys: See no evil, hear no evil, speak no evil.

It wasn't enough.

As the front rank passed the three shrinking against the hewed-stone warehouse wall, a file peeled off and surrounded them.

"Contractual duty," their chief spat.

"Yes, Lord Controller." Brine kept his head bowed, recognizing the tone even without looking to see the rank implied by the man's uniform. "That is, we are returning to take up our contractual duty. This one"—a shake of his head toward Rowan, sagging, less than half conscious and eyes shut, not discreetly lowered like Brine's, and, in imitation of his, Reis's—"is . . . ahh . . . ill, but we hope to have him fit in time for his morning contractual duty."

"Ill," the controller snorted. But he knew, and Brine knew he knew, that it wasn't illness. The stench of the cheap wine Brine had poured over all three of them must have reached even the sensitive nostrils in the sumptuous litter, now swaying slowly past.

"Is that one ill, also?" He jerked his head toward Reis.

"Oh, no, we all have contractual duty soon, he was just trying to help our fellow 'tracted." Brine swallowed and added pleadingly, "Honored Controller, we have a way yet to go, and our contractual duty begins *soon*."

But the controller was staring at them up and down in a way that made it an effort of will not to break and run.

Suddenly he pinched Reis's upper arm in a familiar way that made the man jump; to Brine's infinite relief, he swallowed what must have been an instinctive protest. "Good enough," the controller snapped. He gave Brine the same test, and nodded. "This one seems strong enough to carry your—*ill*—fellow contracted to fulfill his contractual duties. You stay."

Brine stiffened. "I, too, have contractual duties."

The controller spoke the words Brine had been dreading. "My c'holder will adjust with your c'holder."

Brine knew he was doomed. But Reis was ignorant enough to spit out the single protest: "No!"

The controller raised his whip, but before he could slash it down, Brine threw himself between the two men and said hurriedly, "He is hard of hearing, Lord Controller." Loudly, "It is all right, fellow contracted. His c'holder will adjust all with our c'holder. But you must hurry with our fellow, for you must not be late. The controller's c'holder will not adjust for the three of us."

It trembled in the balance, but Reis was now totally burdened with Rowan's weight, and he subsided, half from that, and half from his natural diffidence, hesitance—and the knowledge that he understood little of this world's customs, and if Brine, who *did*, was telling him to go, then go he'd better. And quickly.

The controller was less easily satisfied. "Perhaps my c'holder will adjust for the time of all three of you," he said slowly, running the long, metal-plaited whip through his fingers. "Long enough for me to school proper obedience in that contracted."

Brine bowed his head. "Sire Controller, all shall be as you wish. I only remind you, with all due humility, that no amount of schooling will restore hearing which is no longer there. He but worries for his contractual duty, for he is in charge of the shift during which both I and this other are engaged."

"Humph. In charge of a shift, say you, and he cannot hear to accept his own orders?"

Reis stirred, but had the sense to remain silent.

"Sire Controller, when one has the genius he has displayed in the kitchen, it only matters that he understand his c'holder's preferences. Direct orders can be repeated until they are thoroughly understood."

A snort. "Off with this culinary expert, then." He recoiled the whip to its accustomed place around his waist. "But you stay."

Brine turned to Reis, said with exaggerated emphasis, "You must go, with your apprentice, and hasten that you not be late. I must stay, the lord controller assures that his c'holder will adjust all with our c'holder later."

"Later." Reis couldn't risk too many words; his accent was too different from the local and would give him away.

"Yes, later. I will follow to assist as is my contractual duty, as soon as I have obeyed this controller. Go you now, else you be late and failing yourself."

Reis hesitated. In Brine's eyes was despair. If he was delayed too long, the hue and cry would be up, and he would have no chance at all. And he saw that the other man knew it.

"Go. *Hurry*." Brine repeated.

Reis nodded. It was Brine endangered—or all three of them. "Yes." He risked another sentence. "You hurry too."

Brine smiled. "I will." His eyes added, As much as I can! He turned, said firmly, "With your permission, Lord Controller." A half wink and Brine's hand on his arm gave Reis his clue. When the bored "Granted," was uttered, Brine gave Reis a small push and he sidled past, dragging Rowan carelessly, heedless of his mumbled complaints.

Brine and the controller and his silent squad watched them scurry down the long street, the controller stroking his whip idly, shifting from foot to foot with an odd impatience, for a controller. "He must be a very cook of genius," he remarked.

"Yes, Lord Controller."

"He talks funny. He must be very hard of hearing, to talk so poorly."

"Yes, Lord Controller. It happens that way, so I understand."

"Aye. My mistress's sister had a pretty boy once, also hard of hearing. He talked even more oddly than your shiftboss. It irritated her, so she had his tongue removed entirely. Perhaps your c'holder might do the same with that one."

"Lord Controller, your wisdom is infinite. But it would make for difficulty in the kitchen, could he not issue his instructions. And in the kitchen, his coarse speech and misunderstandings cannot offend our lord c'holder, only the products of his ingenuity tempt his appetite." The controller was standing directly in front of him, but he could see over the man's burly shoulders that the procession was almost past. "If you would condescend to enlighten me what errand or chore I can carry out for your c'holder." Brine was heart-poundingly conscious of time dripping away, wondering if the hue and cry was up yet, or if Rowan's disappearance (and his own) had not even been discovered in the confusion that would—Reis had assured him—follow the firebomb.

"Simple enough. One of my lady's litter bearers sprained his ankle a way back. Clumsy dolt, I'll punish him later. But she has complained that the litter rides unevenly now. You're the right height, and seem strong enough. You may assume the empty pole and bear our lady home. Then you will be dismissed, and I myself will contract your c'holder's controller and make amends for any contractual dereliction."

Brine didn't even suggest that any of the brawny guards could have taken the pole. A c'holder wouldn't think of giving up the prestige and protection of a full squad of guardsmen. And although a contracted could be ordered to any necessary duty—witness his own shanghai—no guardsman would be able to hold his head up after having been demoted to carrying a litter.

In other circumstances, Brine himself would have felt the deepest disgrace, but he was wearing the garb of a common unskilled contracted now, and besides—

Reis was disappearing into the brightening dawn. Brine sighed in relief. At least the other two had a chance. And if he had not too far to bear the litter, perhaps he, too, could—

The attack came without warning. Two guards had come to either side, as soon as the controller started talking. Now all three leaped with the precision of a trained team. Two hands grabbed each of his wrists and he was flung back against the wall hard enough to bring involuntary tears to his eyes. The controller grabbed his head and forced it back and up, fingers thrusting into his mouth so that he choked on them. Reflexively his body bucked, as he struggled to breathe past the probing obstruction. In seconds, there was a single spat order, he was whirled away from the wall, and eager hands tore his clothes away from him. Hands caught in his hair, his head was forced even more painfully back, his mouth still jammed open and blocked by fingers that searched deeper and deeper down his throat.

He convulsed—choking, and desperate—knowing something was drastically wrong, as he fought against his captors. Futilely, and he knew it. Trained in fighting as he was, what chance had he against a squad, even if he hadn't been attacked without warning and held helpless before he could react.

He felt a breath going over his naked body, heard a faint ticking and knew he was being scanned by an offworlder device. Whatever it was, it was run over his entire body, quickly but thoroughly, even down his arms and legs and between fingers and toes.

"He's clean," a voice reported.

"Perhaps." Head strained back as it was, fingers still chokingly down his throat, Brine still felt the sharp bite of the instrument clamped on to his earlobe. Felt and knew what it was, because he had had occasion to use them himself. A baby Truth machine. It could only report yea or nay, not the shades of difference of the big adjudicational machine, but it could catch him quickly enough in a lie. The fingers drew out of his throat just far enough for him to talk—in a fashion.

"Yes or no, contracted, are you possessed of anything that could be of danger to a human or not?"

"Arrghlumph." He tried to explain that he himself was trained to be dangerous.

His interrogator must have read his mind. "Aside from whatever skills you yourself have, do you have anything besides your own muscle and training that would make you dangerous to a human?"

"No." He recognized the formula, at least. Anyone allowed into the presence of a c'holder would go through something similar, although not usually so vicious or so thorough as his own stripping.

"Good." The fingers drew out of his mouth and he was allowed to take a deep breath and lower his aching head and face his interrogator, though the two on either side still gripped his wrists firmly. He was naked and weaponless, and held helpless. He didn't even look down at the mud, where his weapons and the offworld mercy device disguised as a bangle on his belt lay just out of reach. But he was desperate, and as dangerous as a pit viper, caged or not.

The controller, a brawny, muscular man wearing the usual mask, looked him up and down, shaking his head slightly. He clicked his tongue, as at something foolish beyond belief, muttered, "Whim!" and then issued a single crisp order: "Inside with him!"

The hands on his wrists hauled him toward the litter, which had stopped just down the street. The rising Smallsun shone on the insignia on its side, and Brine dug his heels in the mud, not even realizing he was howling, "No!" like some doomed soul on its way to the Courts of the Forsworn.

But two hands on each wrist, and more hands shoving from behind are a potent argument. Almost before the significance of the emblem had sunk in, Brine was falling head-first into the body of the litter, sensuous draperies brushing against his body, and he was tumbling onto a heap of cushions beside a body that was soft and smelled of the subtlest of violets and couldn't be anything but the Oriflamme herself, Medee, the evil.

Willing handmaiden of the c'holder Golden Singh, his apprentice in villainy.

His captor.

CHAPTER 32

From a speaking disk delivered, after some unavoidable delay, to Guildhall:

—To the Lady Navigator whose true name is unlikely to be Jael.

Salutations from the Scholar Epimenides Garibaldi Ryker, Mentator Alpha Class and Professor Emeritus of the University of Plato Ascending in the city of K'ung Fu-tse on the world of Schopenhauer of the Transcendental cluster.

If you are hearing this, I am dead and past the power of any mortal justice. Whether there is an afterlife, as so many human religions have postulated, I take leave to doubt. Either way, I am certain to be discovering the true meaning of dualism.

Suffice it. You do not know me, and have never seen me, but I have seen and know much of you. It is not simple, but it is possible to betray, when one is spared from seeing the fruits of that betrayal. Now I have seen you, and conscience is a bitter specter in my mind.

No, I had nothing to do with whatever tragedy befell your parents and yourself. I cannot know where it occurred, or even when, but I know something of my own victims and you were not one of them.

Nonetheless, you are my retribution, and I accept it gladly, embrace it willingly, if you prefer.

I betrayed, because of my need, and told myself that such betrayals were of no moment, beside that overpowering need.

Until I could no longer live with betrayal, and so came here, where what I need is freely available, and there is never any such thing as betrayal, because there is in truth no honor among thieves.

Yet what has been done continues to exist, frozen in time, ripples spreading out into eternity. The weight of what I have done lies heavy upon me.

It doesn't matter how I first came in contact with the drug

known as Elysium. Perhaps a student made a mistake, and what should have been an ordinary sampling of harmless drugs became more than that. Perhaps I suffered the sin of hubris, and felt myself above the limits of ordinary mortals. Perhaps it was deliberate, an enemy's revenge, a woman's fury. It is of little consequence. I tasted the delights of Elysium and was trapped, then and forevermore.

Elysium, they say, is not addictive. This is simple truth. It has no permanent effect on the body whatsoever. But the mind . . . ah, the mind! The mind revels in inexpressible delight, so that reality by contrast is too bitter, too drab to be borne, and one returns, one is impelled back to the drug-induced paradise of Elysium. When the Elysium fades, life is gray and featureless, its greatest delight a muted, faded echo that causes more pain than joy, because it reminds only of the greater glory available for the swallowing of a single capsule.

I was lost, as are all who taste of the forbidden fruit, with my first experience. It is so compelling that putting it off, for even a single second, becomes a deprivation almost more than any human can bear. Nonetheless, I was able to ration myself, to calculate the precise intervals that I could afford to indulge, without sliding into the normal downward cycle of Elysium takers. As you are probably aware, few habitués of Elysium last more than a couple of standard months. Under the influence, their bodies burn out, they neglect to eat or sleep or renew their energies. They die. Gloriously happy. I lived, if one could call it living, existing merely from dose to evanescent dose.

While I was on Schopenhauer, I got the uncut Elysium the only way possible. I beggared myself, and then I betrayed. Never mind how, but there are ways to obtain large amounts of credit, and I carefully chose those which were the safest, having the least chance of backfiring, revealing my sad secret to my colleagues.

But there is a limit, even for a man to whom only Elysium is significant, and I reached that limit. So I began my search for a world where anything is allowed, where I could indulge myself with Elysium openly, where there could be no true betrayal, because merely living in a world of such unfeigned evil was a betrayal in itself.

I found Rabelais.

I sell my skills here, and I buy Elysium.

And I was . . . content.

Until I looked into your eyes.

I am a Mentator, trained to interpret the smallest clues. I thought I knew what Purgatory was, but I was wrong in that, as in so many other credences. Yet despite all, you are still fighting, while I have given in.

I owe to you, as representative of those I betrayed. I owe you—but now the debt is paid.

And I have broken my cycle. If they permit it, I shall die happy, in another two months or so.

If they do not, I will die the sooner.

Triumphant.

My blessings, woman who calls herself Jael, for what such is worth. And my best wishes. May your luck turn. Either way, I am convinced you will fight and keep on fighting. If there is truly an afterlife, know my anima will surely be watching and cheering you on. Though I am assured you would continue, even if I and a whole universe were striving against you.

Fare-thee-well.

Our lives crossed, now mine is ended, and it is fitting.

The scales are not yet balanced, but I have no more to give.

Salva res est.*

CHAPTER 33

"I'll kill you," Brine snarled, and his hands sailed toward a white throat while beneath him was a lissome body whose utter seduction was forgotten in his flood of sheer hatred.

"If you must," said a soft voice, and his rage-blinded eyes suddenly *saw*. In the dimness of the luxurious palanquin, it would be easy to mistake one sister for the other; but Medee would never have lain unmoving under his attack, she couldn't hold still for a

(* The matter is safe. Terence.)

heartbeat, and her voice was *never* soft. Nor were her hard eyes
gentle and pale as the mists rising from the distant Gargantuas.

He froze, his hands still wrapped around that slender throat.

"If you must," she repeated softly, her breath barely propelling
the words to his alert ear.

His mouth opened and closed. "My—my lady Esme!"

"Yes." Her calm gaze never faltered. Then, "You are the chief
enforcer from the Magistrate Lyhunt's chambers, one Brine by
name."

Too much, too fast. He stared at her, a long pale fragile shape,
the lady c'holder who could have him tortured into infinity, cas-
trated, beaten, or simply chained and starved slowly to death for
her amusement . . . at the lady c'holder who knew him by *name*.
Then he said simply, half a question, "Yes, lady."

"You killed the Lord C'holder Singh's z'par in chambers this
day past." It wasn't a question.

He couldn't breathe. Then, "Yes."

"He's looking for you."

That was it. He rolled away from her, stared up at the palanquin's ceiling decorated with—despite his own past, his leathery
cheeks glowed red and hot.

"My sister's taste"—she propped herself on one elbow to gaze
assessingly down at him—"runs rather toward the obvious, does it
not."

He just lay, defeated. Even knowing what was coming, he
couldn't touch *her*. Medee, yes, he could have wrung her neck like
a chikn, and laughed as he did so, no matter what had been
drummed into his head his life long, no matter what happened
after. But not the gentle Esme, well known among contracteds for
her compassion and vulnerable heart, though she tried to hide it.

She flicked a disdainful glance upward, at the lascivious embroi-
deries. "Quite obvious."

Obvious wasn't the word he'd've used.

"He has your contract now, you know." She ran a finger idly
down his sun-toughened face, from the bushy grizzled brows to
the slight scar that made an irregularly shaped mouth even more
irregular. "If you'd gone back to the barracks he'd have you by
now. He's out looking for you already. But I found you first."

He shut his eyes. "And now you intend to curry favor with him
by turning me over into his hands." A sigh. "Well, you must have
a reason. He has a contract on someone you wish out of his
holding?"

She snorted. "I wouldn't wish to see anyone in his holding. He came to invite my sister to a display of utmost ingenuity. You are to be the star attraction. In a week or so, when he has had time to arrange all exactly as he wishes it." A slight, inward-looking smile. "But he did not notice whom you spoke to after the end of the adjudication—and I did."

Brine looked into the gray eyes smugly complacent. "And you're going to tell me all about it before you turn me over. I thought it was your sister who went in for cruelty."

"He has your contract."

"You said that. Not that I doubted. Knowing him."

"Nonetheless, I have no intention of turning you over."

His eyes widened; he sat up so abruptly she had to duck back or have his head slam into her face. "That's c'breaking!"

"I know." What Jael had been accused of. And the penalty was the same for anybody, contracted—or c'holder. "I want to help you. Exactly what are your plans?"

Then he understood. A typical c'holder trick. They didn't just want him, they wanted whoever had helped him, whoever he hoped, expected might help him. He drew a shuddering breath, fighting down temptation. If they promised him immunity . . . there had been some words carelessly dropped by the freighter-master . . . they might have Jael, too. For both the offworlders, even Singh might be willing to trade.

He opened his mouth—and closed it. Even if he could live with betrayal, you couldn't trust a c'holder. Especially not a twister like Singh. He might, though she was a c'holder, have trusted this woman. But it appeared he shouldn't.

Her mouth twisted, a cynical expression that sat oddly on what should have been Botticelli sweetness. "How can I convince you to trust me?" she said. "If placing myself knowingly in your hands doesn't do it, what will?"

He snorted. "If I lay a finger on you, I know what your retinue will do." It was bred in his bones, that knowledge. She was a c'holder, one of the gods-on-earth. And the wrath of the gods is mighty—and blasting.

She only smiled, and ran a finger down his cheek again, stopping to play in the jagged hole where he had once had an ear. "They're going to kill you anyway. Slowly. They're going to break, torment you, destroy you bit by bit, turn you into a helpless, hopeless, whining, cringing horror. You'll lick Singh's feet for death before he's through, beg for it, grovel, plead, scream—"

A hissed imprecation through his teeth interrupted her. "I know!"

"Think it through." She sat up, pulled her knees to her chin, stared without seeing at the curtains fluttering slightly as the palanquin swayed along. "You've earned Singh's emnity, and he's a bad enemy. Nothing you do now can make your fate worse than it already is, as far as he's concerned. You're free, totally free, in an odd sense—and I'm vulnerable. You can do anything you please, and it won't make things any the worse for you." He was too engrossed in his despair to notice the sideways look out of pale, compassionate eyes.

"Except I'll be a contract-breaker, and doomed in the next world as well as this one." But he wasn't sure he believed much, any more, and there was a tonelessness in his voice that revealed he was merely repeating a lesson drummed in well and early.

"Even that already," she said gently. "You should have reported back, hours ago. Technically, you were guilty of c'breaking the instant you failed to report for your proper shift." He stared at her then, something in voice or body language freezing every muscle. "But you were guilty of c'breaking, in your heart, long before that, weren't you?"

She *knew!* How did she know?

"You were planning to run," she said softly. "I don't blame you. If I had a place to run to, I'd be tempted myself." He made a growl of disbelief. "Oh, yes," she nodded. "Even c'holders have their limitations." Bitterly. "You can't *know*—"

He couldn't. C'holders were gods-on-earth. But if he had to live anywhere near Medee Oriflamme . . . "Your sister—"

"Among other—chains." Again her fingers stroked softly along the jagged scar that ran along his hairline and included what had once been an ear. "Can you imagine what it's like to be a woman, and to know that every man who comes near you sees you as—as a source of punishment, or of power, as a—a useful tool, or something to be feared?"

"Your sister—" he repeated, frowning.

"Glories in her power. Yes, I know. I do not. I would give it up, all of it, if only for one night I could—I could—"

He was a man brutalized by a life of unparalleled viciousness. Yet there was a core of basic compassion in him, humanity undestroyed, and the bleak unhappiness in her touched that core. He laid a finger on her mouth, and smiled, a very male smile, perhaps because, close as they were, he couldn't help reacting to her as a woman. Something in him had been stripped away in those taut hours, and if his mind still saw her as a c'holder, untouchable except by strict order, his body did not. "Hush." His finger moved on petal-soft lips smelling of honey-sweets. "Somehow I can't believe all the men around you saw you only as a—a—"

"C'holder of great contracts," she finished dryly. "Did you?"

He blinked. The time when he had been a pet, an amusement, passed about from c'holder to c'holder as a different one, a delicacy to tempt jaded appetites, had been a time of great trauma. No man who is a man takes kindly to his manhood being used and abused. He had survived by blanking the experience as much out of his mind as possible, both while it was happening and after. Even so, a few larger-than-lifes had been burned into his very psyche, such as the on-her-way-to-being-infamous Medee Oriflamme—but if this woman had been one of the many, he couldn't remember her. "Did I?" he repeated wryly. "You mean I—" A snort. "Lady, there were times when I did not raise my eyes above—I trust I gave satisfaction."

A hesitation, then, "Yes, you were—most satisfactory."

He nodded, but he had been reminded, and once again his eyes dropped. He had worked her motives out. The ultimate titillation, cure for ennui. Being made love to by a man under sentence of dreadful death. A man knowing that every second so spent was a second stolen from— His mouth tightened.

She saw. "Tell me what you're thinking."

He was still much a product of his world: a c'holder ordered, he obeyed.

The slap was loud and echoed in the confined space. "I am not my sister. You may leave for the asking. Say the word, and you will be set down instantly."

"And picked up by Singh's contracteds immediately thereafter."

"Probably. I'd've protected you as long as I could, even at my own risk, but you won't believe that. So—go. The choice is yours."

"Why?"

"Why—oh." She turned her face away. "I suppose, because it has to start somewhere. Because I'm tired of seeing brave people destroyed by such as Singh and my sister. Because—"

"I know of you," he dared to interrupt, "at least by repute. There are none so many truly powerful c'holders here, after all. While you've never, so it is said, abused that power of yours, likewise, you've never lifted a finger to stop your sister or anyone else. You lived withdrawn, apart, shutting your eyes to the usual c'holder games. So I ask again, why me?" He caught the cleft chin, turned her to face him, and saw, with amaze, the dove-gray eyes filled with tears.

"The truth, you would have the truth," she said, and he nodded, suddenly sure that whatever she said, it would be the truth. She licked her lips, and began in a soft voice he had to strain slightly to hear, close as they were. "I was in the adjudicator's chambers this afternoon—yesterday afternoon, that is. I saw— You smiled at the Navigator woman, after. She's an attractive woman, more than attractive; even I, another woman, can see that. But it wasn't just that—that female attraction, with you." He opened his mouth, and she laid a silencing finger on his lips.

"I know"—a small smile—"you're a man. But with her, it was more. You admired her, and respected her, it was all there, plain for anyone with eyes to read. You—wanted her, but despite that, you were willing to give *her* the choice. I'd've done nothing then. Envied you both a little, I think, because you had the one thing I never had, can never have. Disinterested affection offered, as a choice, I mean. And then"—a deep breath—"that slime Zaqanna frightened her into screaming. Odd, that, she didn't strike me as a woman to be so terrified of a man's hands, especially in a situation where there were a dozen or more ready to spring to her rescue. It's not as if he held a contract over her, quite the contrary."

"Navigator's Syndrome," he explained. "She can't stand being enclosed, constrained even for a second. It's not uncommon among the spacefarers, so I'm told. I saw her earlier panic to hysteria at the mere thought of being locked in a cell."

"Oh. I wondered." A small smile. "It seemed—uncharacteristic, somehow. But I stray. She screamed, and the z'par attacked, and you killed it, unthinking. An animal attacked, and you defended, yourself and the woman. But—I know Golden Singh. Once his grief abates, he'll want revenge. And you must know how his revenges run—"

"Yes." He thought of a nameless woman, hair dyed in stripes, dead or wishing she were this very second.

"The woman was safe, for now. But you—you who had done two brave and selfless deeds in the space of a few heartbeats—you would have to pay a bitter price. I—I tried first to obtain your contract. But I've never played the games the others do, I've been satisfied with what was mine, with ensuring my own safety. Singh has options, liens, all about the city. He has—he has you. Once he could lay his hands on you." A shrug. "Nothing I could do, except use my mind and eyes and hope I spotted you first."

"I see."

"I hope so. If you've a safe place to run to, I'll help you. I can't keep you with me, my sister keeps my household riddled with spies. There is a place that would be available, but not now, not soon enough. You can imagine what would happen if *she* found out I was protecting you. To you. And to myself and all who depend on me."

"Yes." He didn't need telling. For him—he'd seen it, more than once. Torture, breaking off to make forced love to a vile creature. The victim, frantic, licking the tormentor's feet, doing anything ordered to stave off the pain, the humiliation, the unbearable inevitable another second, another breath. He'd seen it. The toughest of men broke under it, sooner or later. And this delicate woman—

She mistook his startled jerk for what it wasn't. "You still don't trust me." Centimeters away from him in the sybaritic but small palanquin, she withdrew somehow to a place immeasurably distant. "All right. But know this. I can put two and two together, and so can Singh. And once you're caught—I don't think you'd risk those who were willing to help you. So—" Their gazes locked, hers probing, his revealing nothing. "There's only one place safe, even the wilds would betray you sooner or later. I won't say it aloud, because even now I can't be sure my *dear* sister—but we know who might be able to hide you, safely, long enough. Don't we? Now if you were to say the name aloud, I could turn it in, and that's the only reason I'm talking, isn't it. Trying to catch the other c'breaker. If I let you loose, it's only to find the other guilty ones, through you, isn't it. You won't trust, so out you go. Make your way the best you can. I shan't even wish you luck."

He stared at her. "All right."

She pulled a tiny embroidered belt, and within heartbeats, he was standing alone, the pink light of dawn highlighting a palanquin being borne away with its file of guards.

He caught his lip between fierce teeth, and then, not giving himself time to think, ran.

"You again." The controller was bored. "What do you want?"

"I forgot—tell lady—being transferred—"

"So?"

"Outcity. If the lady would command my services again, she might not—"

A shrug. "If she wants, I'll have your contract traced—"

"She might wish my contract reassigned incity. Now."

"You've a fine opinion of your talents." Had Brine been less tense, he might have correctly interpreted the jealousy in the other man's voice. A sneer. "It's not like her to take a liking for strays."

"Ask her. Or better—give me the opportunity to—persuade her. Now."

"Go your way. I'll contract your c'holder—" Brine had been wearing lying insignia, and knew that by the time this controller did as he promised, it wouldn't matter—one way or the other.

"—and if my lady has by then expressed a wish—"

"It will be too late. Ask her now! I was to go at shift's end. You were to have me here my full shift—so let me have that time, all of it!"

"Tsha!" The man turned away.

"Controller." He raised his voice desperately. "All present have seen you turn me away. I say, the lady may wish the opportunity to keep me incity. And you've dared refuse for her—"

The controller's hand tightened on the whip around his waist. And then, the eyes in the mask promising dire punishment if this was a fruitless errand, if he disturbed his lady against her wishes, he whirled, strode to catch up with the slow-moving palanquin, pressed a small whistle, and, when the curtains parted, trotted to keep up, speaking swiftly. Then he dropped back. "You've less time than to the end of shift. She's a breakfast appointment with the singer Julienne, along with some others. Make the most of what time you have."

This time he was assisted into the palanquin, so that he kept his balance, staring about himself.

She was sitting upright, those eyes of gray as elusive as mists on the hills fixed on him. "What do you want, that you risk what little free time you have left?"

"Little is right. Either way." A grim smile. "I suppose I wanted a memory."

"And since I'm what's available, you'd accept what you thought was an offer."

"No." He made himself comfortable, half lying, half sitting. "I want no more than you're willing to give freely. If only a smile, I'll take it, with thanks. The sight of your face, for that short time, or shorter. Whatever. A light for my darkness. But only willingly given." He reached out, hesitated, ran his fingers along the curve of cheek and gentle jaw, close but not touching the soft, cared-for skin. "On other worlds, they say, a man and a woman can choose freely, to come together or not, to spend their lives together if they so desire, to love and laugh and make children whose destinies they control, until those children in turn go out freely to make their own choices. I'd like that, had I such a choice. But we've only a little time, you and I, such a little time. However we spend that time, let it be the choice of us both, yours as well as mine, freely offered, freely accepted." He folded his arms across his chest, leaned back against one of the supports of the small enclosure. "I've had my say. You can have me thrown out now."

Instead she smiled and opened her arms. "You great fool!"

CHAPTER 34

Lysander!

"Whaa—oh, no! Lady Alizon! How came you here?" The boy, wrists and ankles bound, stirred in the uncomfortable cage-carrier, jogging ceaselessly over the sands of the desert Urquhart.

I'm not "here," Lysander. But thank the Mother I've completed the link.

"Uh? Link?" He blinked, trying to unstick eyelids glued together by dust and phlegm, trying to pierce the shrouded dimness. It was as it had been, a double dozen helpless bodies jumbled together in the woven carrier, stiff with dust, tormented by zingers, thirsty and scarcely able to breathe. The bodies were anonymous, naked and clothed, some female—but none had Alizon's straight pastel rope of hair.

Don't speak aloud. I've formed a link, a psychic link with you, son. I can hear if you only pretend to speak.

"I—I don't understand." A nearby body stirred and grumbled.

Never mind. Not now. I can't know how long the link will last. Listen, Lysander. They—they officially gave you back to us. Only —it wasn't you! But they said he fulfilled your contract.

"Aye, Lady Alizon." He shifted, and multitudinous bruises and abuses creaked. Yet except for the broken arm, which had been ill-set and would never be straight unless a High-T expert rebroke and reset the bone, they had done no permanent damage to him. No physical damage, at any rate; the mental scars went deep.

They hadn't spared him because Singh thought it a waste, but because he simply hadn't had enough time. He liked to orchestrate his amusements, to go from small simple torments to larger ones slowly, shoving his trembling victim one step at a time down the road to degradation. It was time and circumstances that had saved Lysander. First the trial, then Singh's grief, and then the girl with the striped hair, the scapegoat, had proved a diversion. Then the furor over the lost gladiator, and the search for both him and the enforcer who had killed the z'par.

By the time all that was over, Singh was already bored with the boy with the ugly broken arm who screeched in painfully high tones and was really totally unamusing.

But he wasn't giving his one small trophy back to Guildhall, either.

Hence the contract juggling, and, to be sure, the shipping out.

"I'm somewhere in the great desert, Lady Alizon. My contract has been exchanged with someone Singh has dealings with in the far city of La Diviniere. Another such as he, doubtless."

Can you get free and get back here?

"No." Simple truth.

You must! And soon. I'm the only one who can link with you like this, who can help and guide you. And I've had to accept a berth. Lysander, I had to! I must—

"How went the trial of the Lady Jael?" he interrupted. No one had bothered to tell him.

She was found guiltless.

"Ah!"

"Sharrup!" The man next to him angrily elbowed him in the ribs.

Lysander had already learned how to defend himself. He bit fiercely, and when the man howled and jerked, he snarled, "I'll say what I please, when I please. You sharrup!" He had half the man's size, but twice the guts. The other subsided, grumbling. "Go on!"

Not so good. The man Zaqanna triggered an attack of Navigator's Syndrome in her, and she was and still is sore distressed. But he was condemned, for that attack, in his turn.

"And the C'holder Singh, who stood behind Zaqanna?"

(Infinite satisfaction.) *Did not get off scot-free. He lost that which he prized highly.*

"I heard hints. Wish I'd seen. Yet it will not stop his campaign of evil."

No. But that's not our problem now. I want to help you.

"You can't." (But, unknown to either of them, she already had. She had given him back his courage and hope.) He began struggling stubbornly against his bonds.

It was our fault, wasn't it, Lysander?

He continued to strain. "My choice," he panted, "that I find out what I could to help the Lady Jael. My fault that I was fool enough to get caught. Doubly my fault, because I *knew—*"

(Sadly.) *As we should have known.*

He continued to work on his bonds. Invisible fingers, attenuated across the kilometers, helped him. But there was little she could do, over such a distance.

"If I can get away"—he spoke the hope of all prisoners aloud— "they'll list me as dead. The desert claims her own—"

Lysander, don't risk yourself! Wait!

"Here. Or there. Someday I will be back, Lady Alizon. And I will have my revenge." It could have been a child's angry vow. It wasn't.

The join was fading, she hadn't the power, for all her will, to hold it much longer. *I think you will. Guard yourself until that day, Lysander. Use patience, and—*

She was gone. Somehow, he knew emptiness, where there had been presence.

And yet—she had left a gift behind. He had always had a sense of direction, of where he was; this was a common necessity, a basic need for all Navigators. Now he had more. He had a world view, of the whole planet Rabelais spread out like a three-dimensional puzzle, and he a tiny mite moving across the surface of the rolling dunes of the desert Urquhart. He knew where he was, and where the cities were, and the oases, the smallest supplies of the precious water. No normal person, even a desert dweller, could expect to survive the endless dry sweeps alone and naked. Lysander would at least have a chance.

"I will be back," he repeated aloud. Oath, promise, threat—he knew he would. One boy-not-yet-a-man against an entire world. In that dedicated second, he wouldn't have taken odds on the world.

CHAPTER 35

Reis had thought the worst part of the nightmare was when he had to walk away from Brine, dragging Rowan, semi-conscious, through the mad world where slavery went under the guise of freedom, but he had been wrong. He had stumbled through horror, grimly putting one foot in front of the other, Rowan a dead but complaining weight on his shoulders. On and on, like one of those dreams where a dire fate pursues, but you run endlessly on a treadmill, never getting anywhere, and hot breath curls the hair on the back of your neck.

On and on—until he saw the clean lines of the *Scalded Cat* before him.

It was inside the *Scalded Cat* that the *real* nightmare began. He hauled Rowan to the sick bay, laid him on the diagnostic table—and got his first good look at what he had thought in the dimness were simply bruises, saw the still raw wounds where the younger man had been literally scalped, and the other mutilations. . . .

He turned and vomited.

He was still shaking some interminable time later, when Brine strolled up to the ship, cool as if he had been out for a pre-duty breath of fresh air, and was admitted. The now ex-enforcer took one look at Rowan, encased in the medimachine, and nodded. "He was scheduled for short and sweet. Lucky you grabbed him in time."

Reis didn't say anything, he merely checked that Rowan was totally under, in a state of dormancy that would keep his wounds—the areas where his hair had been were literally putrid; he would have died of infection fairly soon, regardless of what his fate in the arena had been—at least from getting worse, until he could get to a High-T hospital and be fixed. If he could be, his brother couldn't even be sure. But Reis had for once made up his mind: Cargo or not, he was begging or stealing fuel and taking off from this primitive horror of a world. And if he had to sell the *Cat* at the other end . . . too bad. . . .

And if they came looking before he could take off, too bad for *them*. . . .

The charter came through first. In a hurry, they were, but not in so much a hurry that Reis couldn't see what kind of example Zaqanna made. Quite an example. Hardened as he thought of himself, Reis knew he would never after be able to think of what little he had seen of Zaqanna's public painful end without a shudder. Little brother, he muttered to himself as he turned away, back to the *Scalded Cat* and freedom, your suffering has been paid for—in full.

Who would have thought that combining revenge and justice would have paid so well?

The trail to Rowan, so cold, such a tangle of contracting and subcontracting and assignments . . . he could never have unraveled it. But now—the routine of take-off enfolded him, and it was some time later that he could sigh, pat the ship's thrumming outer hull in content, and lose himself in the easy pattern of the voyage.

The paid-for voyage. The charter. And, best of all, the charter to Starroads, the most advanced world in the whole quadrant. If they could hope to cure a mind-damaged Navigator there, maybe they could cure Rowan, too. Physically, for sure. But whether the mental scars of mutilation, of gladiatorial training could be as easily dealt with . . . But that was a problem for another day. For now, he was on his way, with enough profit from the charter to hope to be able to get the best, even after the losses on Rabelais.

Reis patted the hull again. Even the extra passenger might prove to be a bonus; he might be trainable as crew, he was eager enough to learn. If not, Reis decided, there'd be a decent ground berth on Starroads, that's the least we owe him.

If that red-eyed boy doesn't lose us halfway, that is—

"Reis!"

He turned, to see his first pilot, who also doubled as medical officer, though any of the crew could do routine med service, hurrying up behind him. "Reis, I've been wanting to talk to you. It's the Navigator—the woman."

"What's the matter, Damask?"

"She's reacting badly to forced unconsciousness."

He frowned. If anything went wrong with his precious cargo . . .

He and Damask consulted with the albino Navigator, the closest thing they had to an expert on Navigator's Syndrome.

Nikady wasn't encouraging. "You say—that's bad, really bad. You see, sometimes, they fight against anything that holds or binds or—or anything. They destroy themselves, fighting . . ."

"But if we shut off the machine, and she awakes to find herself aboard a ship, she may go permanently, incurably insane."

Nikady flinched. "If you leave her under, she may not survive the voyage. Master, I have no easy answers for you. I wish I did." His pink young eyes shone, as if with unshed tears. "For her sake, I wish I did."

Reis went in to the sick bay and watched her, twisting, fighting —it was supposed to be impossible—the machine, the outside control. He brushed the tiger-striped hair away from the pale forehead, and she seemed to jerk away from even that gentle touch. For once, he didn't hesitate, his hand didn't stretch toward the pocket with his lucky piece in it. "Bring her out of it."

Within seconds her eyelids fluttered up to reveal blank, mindless eyes.

But not mindless long. She lay, very quietly, while intelligence and character seeped back into those long, gray-green eyes. Her lips opened. "We're—aboard a ship. Yours, Master Reis? Who's navigating?"

The albino moved from behind Reis's bulk. "I am. Greetings, sister. How do you feel?"

"Tired, thank you, brother." Her hand brushed against his and fell back. Again her eyes caught Reis's. "A wise selection, master. Yours or the Old One's?"

"Agreed between us. You are a mere passenger this trip, Navigator Jael."

Her eyes closed. "You are the master—master." Almost, it was sly mockery.

His forehead writhed in an unconscious frown. She was too calm, too composed, too integrated. Could several days of enforced rest have improved that screaming, convulsing hysteric to this? Her eyelids flickered one last time, her lips curved into a gentle, subtle smile directed at him—and he *knew*.

That Personal hadn't landed in his cup by accident.

What Starfirehell she must have gone through, waiting, wondering which way he was going to jump.

The risk she took! That his hatred of Zaqanna would be greater than his fury toward her.

How great her own rage and frustration must have been, when, after all her efforts, Zaqanna seemed about to wriggle out of her carefully set, painfully baited trap.

Except he hadn't. He'd trapped himself, condemned himself when he triggered her attack of Navigator's Syndrome.

Or . . . had he?

Was it real, that attack, and now controlled or wholly false—or some mixture of the two? He'd never know. She might not know, truly, herself.

"Navigator," he said softly, "I heard someone ask once what one could do about evil, widespread and deeply entrenched evil. I had no answer to give then, but since I have learned—*much*. You fight it, Navigator. You fight it relentlessly, unstintingly, with your weaknesses as well as your strengths, with every weapon and wile you command. You fight"—his low voice held admiration—"though you know it grows far faster than you can possibly conquer it, and someday, inevitably, it must win and overwhelm you. Yet still—you fight."

Silence, except for the sound of regular, even breathing.

He left her with Nikady the albino standing worshipful sentry-go.

But as he went through the door, he heard, so soft he might have thought he imagined it, except he knew he hadn't, "You forgot—*trust*."

ABOUT THE AUTHOR

Jayge Carr has a degree in nuclear physics, and has always been interested in science fiction. She has published short stories in many magazines, and is the author of a previous novel for Doubleday, *Leviathan's Deep*.